STORM THE CASTLE

MARRY THE SCOT #1

JOLIE VINES

WWW.JOLIEVINES.COM/NEWSLETTER

Paula - "I loved this book! It had all that I would expect with **hot Scots and rambling castles.** I had to giggle when I discovered that I was reading this book with my own manufactured Scottish brogue! Can't wait for more."

J. Saman, Bestselling author - "Jolie Vines has fast become a **one-click author** for me!"

Zoe Ashwood, author - "I'm impatiently waiting for the next book - I just know it'll be **another sizzling story** from Jolie Vines."

Viper Spaulding - "(Hero) is an amazing work of art, highly recommended for anyone looking for a **modern-day Highlander to swoon over.**"

Chikap09 - "I swear, every time I pick up a Jolie Vines book I think: this is him, **my favorite hero**, no one will be able to top him. And then I read the next book and the process begins again."

Pam Graber - "If you haven't read the other books in the series Marry the Scot, you should really start with Storm the Castle, then move on to Love Most, Say Least before diving into Hero. **I cannot wait to see what Ally and Wasp get up**

to in their stories! I've enjoyed the first three books immensely!"

Carmen Davis - "Jolie Vines is an amazingly talented writer. I am so **completely obsessed with this series** and so madly in love with the characters. Each book gets better than the last and when you start off with a 5 star? There just aren't enough stars. I can't wait for the next book in this series and anything else Jolie Vines writes."

For N and M, my very own happily ever after

Storm the Castle (Marry the Scot, #1)

"Come, lass. Get on a plane with me."

After a business deal goes awry, Laird Callum McRae is in over his head, struggling to keep his castle afloat. He knows exactly what he has to do to save his family of brothers. Collecting a debt from the corrupt man who swindled him is his only mission. But when he meets a compassionate and determined woman, his plans change.

Now, he needs to get the girl while confronting her father...

Mathilda Storm will do anything for her sister--even if it means entering into a contract for a loveless marriage. After all, it will solve her family's problems. But she doesn't count on meeting a broad-shouldered, rugged Scottish laird. And resisting him is harder than she imagined.

As the chemistry between Callum and Mathilda ignites, Mathilda is torn between her desire and her need to help her family. Can the practical daughter marry the Scot without losing her heart along the way?

Storm the Castle is the first in a major new contemporary romance series. Set in the gorgeous Scottish Highlands, this story of big love brings Highlander romance into the modern day.

A LETTER TO MY READERS

Hello lovely reader!

The *Marry the Scot* series is complete with five novels available. All the men of Castle McRae have found happily-ever-afters with their lasses.

There are **boxed sets** available here.

Audiobooks are here.

The series was so popular that when I asked my reader group what they wanted me to write next, they voted by a landslide for more Scots.

I obliged, and the *Wild Scots* series picks up a new generation of Highlanders.

Enjoy your immersion in gorgeous and modern-day Scottish romance and be sure to **add yourself to my Facebook reader group!** We often carry out read-alongs and polls.

I'd love to have you stop by.

Jolie x

A WALL OF MAN

*M*athilda

As a little girl, I'd dreamt of hearing the words 'Marry me'. Soft music playing in the background and a ring offered from my lover's eager hands. This, of course, was before my closest example of marriage became a warning rather than an inspiration.

My childish, rose-tinted vision had never involved me standing in the corner of a glittering conference, freaking out over the proposal I'd just received.

Dominic Hanswick, my father's business partner, had watched Dad leave then taken me to one side. He'd been polite and concise as he'd laid out his terms. "Marry me, Mathilda. Save my reputation. Save your sister in the process. Think about it. I'm sure you'll find it a reasonable idea." He'd offered it so easily then he'd smiled and moved away through the tables, murmuring pleasantries to colleagues.

A business deal, he'd called it.

Who said things like that?

My head already ached like I'd been in a hit-and-run, the

dreadful lunch I'd had at my parents' home still forefront in my mind. Scarlet's behaviour was the only reason I wasn't laughing this off.

Shocked, I'd barely asked Dominic any questions, but now dozens came to mind. God, he wouldn't expect me to sleep with him, would he?

I needed answers, and standing around in my flat sandals wasn't getting me anywhere. My job for the evening was done—I was only at the event as a favour to Dad, meaning I could leave and return to my hotel, but this had thrown me for a loop. With a calming breath, I left the safety of my alcove and crossed the hall.

"Mr Hanswick?" I tapped the shoulder of his smart suit, and the man turned. My would-be fiancé was a businessman, a senior partner with Storm Enterprises, the conglomerate my father ran. He was smart, had the stout figure of a man used to finer things, and at forty-two, seventeen years my senior.

Overall, Dominic was not what I had in mind when I'd envisaged my groom.

"If you have a moment, I need to ask a quick question." A vast understatement. I backed away from the group, smiling at people important to my dad. The model of a dutiful daughter.

Dominic excused himself and followed. His brow crinkled. "You have my business card. Set up a meeting, and we can talk through the finer details."

Right. And yet, "You said you wanted a marriage of convenience. In name only."

He glanced around, presumably to make sure we were out of earshot. "Naturally."

"What happens if I want to date someone?" Why was that so important? I hadn't dated anyone in months.

He sighed. "The point of selecting you, Mathilda, is that

2

you're young, single, and practical. My home is big enough for us to live separate lives: you with your sister on one side, me on the other. This arrangement works for all involved. As for other...needs you might have, sleep with whomever you choose, but I'd recommend you stick to one-night stands. At least until we near the end of the five years. And for Heaven's sake, be discreet. I've had enough scandal to last a lifetime, and a cheating wife would set me back to square one."

"I see." I nodded along like this was anything other than insane. I knew Dominic had been the subject of press attention. He'd had an affair with a high-profile, married politician, and the newspapers had made a meal over it. Dad had ranted about the effect it had on Storm Enterprise's shareholders, so I knew Dominic was losing money fast.

Getting married would fix his reputation and save his bank balance.

None of this was my problem.

Scarlet's emotional health, on the other hand, was. Her chance at having a good future.

As if sensing my reticence, the man leaned in. Even though I was in my flats, my six-foot height meant I was looking down on him. "Your sister is off the rails. You can help her. Why wouldn't you do that? Your father will let you take her in if you're married, am I correct?"

How on Earth did he know that? I gave a slow nod. From behind me came the clamour of raised voices. Dominic's attention shifted to the source of the commotion, and his eyes widened as if in recognition. He gave me a short bow. "I have to leave. Call my assistant to set up that meeting, and we can finalise the arrangements. Just don't take a time over it. It serves us both to arrange this as soon as possible."

Then he was gone.

Rotating, I spied a vacant table in a dark corner. On the way, I grabbed a glass of water from a waiter then found a chair and laid my head back. My sister, Scarlet, nearly arrested again last week, worried me to death, and clearly Dominic knew enough about the situation to determine which buttons to push. It was the solitary reason I'd have to say yes, saving her skin and, separately, his, and why I hadn't yet laughed him out of town.

Not that I would do anything quite so unladylike.

A surge of frustration filled me from even entertaining the idea. I didn't want Dominic. He'd called me practical, and I was, but what about chemistry and heat and passion? I wanted more than the lacklustre relationships I'd so far suffered in my twenty-five years on the planet. Beth, my best friend, made a robot-Mathilda voice when I was being ultra-efficient, but inside I was like everyone else: desiring that overwhelming romance. The breathless appetite-quenching satisfaction that came from sex with someone I loved.

The love stories I devoured couldn't all be wrong.

If I took the marriage deal, on whatever terms, I wouldn't have the chance to find out. Then again, who's to say I'd ever find this relationship utopia. My last boyfriend had cheated, after all. Maybe a sham marriage and one-night stands could work. Passion based on the purely physical was better than nothing.

At the entranceway, a distance across the open hall, two men emerged through the crush. Both tall, the men carried a watchful air as the event's patrons left a moat around them, and my interested gaze skipped over each as they shook off the security staff.

The dark-haired younger man had the kind of looks you could stare at for an hour and praise God for pretty people. But it was the man beside him who caught my attention. And held it. Because *holy hell.*

Not only because of his size—he was one of the tallest men I'd ever seen—but for the way people orbited around him, and how he held his powerful, large body with ease as he reached out a long arm to take a glass of what appeared to be water. He gave the waiter a polite nod, and I warmed inside.

Lifting my drink, I tried not to stare. *"Good luck with that."* I imagined my friend's stage-whisper. If only Beth could be here to ogle alongside me. She'd nab a cocktail, rest her chin on her hands, and goggle freely.

The room lights flickered over the doorway, as if showing off for the big man, and a lick of interest curled in my belly.

Power impressed me. I couldn't help the fact.

Then, like I'd switched on a neon light that said "Look over here, big guy!" the man's gaze swept over the busy space and locked onto mine. I started, but he didn't move on as would be proper. Instead, he angled his head and ran an attentive glance over me. A fair eyebrow raised, appreciation lightening his serious expression.

The babbling noise of the room ramped up, and I dragged in a breath. Heat snaked under my high-necked dress, maybe from the intensity or maybe from the humidity, and I tore my gaze away, fidgeting on the chair. *Wow.*

If I was to ever try a one-night stand, he'd be top of my list.

Then my head panged again, and I winced. My cue to leave. From my bag, I extracted my phone to book an Uber, and on the screen, a message already waited. Beth.

Testing testing, are you still alive? Did your dad make you do a speech?

I tapped out a reply.

Luckily, no. But he did tell a bunch of his colleagues that I'd be working for him soon. I should've just come home after lunch.

I'd journeyed to London this morning to see my family, and I could've been on the first train home to the house I shared with Beth. Instead, I'd gritted my teeth through an awful lunch, politely kissed my mother goodbye, booked into a hotel, then attended Dad's product launch. They thought I was getting the late train, though I hated travelling at night, otherwise I'd be forced to stay at my family's home. The mere thought had me shuddering.

Beth shot back an answer as Uber gave me a twelve-minute wait time.

Ugh, I'm sorry, honey. Want me to come get you tonight?

It was a generous offer, and a long drive, but I was too rattled by Dominic's offer and by no means ready to talk about it. Beth would expect me to be miserable as each visit to see my family took me a week to get over. But this... I needed to sleep on it.

Readying to leave, I let my gaze seek out the big man one last time. From first appearance, he wasn't the type of guy I'd usually find interesting. Rougher, less refined than a standard city-dweller. At a black-tie event, he was wearing jeans, so I guessed he was in the wrong room at the conference centre. He was a tourist, maybe. Though the way he and his friend had entered the place felt more purposeful than happy holidaymakers.

A mountain man, I mused, sliding my phone into its pocket in my bag. Used to harder living and working with his hands. Maybe he had a shack somewhere he emerged from each morning to cut wood and fetch water from a stream. He'd go swimming in a river some days.

Naked, obviously.

I grinned at my own fantasy, the levity of it the most exciting part of my evening. But my search of the event space was fruitless. The shy-looking model-type stood with his back to the wall. The interesting one had vanished.

More disappointed than I reasonably should be, I took a final sip from my water then eased myself up from the table. But as I stood, the strap of my sandal snapped, and I stumbled. My purse swung in a wide arc, knocking straight into my glass.

Down the glass fell, cracking on the seat. It shattered and rained razor-edged pieces over my feet. "Shit!" I squawked. And there was me, proud of how little I swore.

I danced away, but in the process, wedged my ankle against the chair leg, trapping a piece of glass. It stung. With a wince, I fell back onto the seat and clutched at my foot, losing my shoe. A sliver of glass stuck out from my skin. I touched the edge and nearly fainted.

Blood welled, and my head swam.

"What's happened here?" a deep voice sounded beside me.

I peeked up. And up.

It was the man. A *wall* of man, looking down at me. Sweet Jesus, he had to be close to seven feet tall. The top of my head wouldn't even reach his chin.

I opened my mouth and managed, "Be careful, there's glass. My drink fell."

Then, with the worst timing, a flood of emotion came over me. My evening had turned absurd. My tiny, stinging injury was nothing compared to the impossible offer my father's colleague had made me. Worse, I couldn't think of another way to help my sister than to accept him.

Marry someone I didn't care for.

Add to that the embarrassment of being a klutz in front of the most impressive man I'd ever seen, my horrible headache, and nausea from my lack of food, I wanted to curl up in a ball.

That was it. My head reeled double-time, my foot panged, and my brain checked out.

Like in an old-style romance novel, I swooned, and everything went black.

IN STATURE AND IN FIRST
IMPRESSIONS

Mathilda

My mortifying blackout lifted as my forehead tapped my knee. If it wasn't for the warm hand on my shoulder, I would have toppled from my seat.

"Hey! Whoa, I've got ye. Keep your head down, lass. Like that. Lean on me."

I kept my eyes closed for a glorious second, letting the stranger support me. Then I cleared my throat and sat up, forcing a smile, though blood trickled out of the wound on my leg. I needed to get back to my hotel.

If only the room would stay still.

"It's just…it's a tiny cut. It's nothing. I'm just a little dizzy."

"Nothing? You're bleeding, and it scared you. That must hurt," the man decided as he knelt at my feet, ignoring the glass under the knees of his jeans. His accent was Scottish. A Highlander. "Christ, there's a wee piece of glass stuck in there. Will you let me take a look?"

Sarah, the floor manager Dad often employed for such events, emerged from behind the tall man, a brush tucked discretely at her side.

She gasped, taking me in. "Mathilda! Oh, blood!"

The big man huffed. "Aye. She's cut. Will ye fetch a first-aid kit?"

Sarah eyed me again then darted off, barking into her headset. The man indicated his blond head to my ankle, seeking permission to touch me. This time I nodded, relaxing a degree while he applied pressure to the cut, his thumb and fingers closing on my skin. I barely felt him whip the glass out.

"Done." He continued his ministrations, checking my skin. "Mathilda, then? I'm Callum McRae. Pleased to meet you."

"Likewise," I managed. "Thank you. I'm not afraid of blood. I didn't eat much today, that's all." I hadn't taken a bite at lunch with my parents. Not that either of them noticed. And this evening, since Dominic's bombshell, I'd been in a state.

The man made a noise of disapproval and, not wanting to look at the cut in case my brain flipped again, I watched him.

His hair was pale blond, curled into small whorls on top like he'd run his fingers through it over and over. It appeared rough-textured, as befitted the mountain man my imagination had made him into. The squareness of his jaw could be used as a model for angled tools.

Was he pretty? No. But the utter manly ruggedness of him was deeply attractive, and his kindness was soothing in the way of an old friend.

A thought entered my mind that I really should enjoy this if I could. Maybe try to smell his aftershave. Notice more than the bare rudiments of his features. But inwardly I'd flushed cold, picturing Sarah scandalising the staff with my mini accident. The boss's precious daughter being hurt on their watch. The drama.

I was one phone call away from Dad showing up.

The last thing I needed was to stay in my family's house overnight, which he would insist on if he knew I was still in the capital. Tomorrow, I'd journey the hundred and twenty miles back to Bristol, to my home, and if I could get away without seeing either of my parents again for a month or two, my stress levels would thank me.

Taking a deep breath, I pulled myself together. Time to go.

"Mr McRae. Could you help me up?" I extracted a pack of tissues from my bag to mop up the blood. "I've ordered an Uber. It'll be outside soon."

"It's Callum. And your cab will wait and so will you. We'll stop the bleeding first. Patch you up. Keep to your seat until you're steady again."

I opened my mouth to protest, but the stranger gave me a stern look and, *sheesh*, it stirred something deep in some recess of my brain. A sensation that took away the insult of being ordered around, and instead spoke of protection and care. Of doing what he said because he had my best interests at heart. My blood on his hands and him not caring because he only wanted to fix me.

It made me want to bat my damn eyelashes.

As if he could read my mind, a small smile pulled at Callum's lips, and he tutted and shook his head. Then he took my packet of tissues and began carefully cleaning my injury. I sighed, my skin tingling everywhere he touched. A knight in shining armour. Where was he when I was free and single? Well, I still was. I hadn't officially accepted, but what choice did I have? At least Dominic hadn't reappeared.

The Highlander's touch was gentle.

Warm. He was very warm.

"Here!" Sarah returned with a white box, a red cross emblazoned on it. With one hand, my hero took it—as, somehow, he'd gained complete control—and in a minute had me cleaned and bandaged up. I rotated my freshly wrapped ankle on his instruction.

Callum worked his jaw as he regarded his efforts. "I dinna think it needs to be stitched, but you should get it checked all the same. Glass can stay in the skin. I'll take you on to a hospital, if you care to go."

"I...no. Thank you," was all I could say, my mouth too stupid to produce better words.

Sarah had finished sweeping up the glass, and she turned back to me with wide eyes. A spark of panic lit her eyes. "Hospital? I really think I should call your—"

"No!" My brain reengaged, and I cut her off. "It's not necessary. My ride's here." I waved my phone in a desperate attempt to convince her not to contact my dad. As if to prove how taken care of I was, I placed my hand on the big guy's arm and turned my attention to him. "Mr McRae? I'd really appreciate your assistance a moment longer."

Two strong hands landed on me as I wobbled to my feet, my sandal now acting as a slip-on, though I hadn't yet forgiven it for causing the debacle. Of all the footwear I could have worn, the elegant and slender-heeled sky-scraper beauties I coveted, bought, but hardly ever wore, an almost flat pair were the ones to fail me.

The man took my elbow and laid his other hand on my hip, while my forehead landed on a solid shoulder. I righted myself, my cheeks burning.

Well, damn.

"Come on, woman," he murmured and then led me away.

In the weirdest twist of my fun-filled evening, I, self-contained and independent Mathilda, would have followed him anywhere.

* * *

*O*utside, the damp and chilly February night licked my shins. With Callum's assistance, I made my way over the road to where my Uber idled. No pain affected my ankle, but I liked his help and wanted to cling on to it for a few moments more.

Men like him didn't come around very often, and I'd never see him again.

"Thank you," I said as he leaned in to open the door for me. "This was a strange evening, but you made it better."

Under the bright city streetlights, Callum's eyes shone blue. Pale, like his hair, and like his Celtic skin tone, but there was nothing weak in their intensity. He didn't speak.

"Do you often save damsels in distress?" I was flirting. Why was I flirting?

"If only I had the time. I made an exception for your grave injury," his low tones teased back, and I liked it. A lot. "Mathilda what?" he asked after a beat.

Ah, my surname. I had a standard response I gave to strangers—my mother's maiden name. My actual name, Dad's name, was too recognisable. Instinctively, I replied, "Mathilda Jones."

My mouth felt full of cotton wool, like the version of me I presented in order to protect myself had turned into an untruth. I didn't want to lie to this man.

"Bonnie name." His lips quirked in a half-smile.

We stood together. His broad body blocked the cold wind. The sheer warmth coming off him, rolling waves of heat, wrapped around my skin as he inched forward. For some reason I couldn't drag my gaze from his lips.

The idea of a one-night stand crossed my mind again. No, I wasn't that bold.

Then Callum's brow creased. "If I was staying longer in England, I'd ask for your number, Mathilda Jones."

I clutched my arms against my silky jacket. "If I was available, I'd give it."

Understanding settled between us, a cooling that had nothing to do with the weather. He inclined his head to the venue's entrance. "The man you were with—I saw someone walk away from you when I came in. It's none of my business, but what kind of man leaves his woman to go home alone? Does he even know you were hurt?"

His almost prim tone had me chuckling. "So you weren't just passing by when I cut myself?"

Callum huffed. "Are you asking if I worried when I saw you being abandoned? Aye. You went to sit down alone and you rubbed your head. You looked vulnerable, and that was all wrong. Did I also plan on talking to you because you're the most beautiful woman I have ever seen? True. I did."

Mmph. Sold, ladies.

I had a real problem with the whole hero complex, and of being the heroine wanting to be saved. So much so I needed to stamp it down and contain it as a fantasy. Ever since I was a girl, I'd dreamt of a man sweeping me off my feet and stealing me away to his stronghold. Protecting me from my father and taking my new baby sister with us. It was so anti-feminist, so backward in every way, I needed to make my life move forward. And yet here, standing in front of me, was the kind of guy who fit that image to a T, and I'd never been more interested.

Callum blew out a cloud of frosted breath. "Sorry for the flattery when you dinna need it. I dislike false pretences and can be overly honest. Sometimes brutal."

"I like brutal honesty." This stranger had my senses piqued, and now I wanted to stall. To talk more. "The guy... My life is complicated in a number of ways." I stopped myself, because I was in danger of spilling the whole story and I'd barely got my head around the offer. I was desperate to share it with someone. But Beth would rightfully lock horns with me, and my dad would blow his top. No one else knew me well enough to help.

"Complicated," he repeated. "Aye, I know that feeling well. I've enough to manage until I'm a hundred."

"Yet you helped me."

"How could I not?"

Easily, for most people. But not this man. I wondered... No, I had no right to wonder a solitary thing. Wondering only led to finding answers, and I needed ignorance.

Walk away, Mathilda. This hero isn't for you.

"Goodnight, Callum McRae. It was a pleasure meeting you."

He watched me for a long second, the look on his face one I couldn't read. Then he handed me into the car, and my driver sped us away into the winter's night. Out of the rear window, I watched the biggest man I'd ever met—both in stature and in first impressions—disappear.

3

FIRE

*M*athilda
The ear-splitting sound of a horn fractured my dream. I bolted up in bed, clasping the blanket to my chest. Then I clutched my hands to my ears instead because *oh God* that was loud. The fire alarm?

The long, piercing siren wailed from the hall and repeated through the building. Above my hotel room door, the emergency exit poured green light into the dark. Footsteps drummed outside.

Ugh, I was going to have to get up. I'd been having such an interesting dream, too. Of a wonderfully tall man who threw me over his very broad shoulders.

Nng.

Throwing on a long sweater over my sleep shorts and camisole, I jammed my feet into my winter boots, grabbed my key card, and left the room. People in various states of undress tied on white hotel robes or shrugged on coats as they entered the stairwell. I trailed after, debating turning back for a coat. But it was too late, and the flow of the crowd was against me.

Chilled air crept over my bare legs as I descended the internal concrete fire escape. At least if there was a fire, it couldn't be burning that hard. The emergency exit led me into the bitter winter night, and I shuffled along with the crowd, cursing myself for not grabbing warmer clothes.

Hotel staff ushered us to an open pavilion between tall office buildings. The wind whipped my hair and numbed my legs. I buried my chin in the collar of my sweater and hugged my arms tight around my body, but there was no avoiding that cutting, needle-like wind.

"Mathilda?"

That accent... I looked up to see none other than Callum McRae approaching, his friend at his side. My mouth dropped open. The men were fully dressed but obviously part of the evacuation, Callum's hair tousled on one side like he'd just leapt from his bed.

My dream loomed large in front of me, and he stared back like I was a mirage. "You. You're staying here?" I uttered.

"We are. Of all the hotels in the city..." He blew out a breath then twisted around and beckoned forward the dark-haired man. "James, this is Mathilda Jones. Mathilda, my friend James Fitzroy."

The younger man waved a hand. "I hope your ankle is improved?" he asked. His accent was only faintly Scottish, and well educated. I didn't know why I expected another Highlander. Maybe I'd heard Callum's gentle rolling Rs and decided all men should speak that way.

I nodded, still slightly stunned under my layer of cold. A shiver rippled over me. "And you're staying here," I stated again to Callum, like I needed it confirmed for the record. The hotel was only a few streets from the venue, but even so.

At the front of the crowd, a hotel staff member made an announcement, though it was impossible to hear over the whine of the wind. I'd seen the panicked-looking night manager hand over her walkie-talkie and disappear down the hotel's side alley a moment ago, and I gnawed my lip, guessing we might be stuck here a while. Callum's friend made a gesture then strode over to hear the news, leaving us alone.

Callum moved closer. "When your cab left, I thought I'd never see you again."

"You wanted to see me again?"

"Aye. Regardless of what we said. The alarm woke me from a dream about you."

Was it as racy as the dream I just had?

This was so strange. We watched each other. I shivered, violently this time, and Callum's eyes narrowed. In a swift move, he stripped his jacket from his shoulders and swung it around mine.

"Oh! You don't have to do that," I squeaked.

He pulled the lapels in then took a step away, his lips pursed. "It's three in the morning, and you've been forced from your bed by some arsehole pushing fire alarm buttons. The cold doesn't bother me, and you're half frozen. It's the least I can do."

Actually, I could huddle into your huge frame, rub my cheek against your ribbed sweater, and purr like a kitten. That would do nicely.

I snuggled down into the warmth of his coat and breathed in the scent of him. This was better than the dream.

"I don't like that you're cold," I murmured, my rigid muscles loosening as warmth crept in.

Callum blinked, as if surprised someone cared how he felt. "Did you manage to eat?"

"Um…" I wasn't one for missing meals, but after the event, I'd sat on the bed in my hotel room and, instead of ordering food, called my sister. At the dinner earlier in the evening, she'd been quiet to the point of withdrawn. I knew why, but we hadn't talked about it around the table.

A few days before, Scarlet had been caught shoplifting from a London boutique. Such an obvious cry for help, because she didn't want for anything. My parents gave her money, clothes, and whatever she needed.

Except for love.

Luckily, the store attendant knew Mom—a frequent customer—so Scarlet hadn't gotten into serious trouble.

"I love you," I'd told her on the phone. She'd still refused to talk about the incident, probably because I wasn't the one she'd try to make listen. "Everything will be all right."

"The day I'm old enough, I'm moving in with you."

How could I answer that? It only made my resolve to help her stronger.

James returned. "A false alarm. They're waiting on the fire official to approve the stand-down and let us back in."

Behind him, waiting by the trio of fully lit fire engines, a bulky-suited firefighter tapped a clipboard. My gaze narrowed in. The woman would need to speak to the night manager before we'd be allowed to return to our beds. The night manager who I'd seen vanishing down the side road, heading toward the front of the hotel.

I couldn't ignore this hotel's disastrous planning.

"I'll just be a moment," I murmured and crossed to where the fire official stood. The hotel receptionist waiting beside her had wide eyes and hopped from foot to foot.

"I really don't know what to say," he squeaked.

The fire official huffed. Over my shoulder, I sensed Callum sticking close.

"Excuse me." I smiled at the receptionist. The man glanced at me, above me, then away, his gaze searching the crowd.

"We can't let you and your husband back in yet. I apologise for the wait. We're doing everything we can."

"I'm not married, but are you looking for your night manager? Presumably, we're all waiting on her."

The guy's attention snapped to me. "Yeah. She's not answering her radio."

"One of your colleagues has the radio. Your night manager walked that way a few minutes ago, perhaps to check the front exit." I pointed in the right direction. "I suggest to speed things up, you could go and retrieve her yourself?"

The man blinked, relief replacing the anxiety on his face. "I'm just going to—" He took off down the side street.

I nodded at the grumpy firefighter—at work, I coordinated with emergency services all the time, so I knew the drill—and turned to Callum. Standing right behind me, as I'd suspected.

"Wouldn't want you to be cold for longer than necessary," I murmured.

A smile curled his lips.

See, when I gave up on the notion of being rescued, when that childhood dream was obliterated by real-life experience of how hard the world could be, I learned that every single person has to shift for themselves. Take responsibility for their own success within their individual circumstances.

In my own tragedy, I would be the one to sweep in and slay the dragon, and I didn't need anyone else's help.

After a minute, the receptionist returned, the flustered night manager in tow. She babbled about waiting in the wrong place, but the crisis was over. A paper was signed, she waved us forward, and the frozen, miserable crowd moved.

Callum fell in beside me, and we travelled back into the light and relative warmth of the lobby. Inside, I slipped the heavy jacket from my shoulders and returned it to its owner.

"Have breakfast with me." Callum ran his hands over the collar of the coat as if he'd enjoyed me wearing it, and my stomach gave a pleasant flip.

"I need to leave early. To get home to Bristol."

"Please, madam, sir, return to your room, we need to keep clear movement through the lobby," a different receptionist said, making the same assumption that Callum and I were a couple. Perhaps we looked good together.

"I'll be here until nine. Change your mind." Urgency crossed Callum's face, and I liked it, the effect I had on him.

God, I wanted to agree. But I needed to nip this in the bud. No matter how much I liked his manners, his competence, his face, and his damn scent. It had soaked into my clothes, and I smelled of him. Like I'd been marked and claimed. I liked too much too quickly, and it was obviously a stress response. The chemistry he made me feel. The rush in my blood and the ache in my centre.

"Goodnight, again. I'm going to bed."

"Fine, woman. You do that. Dream of me," he called in that sexiest of accents. "You can pick up where I left off."

Well, wouldn't that thought keep me warm for weeks?

* * *

The next morning, I stood, poised, in the Continental Hotel's lobby, the scent of brewing coffee from the breakfast service no distraction from the fresh hell of the digital notice screen's scrolling message.

No trains.

The derailment of an empty passenger train in the early hours meant all rail services to Bristol had been cancelled, and my rapid check of the coach websites told me their seats were fully booked.

I was stuck in London. After my rude awakening in the night, luck was in short supply.

Guests busied in and out of the revolving doors, breaking around me in a frothy, frowning tide. No sign of Callum McRae, but that was good.

Probably.

To avoid being jostled, I stepped aside and perched on a leather chair, resigned to calling a cab though not relishing the exorbitant price they would charge. I'd been raised in the comparative lap of luxury, but I lived on a budget I earned myself and disliked frivolous spending.

As I unlocked my phone's screen, my device buzzed in my hand. 'Beth', the screen read.

"Saw the news. I'm already on my way. Borrowed your car," my friend chirped after I accepted the call.

A grin crept over my face, and I patted the handle of my wheeled suitcase. It was 7A.M., and Beth's Friday night job in a fast food restaurant usually kept her out until late. I'd discounted the idea of calling her to come get me as she hardly slept as it was. "Didn't you work until the early hours?"

"It rained cats and dogs all night. The place was dead by ten, and Kendra sent me home. What a crock, because man do I need the money. Listen, I'll be an hour and a half, so text me the hotel address and have a luxurious long breakfast until I get there. We can sing songs from musicals all the way home. Even the creepy women-stealing one."

She meant *Seven Brides for Seven Brothers*. I loved that movie. It might have had something to do with my obsession with mountain men.

"Wow, you must really have missed me."

"Or maybe I just want an excuse to drive the Audi? I'm burning up your tyres on the motorway as we speak. You said it was due a new set, right?"

We both snickered, and tension eased from my shoulders as we said our goodbyes, but when I hung up the call, my phone vibrated again, somehow more aggressively this time. 'Dad', the screen read.

Oh, boy. The yelling started as soon as I uttered a cautious, "Hi?"

Dad commenced. With hardly a breath drawn, he covered how embarrassed he was to hear about my accident second-hand. Then he got down to business. "Worse, Mathilda, is that you took silly risks! You left with a stranger. Did I raise you this way? You should be looking to settle down and be respectable, not—" He continued on about my mystery man.

That confused me for a second—as much as I loved my dad, he had set ideas on dating which he'd force fed to me since I'd become old enough to notice boys. Then I worked it out. His floor staff would have mentioned me leaving with the big Highlander. Heh, let him chew over that description. No wonder he was rattled, as a matter of principle, Dad always hated men bigger than him.

My father's words remained distant in my ear while I recalled the acutely pleasant sensations of being taken care of by Callum McRae.

My father finally calmed and asked, "And where are you now?"

"My hotel's lobby." I bit my tongue, but it was too late.

"I see. Since you're still in the city, you will come to my office. Dominic Hanswick is here for a meeting this morning. We'll be discussing the marketing of the new label, and I want you to be a part of it."

Storm Force was a new line of spirits Dad had dreamed up. His next big thing. Expensive, top-end single malt whiskies, boutique vodkas; classic tastes, select distilleries, exclusive prices. He wanted me to work on the marketing, but I'd need to leave my current job to have the time. He hadn't approved of my events coordinator career choice, which I adored. Dad assumed I'd join his company at some point. It was getting harder to say no.

I dreamt of creating my own business, but I needed to keep Dad happy for Scarlet's sake.

"Storm Force's portfolio has changed since I told you about it. Dominic has lost investors, following his troubles, so we've reduced the expenditure. You'll find it a challenge, and I know you can help. What time will you be here?"

I opened my mouth, but no excuse was forthcoming. The very last thing I wanted this morning was to sit opposite Dominic, with my father in the room, talking strategy but being secretly cajoled into a marriage by one man and a career I didn't want by the other.

Dominic's troubles made me pity him, but I also thought him a fool and a single-minded, selfish man.

Yet I had no reason to refuse Dad. No alternative came to mind.

Then a warm, pleasantly scented breeze hit me, and I raised my head to see the glass door to the gym swing open.

A man emerged—James, the dark-haired man who'd been with Callum last night—then a hot and sweaty Callum *oh-would-you-stop-it-with-the-muscles* McRae loomed large behind him.

Fate, if I believed in it, was trying to tell me something. This time, I was going to listen.

4

I'VE ONLY JUST MET YOU

*C*allum

It was official, I was careening full pelt toward a heart attack before I reached thirty. Probably within the next hour at this rate.

After travelling all the way to London on the hunt for a businessman who refused to return my calls, I was going to have to jump on a plane back to the Highlands. A different pursuit in mind.

The twins, my sixteen-year-old brothers who lived under my roof, were up to no good.

They'd left their ma's house where they were meant to stay put for the weekend and neither of them were answering my calls.

I'd cut their bloody phones in half when I caught up with them.

They've scarpered, over to you, read the text message Patricia sent half an hour ago while I'd been flat on my back hefting weights, and now she wasn't answering me, either. I pictured the woman finding her spare room empty, rolling her eyes, and returning to her snug bed with her new husband and new baby daughter. Not that I blamed her. The boys drove me to distraction, but I had the space and time for them. The havoc they'd wreak on her neat Edinburgh home would be second only to a hurricane dropping by for tea.

The twins would give a saint a stroke.

"For fuck's sake." I sent yet another message as we readied to leave the gym. "We're going to need to go back early. Check flights, will ye? I'll call Gordain and see if he's around to go chase them down."

James made a humming noise, staring at his own phone. Then his eyebrows pulled in. "No need. They'll be home before we get there." He pushed the glass door to the gym open ahead of me, and we entered the cooler reception. "Look. Ally shared a picture of his coffee. The location reads Pitlochry. They're driving back."

I blinked in surprise at the screen held in front of me. For one, that my friend had social media accounts. My youngest brothers were rubbing off on him. For two, he was right. Pitlochry was on the way home to the Highlands from Edinburgh. The twins were heading back to the castle.

My pulse rate reduced a dram, and I made my mental search party stand down, but I huffed a breath in frustration, trying to dislodge the fear of them getting hurt. "Aye, but that's nae the point. I told them to stay. It was two days. Not even that. How hard is it for the wee beggars to follow orders?"

James chuckled, and we made our way across the lobby. An arsehole in a suit, importance stamped all over him, tried to get in my way, until he looked up and thought better of it. Good, because I wasn't in the mood. I glared, and the man ducked around me. I had a shower and a hearty breakfast in mind, to power myself up for the day ahead.

Then my friend laid his hand on my arm.

"Do you recall what you said this morning?" James placed the words carefully, something like enjoyment playing over his face and into his formal speech. Now, I knew he was changing. In the first weeks of him living with us, I'd barely got him to crack a smile. Now, a few months under my mentorship, he was almost grinning as he said, "That I wasn't to let you make a fool of yourself over the woman who'd told you no twice?"

I drew my eyebrows in. What was he getting at? Mathilda had said she was leaving early, and I hadn't chased her down despite every bone in my body telling me to.

Then my heart jumped as I caught his drift and I swung my gaze around. Holy Christ on a bike. Sitting pretty at a low table was Mathilda. *Still here.*

Adrenaline jolted me.

I cleared my throat. "Forget what I said. Do you think… I might just…"

"I'll keep trying the office number. Why don't you go and say hello? Maybe it will be third time lucky." James patted my shoulder and headed over to the stairs. I didn't need telling again. Ideas of taking an earlier flight home to bash my brothers' heads together left my mind like they were never there.

My strides ate the ground.

It didn't matter how complicated my life was—I wasn't lying to her when I'd said I'd no time for anything, let alone asking out a beautiful woman who lived in a different country—I knew when I'd made a mistake. I was more than man enough to admit my faults, and I knew to listen to my thumping heart.

My hands had shaken as I'd tended to her poor ankle. My pulse had raced when I'd placed my coat around her while we'd waited in the cold.

She'd been in my dreams, before and after the alarm.

Pretty eyes and long legs I couldn't avoid noticing. If that wasn't a clear enough message, who knew what would be. I had let her walk away without even trying. Not good enough. Not by a mile.

At the last moment before I reached her table, I recalled I was wearing my gym clothes. Skin tight Under Armour. And I was sweaty from my head to my balls from working the weights.

I stopped two feet away and linked my fingers in front of my shorts. Mathilda's polite smile of recognition broadened with amusement, and she held up a finger to pause me while she finished her call. Shame to say, but I hadn't noticed the phone in her hand, only the blonde spiralling curls of her hair and the way they tickled the curve of her neck.

"You're still here. My damsel in distress," I murmured.

"Sorry, Dad," Mathilda spoke into the phone. "I'm not free this morning. There's someone here I need to talk to. Bye."

With an over-emphasised action of irritation, she cut off the call even though I didn't think the other person, her father, had finished talking. Mathilda tossed the device into her bag. Then she drew a long breath.

So, her da was a problem. I logged the information away.

"My knight in shining armour. Looking a little warmer now."

I had any number of troubles. From the backtracking bastard I'd force one way or another to meet with me today, to two missing teenagers, but my priorities shifted as Mathilda gestured at the too-small chair opposite her.

The invite couldn't be ignored. I dropped into it. The fake leather creaked, and my muscles bunched.

I bounded right back up.

"If I can shower and change in ten minutes, will ye still be here?"

Mathilda blinked.

"Whatever your plans are, shift them. Have breakfast with me," I demanded, aware I was looming over her and barking orders. What the hell was wrong with me? "I mean to say," I started, casting about for better words, but she held up a hand.

Her face, finely made and with schooled features, tipped up to regard me. Humour lit her eyes. "Did you just ask me out again? Even though I've turned you down twice?"

"Aye. I ken what you're going to say, but I have to ask. Persuade ye, somehow."

"I told you I can't date."

"Neither can I. Come anyway. Tell me why." I had a burning need to know what her complications were. A compelling urge to fix them.

I'd been a big man from the time I was a thirteen-year-old boy, and now I had all the eloquence to match. It was like I'd never met a woman before. She'd send me away, and rightly so.

"Ten minutes, Mr McRae. I'm free for an hour. But it isn't a date. Just breakfast."

Time slowed, and my pulse pounded in my ears. Was that…? Had she…?

"Hadn't you better get going? Don't keep me waiting."

Fuck me. She'd agreed. "I'm a lot of things: stubborn, impulsive, and overbearing," I said in a strange amount of oversharing. "But I have never, ever let anyone down."

She fought a smile and checked an imaginary watch on her bare wrist. *Right.* With a long last look, I was away.

* * *

*M*athilda kept her cold fingers in mine as we entered a half-empty hotel restaurant, and I had the urge to pull her into a hug to warm her bones. After

I'd flown down the stairs, I'd taken her hand like I'd had no choice, leading her through the foyer.

A chirpy waiter seated us by the window, looking out on a dirty grey street, and my pang of missing home grew stronger. My mountain, my loch, my open space and sky. I wasn't suited to being in town. This wasn't what I was built for.

The lass lived in a city. Bristol. Almost the farthest city in the opposite corner of the United Kingdom from mine. But I was never a man to be daunted by obstacles. And at least it wasn't the U.S.—I'd picked up a hint of an accent.

"You have a bonnie lilt to your voice. Not solely English."

"You can tell? My mom is Californian, though we've always lived here. Dating would be even more problematic across five thousand miles."

With a huff of a laugh, I placed my phone next to my cutlery, and Mathilda eyed it.

"I dinna mean to be rude, but I've a need to keep my phone in sight. I'll ignore it for all but one call I'm waiting on." The twins had yet to open my messages, but when they did, they'd know better than to ignore me.

"Work?"

"Family. A wee problem I'm trying to sort out."

Her shoulders lowered, and she slipped her smart coat from her shoulders, tucking it on the chair next to her. The waiter reappeared and took our order and, as he left, Mathilda checked out my hand as I replaced the menu. Sneaky. I caught her eye and bit my lip, enjoying the hint of pink that flooded her cheeks.

"You said family, I heard wife. You're not married, then?"

"Never tried it, but I've only just met you. Give me a chance," I joked, but the pensive look she'd been carrying since the lobby intensified. It hadn't even occurred to me that she might be hitched, as I'd say she was a few years younger than me, but I slid my gaze to her hands to carry out the same check.

Bare. Good.

Eight years ago, at eighteen and scarcely a man, I'd become laird and master to the McRae ancestral estate, only my instincts and brawn on my side. With three younger brothers, a stepmother on the brink of a nervous breakdown and near bankruptcy from Da's death, I still held it together.

Instincts kept me going and served me well. They could not be wrong for the gorgeous woman in front of me who regarded me like I was a puzzle she had to figure out.

"I'm not married either. But," she took a breath and turned her attention to the street, like it was easier to address the bundled-up passersby, "I might choose to be soon. That's what I meant when I said my life was complicated and why I won't lead you on. Why this is just breakfast and not a date."

As that sunk in, she rolled her shoulders then met my eye.

"I received a marriage proposal last night. And I'm running out of reasons to turn it down."

* * *

*W*ith my hot head occasionally getting the better of me, I sometimes spoke before I thought, but ninety-nine times out of a square hundred, my gut feeling was right. Which was why, for the life of me, I couldn't understand what Mathilda was talking about. "Why did your boyfriend ask if he wasn't sure you'd say yes?"

"The man who offered me marriage is not my boyfriend. I hardly know him."

I had no idea what to do with that information. "The way I see it, you meet someone, do or dinna fall in love, want to stay with them forever if it's the happier option. Where in that is marrying a near stranger?"

She gave a self-conscious laugh, a hard little *ha*. "When there's a reason for saying yes that outweighs the negatives."

Our coffees arrived, but I could only stare.

"You've got to give me more than that."

Mathilda raised a curved eyebrow. "Do I? I've already overshared on an intensely personal problem I have no idea what to do with. How about you share something now. You live in Inverness. What do you do there?"

She picked up her fancy coffee and blew on it, and I could see the topic was closed. *For now, lass.*

Still flummoxed, I made a rash decision. If you wanted something, you went all in to get it. I wanted to know Mathilda better. I liked the small window into her personality I'd seen, and Christ was she beautiful. Armies of men could die trying to score a kiss from those lips.

"I live near Inverness, not in it. Forty minutes south. I'm an estate owner."

"What kind of estate?"

Here goes nothing. From my wallet, I took out one of the business cards I'd had made, and I offered it across the table. Mathilda eyed me then took the wee white card, the castle embossed under dark grey type. My full name in a solid font.

"Laird Callum McRae of McRae Castle and Estate. Laird?" She sat back, her mouth open. "Is this for real?"

"Aye."

"Did you buy a place and name it after yourself?"

I barked a laugh that had heads turning. "Nae. The name was given to me in the same way my birthright was."

"You're a laird. A Scottish lord. You're single, and you live in a castle. With stone towers and crenelated walls? Safe from marauders. Do you swim naked in the loch and fight dragons in the mountains on the weekends?" Mathilda's voice sounded strained.

"All apart from the dragons, aye. One of my brothers and

31

I go out on the mountain rescue once every month or so, but naked loch swimming is a rarity. The water will freeze your b— Er, well, it's cold all year round."

"And I ran into you at random. Jesus." She tipped her head back and spoke to the ceiling, mouthing something like, "Why couldn't I have met him last week? What is wrong with the world?"

I suppressed a grin and sat more comfortably in my seat, enjoying her reaction. I'd never before used my title to impress a woman. I'd never had the need.

Mathilda didn't seem the sort of woman to be easily moved.

"My turn for a personal question, now. The marriage proposal you had... I get that ye dinna want to talk about it, but why the confusion? Can I help you with a reason to say no?" Then, because my mouth had the habit of speaking before I could think, I said something daft. "Because here I am, waiting on your every word since I first laid eyes on ye. Fate keeps throwing us together. We ought to listen."

Mathilda returned her attention to me, that same hesitation replacing her mirth. "You know, I thought about fate when I saw you come out of the gym. But you told me you weren't available either."

"Because of where I live, and my lack of free time. That doesn't mean I wouldnae change my world for the right reasons." More daft talk, though honest. I'd loved once or twice before, but as a lad. Testing out the emotion and growing the capacity. Even then I knew the real deal would floor me and have me on my knees, offering my life up to the lass who'd stolen my heart.

"I considered having a one-night stand with you." Blooms of colour stained her cheeks. "To see if I could give up on intimacy and focus on the purely physical. The marriage I was offered would include separate beds, of course."

Some fucker had turned up the heat in the restaurant. I pulled at my collar. "Christ. But you decided against it."

"Yes. And if it wasn't for this," she gesticulated between us, her hand weaving in the air and wafting the steam from the mugs, "I wouldn't have said anything at all."

"What do you mean by this?" I made the same hand gesture, but once, and slower. My voice hoarse.

Her cheeks grew darker. "Chemistry. I don't know."

Shite. She felt it, too. It wasn't just me. The impulse that had me wanting to pull her in. "The way I can feel the presence of you across the table though we're not touching."

"Something like that."

My phone buzzed on the wood in front of me. I ignored it, unable to look away from Mathilda.

"You were waiting on a call?" she said faintly, and I relented, dragging my gaze away.

"Patricia. That's my boys' mother. Oh fuck, what now?" With a grimace, I answered the phone, unwilling to let the world back in now I had found a reason to leave it.

"Callum!" Patricia's shrill voice deafened me, capturing my full attention. I moved the device an inch from my ear but still heard her perfectly when she yelled, "They took Grant's car. The wee swines stole my husband's car right out of our garage. They are out of control, Callum, and I hold you responsible!"

5

BRIGHT, AND MADE OF DISAPPOINTMENT

Mathilda

Callum McRae had children. The mother of his children had called, and he'd sworn a few times then leapt to his feet, stomping away to take the call in private.

Did it matter that he had kids? An irrational spark of jealousy flared. I liked so much about him. Every word he'd said had painted a picture of responsibility and of a traditional man. Homeowner, landowner, a damn castle owner, it had lit me up like a pinball machine.

But whoever wanted him had to share him with another woman. The degree to which I disliked that almost took my breath away.

The bell over the restaurant's external door nearly came off its hinge as Callum thrust his way through. He fell into his seat opposite me, dialling another number on his phone.

"I'm sorry about this," he muttered, stabbing at the screen. "I have the care of my youngest brothers, and they are a force to be reckoned with. This weekend they were meant to be staying with their mother, but they took off in her new husband's car. He's a wet blanket but he's mighty angry as he needs the car for work tomorrow. I dinna know what gets into their heads. It's Ally, obviously," he continued, half to himself. "Always the ringleader. Wasp goes along with him for a quiet life, but he knows better."

Brothers. Not sons. No baby mama. Well.

The call on his phone connected, and the video screen activated. A young man's face appeared, grinning broadly under a shock of blond hair, a pair of headphones slung around his neck. "Cal!" he yelled over the grumble of an engine.

"Dinna you give me Cal. Where the hell are you?" Callum barked.

"Eh? About an hour from home. We're making great time. Wasp's behind the wheel, so don't you fret, I'm not yakking and driving." He panned the camera around to an identical boy, though with shorter hair, sitting in the driver's seat. Wasp, I presumed, gave a salute and returned his attention to the road.

Callum drew a breath. "Alasdair Maddock McRae—"

Ally reappeared on the screen. "I know what you're going to say. About the car. But we have a plan."

Their older brother ground the heel of his hand into his forehead. "Do you, now? Besides thievery, potential arrest for not having a full licence, the stack of firewood you'll chop to work off your debt to the family, the heart attack you'll give me—"

"Aye. All that." Ally waved a hand, clearly not listening. "Fitz was going to collect us later, so tonight we'll drive back in convoy, give Grant his seriously shite ride back—honestly, Cal, if we had a grannie, she wouldnae be seen dead in this— then Fitz can bring us home. Genius! Ma was planning to stay home today, so it made no difference to them."

"Are you kidding me?"

"Don't pretend you thought we'd stay. They sit in front of the TV. All day. And Lily is cute, but she's a baby and boring as—"

Callum's hand dipped, and for a moment, the screen rested on me.

"Is that a lady you're with? Who is she? Hi! Woo! Put her back on screen!"

I couldn't help it, but I laughed. At Callum's dramatic huffing, at the boys and their ridiculous antics and their complete lack of fear. It told me so much. I had no idea how their brother came to be their carer, even if I could guess with their mother having a new husband and baby, plus him owning a castle so presumably having the space, but the boys obviously adored him. And ran rings around him.

Callum McRae: the responsible hero. Raising a family, being the one in charge, trying to keep them safe. The stranger in front of me became fully fleshed. My imagination projected a baby on each arm and a castle at his back. I was screwed. Totally and utterly.

"Wasp, did ye see? Cal's big meeting was a front. There's no bad guy doing him out of a deal. He snuck off to London to see a lass. Listen, woman! He might look big and impressive, but he's a terrible snorer," the boy yelled. "His temper in the morning is like a barbarian with a migraine, and he's got the worst smelling feet."

To my even greater amusement, the apples of Callum's cheekbones grew pink. He sat up straight and barked at the boys, giving them orders to drive safely, stay within the speed limit, and go straight home. After he hung up, he sent a couple of quick messages then stuffed the phone in his pocket. He closed his eyes for a moment, then returned a sheepish gaze to me.

"I've blown my chance of impressing you, aye?"

"Is one of your brothers really named Wasp?" I asked, not willing to admit how much the opposite to his statement was true.

"A nickname. There's four of us, five, if you include James, who we've adopted. I'm the oldest, then there's Gordain, he's in the RAF, so not at home so often, then William and Alasdair are the twins. Wasp and Ally."

"And they drive?"

"Aye, have done since they could reach the pedals. It's necessary where we live, but they're sixteen, so have a year until they are legal. But you can see how well rules work with them. I spend most of my days fretting after their safety."

"I've got a younger sister," I blurted.

Then that was it, our food arrived—a feast of sausages and bacon for him, eggs benedict for me—and we settled into an easy conversation. I kept my cards close to my chest about my family, but confessions about work and my home life flew off my tongue. The joy of working in events and how it suited me to the core. It was like I'd known Callum for years, not for a total of twelve hours.

His eyes lit when he talked about his home. They shone with warmth when he grumbled about his brothers, and my heart swelled for a specific reason. Ally and Wasp were obviously half brothers, not full blood. Yet not once had he referenced the split. At no time did he distance himself from them and their mischievous ways, and the extent to which they were a family was clear.

It almost broke my heart to hear.

It was oh-so unalike to my experience. To the rot that ate away at my family's foundations. The difference was stark and highly addictive. I wanted to see them all together, witness the bond, and work out how it was done.

By the time my phone buzzed in my purse—Beth, with a

ten-minute warning—I didn't want to leave. Fancy that. Of all the big man's attractions, his family life had me reconsidering my plans.

Wait. Was I having second thoughts?

Dominic had laid his cards out in his proposal. His tone had been brisk. "What is the girl, thirteen, fourteen? Five years married to me, with her living at your side, then she'll be an adult. You, in turn, will save my reputation, and all you need to do is follow a few simple rules. Don't you see? This is in both our interests. Your father trusts me. You can have everything you want."

Dad didn't trust anyone, not really, but Dominic was right in everything else. And in exchange, he'd get his reputation repaired. Marriage to me would smooth over the damage of his affair, and his status with his shareholders would be restored.

But then there was Callum. I still barely knew him, but my body and mind had already started to attach. He invited it, like he could take care of me.

My father had his old-fashioned ways. His conservative view on young women and their sex lives was the main reason he wouldn't allow Scarlet to move in with me and Beth, some wild picture in his head of us having men over to stay and all kinds of debauchery. He'd point blank refused my request to take on Scarlet, even though he loathed seeing her every day. Even if it cut him to the bone and caused infinite damage to my sister's self-esteem. Caused all kinds of negative behaviours I needed to stop.

Mom begged me to never ask again.

I so desperately wanted to fix it. For everyone.

Callum and I left the restaurant, with me insisting on splitting the bill, though the argument left him adorably cranky.

James, his friend, waited in the lobby. He offered us a shy, polite smile. Callum beckoned to him, and we walked together out of the rear hotel exit, Callum wheeling my luggage.

"Any luck?" Callum asked.

"I got through to the office. They wouldn't allow me to book an appointment, but they are open even though it's a Saturday. I believe the best approach will be to show up on the doorstep."

At the end of the street, my red Audi came into sight, Beth behind the wheel.

"You never told me what you're doing in London," I said to Callum as I waved to Beth.

The car accelerated up the road and halted abruptly alongside us. A wide parking space yawned, but Beth didn't pull in. She slid the window down, and a show tune blasted out. 'Sobbin' women' from *Seven Brides for Seven Brothers*. I grinned, and she cocked her head.

A devilish look filled her gaze, and she eyed the space, the width of the road, and the empty street. "You didn't say there were men here. Whoa, mama."

"Beth," I warned. She was planning something.

"Be right back."

The Audi screeched off to the end of the access road, tyres squealing, Beth pulling a smart U-turn. I heaved a sigh. I should have yelled after her that she couldn't pull this kind of stunt in London, but it was too late.

"Gentlemen, meet Beth," I murmured, bracing myself a little. "Don't be alarmed."

Either side of me, the men stood taller, their eyes trained on the red car.

As the Audi sped back up the street, Callum inched closer, placing a hand on my shoulder and reaching out to do the same to his friend.

Then Beth slammed on the brakes and pulled her trademark stunt—a one-eighty degree turn to spin the car around and precision slide it into the narrow parking space. Road grit spat. Smoke billowed, and my closest friend in the world beamed from the bouncing driving seat, chuckling at her cleverness.

"Christ," muttered Callum. His arm had slid around my shoulders, holding me to him, and the other was now clamped on James. To reassure him? But when I glanced at the younger man's face, I recoiled.

His handsome features had twisted in fear, and he held himself so taut, he looked like he'd snap. "What in God's name— What the hell did you do?" James shouted, red flooding his face, terror contorting his words.

"Steady," Callum murmured. "It was just a stunt."

Beth popped her door and hopped out, all five foot nothing of her. Her wild brown curls swept over, and her holey black jumper slid from her shoulder. "Huh? That was epic. I nailed it."

James found the use of his muscles and spun on his heel, marching into the hotel.

"Shit." Beth's face fell and she tracked James's flight path. "I didn't mean to scare anyone. I was in total control. And no way could I resist that chance." She bounced over to where I waited with Callum. We exchanged a swift hug.

"This is Callum," I said. "And that was James."

"He'll be all right." Callum glanced at the hotel, but worry clouded his gaze. "He's nae great with noise and drama."

"I'm just going to—" Beth pointed finger guns at the lobby, then strode off. "Want a coffee for the road?" she yelled back, reaching the doors.

After I refused her offer, careful fingertips touched my face, and Callum brought my gaze back to his blue eyes. "I want to see you again." He placed his words as if they were individually weighted. A little too heavy. Not quite balanced.

My pulse fluttered. "I want that, too."

A smile made of relief and something else pulled at his lips. "Finally, she admits it. You have my card. My number. Will you use it?"

Conflict flipped my stomach, but yes, I was going to call him.

Like I even had a choice. He wasn't the sort of man Dad would easily tolerate, but everything else about him was perfect. Dominic's proposal suddenly became a joke, and all I could see was the big man at my side. He was too good to be true. He seemed to want marriage, and he was everything I'd ever dreamed about.

I stopped the *whys* and *hows* in their tracks and inclined my head, and he ran his hand down my arm and interlaced his fingers with mine. Blood rushed to my head. Heat pooled in my belly.

No. No choice at all.

"Good." Callum held my gaze. "Now, you asked why I was here. I'm in London to confront a man who owes me money. On my estate, we have a distillery, and a year ago we had a big order for whisky. The sort of order that would keep the wolves at bay for years to come. The bastard reneged on the deal. Offered me half what he promised."

Cold slunk into my veins.

"I dinna believe in lawyers and waiting around, so I'll see him and force him to explain. Tell him what his decision will do to my family."

No, it couldn't be.

"He's an alcohol distributor?" I could barely utter the words.

"Aye. Maximus Storm, if you can believe the name. False, like his promises. Like the small print on his contracts. He's the worst kind of charlatan but he met his match when he crossed me."

Dad had done this. His new venture for selling top-end spirits. Oh God, it was Dominic's fault. His reduced investment. All because he couldn't keep his hands off a married woman.

Callum continued, naming my father's faults one by one, exposing each one like I didn't already know them. Hadn't lived with them and excused them my entire life.

Every word cut deep, severing the tender little bond I felt for the big man and his wonderful world. The nicks bled, but I kept my face unaffected. Because what was the point? I couldn't tell him.

He was right. In everything he said. But it was my dad, and Callum didn't understand what my father had been through and why he was so ruthless. How the bottom line always came first and how all his deals had clauses to keep him safe.

Why I loved him and needed him onside. For Scarlet, but for Dad's own sake, too.

Callum wasn't an option now. I had to walk away.

I really was stuck with Dominic.

Beth reappeared in the entrance to the hotel, James at her side. She tripped as she peered up at him, and James caught her. Beth beamed, gave him a hug, then darted over to the car.

The dark-haired man stood there, frozen, his face impassive. But his hand hovered over the place on his arm where Beth had clutched him.

"I need to go," I murmured, looking anywhere but at Callum. Then I swallowed the hurt and forced a smile, bright and made of disappointment. Callum spoke, his words low and entreating. I didn't hear a single one. Didn't focus on the face which represented childhood fantasies and made-up worlds. Because that was all they were. And I had reality to handle.

Then we drove away. I set my face and got on with my life.

6

FATE OR LUCK, GOOD OR BAD

Callum

The cement I'd been hacking out of the joints of the castle walls for weeks was destroying my fingertips one by one. A miserable job, though essential to stop the creeping damp eating away the ancient stone. Even the twins were quiet, suppressed by the ever-present Scottish drizzle we were working to banish from our home.

"Call it," Ally whined from above me on the dripping scaffold. He hefted the tub of high quality mortar we were using to refill the gaps. "For the love of all that is holy, can we be done for the day?"

I straightened my aching back and surveyed our progress. The five of us working on it, with Gordain home for the weekend, had the task almost complete. The kicker was, I recalled my father putting in shitty cement when he was laird and I was a wee boy. I'd learned at his knee how to cheap out on your responsibilities and fritter your income away on gambling and drinking. How to die, leaving as much turmoil and disaster behind you as you could. An estate poised to take a nosedive into being sold.

One son in custody and the others fighting for his release.

Da and I were two very different men.

I was doing it right this time, the walls, putting in breathable lime mortar and readying for the den's custom-built windows to get us watertight. But money didn't grow on trees. After the Storm Force deal had been signed for my whisky, I'd ordered the pricey windows, alongside upgrading the distillery which cost a bomb on its own. The estate pulled in money from the small businesses like the distillery, from rents, government land subsidies, half Gordain's salary, and whatever I could earn, but it was never enough.

Now, to afford my bills, I'd had to do something about the debt owed me.

Last week, I'd made a final decision about Storm Enterprises and their breach of contract. They'd given me the same line over and over about shifting profit margins and it being my fault for not reading every minuscule detail at the back of the pack. Call me old-fashioned, but if a person looks you in the eye and shakes your hand on a promise, as Storm Force's Dominic Hanswick had on his visit, failing to deliver it was on them, not on you.

The cowards refused to meet with me in London, which left me no choice. I was taking action against Maximus Storm and his cronies. Pride was at stake, let alone the security of my family.

"Come on, Cal. If your mind wasn't away with a certain fair-haired lass, you'd let us finish up."

"We're done." I ignored the painful quip. "There's too much to finish before dark." Tomorrow morning would see this particular repair complete. Thank God.

A collective cheer went up from my brothers, and we downed tools, dragging tarpaulin over the drying mortar and the holes we'd made in my poor castle's walls. Inside the great hall, the twins tossed their coats on the stone hearth in front of the roaring fire, shucked off their boots, and took off up the stairs.

I'd complain at them for leaving a mess, but it was all I'd been doing for the past month. Since a certain lass had ghosted me, throwing me into a miserable mood.

Gordain pitched a sodden hat into the steaming clothes pile then rubbed a hand over his shorn head. "I'm away tonight. After dinner."

"You've been called back?"

"Aye. I'll not return for a few weeks. But…when I do, I should know my streaming."

His career stream—the selection process for pilot—was almost up. I clapped his shoulder, harder than I meant from the nerves. *Christ, please let him get it.* He was due a break. "Let me know."

"I will. As soon as I do."

My brother, the second of us, served in the RAF, and had applied for a hard-sought-after training programme to fly search and rescue helicopters. With both of us volunteering for the Cairngorms mountain rescue, the career was a natural fit for him. Despite being a military man, my brother was not bloodthirsty, and saving lives, rather than taking them, suited him well.

Though excellent at his job, the man needed focus, and I worried for him as much as I worried for the twins. If they streamed him to rotary, as he wanted, we'd all be relieved.

"Did you reply to Lachlan?" Gordain took an armful of split logs into the enormous fireplace and tossed them into the flames. The fire leapt, feeding greedily. We had a thing over never letting it go out. A superstition, you could say.

"Nae yet. I'd planned to burn his letter and send back the word 'No' written in ink made from the ashes," I grouched.

Lachlan was kin. Our father's cousin, who Da had

despised and who held the same opinion in return. A man I respected but had quarrelled with over land rights, his property, and mine sharing a quagmire of muddled borders. I'd gone to his door in a mood and ended up rowing with the man, my temper taking over my mouth.

We hadn't spoken since, though he'd sent us an invitation to the lavish party he was throwing for his fiftieth birthday. A true Highlands event with games and bagpipes, knowing him. The twins were desperate to go, but I was in no mind to bend to Lachlan's will and accept his hospitality. He had an idea to be a father figure to me, and it rankled my pride.

My brother coughed. As I looked again, Gordain's square jaw was set, mischief in his eyes. "And are you going to tell me about the woman before I leave? Dinna wave me off. You've been a bear with a sore head since your trip to London. The twins have more punishments than free time, and you've never been this hard on them before."

Behind me, James huffed a laugh. "They did steal a car."

I shrugged my jacket off, taking my padded shirt with it. Every muscle ached from either the work or from holding myself stiff to prevent from freezing. Scotland in early spring was not the ideal time to do the repair work, but it was that or suffer the creeping damp. I pointed at our friend. "What he said."

Gordain rolled his eyes, switching his attention to James. "Hey, Fitz? Did you meet this mystery lass? Give me the story. Ally's a terrible gossip, but he has none of the facts and he only caught a glimpse of her face."

Ignoring them, I moved around, picking up wet clothes and draping them on the iron drying mount some ancestor had installed inside the opening to the huge fireplace a century or so ago. We had a modern laundry room, but the fire burned so why not use the heat for clothes that already smelled of the outdoors.

"I'm not sure I can help, aside from thinking her very pleasant," James said, and I kept busy at my task, my cheeks burning from the blaze. Only the blaze.

"She pretty?"

I peered out of the corner of my eye. James put up a hand as if to deflect the question. "I'm not answering that. I have a feeling someone might get defensive should I comment on her looks in any way."

Gordain was being deliberately provocative, but I'd not spoken about Mathilda to anyone and I suddenly wanted to. The rejection hurt, and it really shouldn't, as what time had I had to form an attachment? But I had, all the same. I'd dreamed up a life where I had someone of my own. Typical Callum, nought to sixty in a heartbeat.

With my family, I tried to hide my concerns about the estate, our bills and debts and the worsening state of the castle—as soon as we repaired one wall, another pile of stones crumbled—but to have a sympathetic ear, a hug, and a bit of reassurance... I wanted that.

And I'd made Mathilda into that woman. She worked in events, and it had set me to thinking as she'd described what she loved. We didn't use the land or the castle enough in that way—too far from my comfort zone to make any sense of it—and it was crying out for someone with that expertise to run a business here. To make use of the space and the history of the land and the old building in a way I never could. See, I'd even found her a role of her own. Something I thought she'd like.

The depths of my own pathetic need yawned in front of me.

I barely knew her, but I missed her. At least the idea of her.

It was a deeply uncomfortable feeling, being vulnerable, and I rarely allowed it, but Gordain and James were my closest allies, my seconds-in-command, if a man could have two, and I needed to share this wedge inside my chest.

"I thought she seemed pretty taken with Callum, but I know next to nothing about women. She had a friend, this insane driver—"

"Mathilda never called me," I blurted, interrupting James as I stepped away from the heat. "She took my number. I should have asked for hers, but then if she wanted to see me again, she'd have called. Ye ken? So it's a waste of time me thinking about her."

Two men, James with a shock of dark hair and Gordain with his blond and shorn, regarded me. Both were better looking than me, I was man enough to own it, but I thought I at least had something in my favour.

Mathilda had seemed attracted, but obviously not enough.

"Maybe she lost your number?" James offered, because he was kind, if entirely naïve, after the shitty life and gilded cage he'd suffered before he'd come to us.

"She could have found me. Searched for the castle online. It's hardly a secret."

Gordain ran a thumb along his jaw. It was growing dark in the hall, with no one having put the big lights on, and fire-light illuminated my brother's features. It softened him a wee bit. "What if there was another reason keeping her from calling? Some sort of misunderstanding. Are ye just going to leave off and forget you ever met her?"

That didn't sound like something I would do.

"That does nae sound like something you would do," my brother echoed in the way of a challenge.

"She did have a lot on her plate." I adjusted Ally's coat on the frame. He'd torn the sleeve. For fuck's sake, he could bloody well sew it back up. "But I can't be chasing after

49

someone who doesn't want to know me. It wouldnae be right."

"Only if you're sure that's her intention." James, this time, like the two of them would do anything to lift my brooding.

Was I sure? Not a bit, and that somehow made me crosser. That was enough sharing for now. I grumbled, "Are you two making dinner?"

Gordain saluted. He'd been teaching James to cook. Having brought the man into our lives, he felt a responsibility to him, though the contract of mentor was mine.

James's quiet, enigmatic ways had brought out the strong sense of brotherhood in all of us, and in the months he'd been here, we'd adopted him into the family. It was an uncomfortable feeling to think he'd leave us when his contract came to an end. I liked my people close. I needed that surety.

My brother and my friend set their boots toward the kitchens, and I strode away, running up the two internal staircases to my solar—my suite of rooms at the top of the castle. As I entered, my frustration about Mathilda grew. What if she'd got married? The idea made me sick to the pit of my stomach. But I knew it couldn't be true. I knew people, and she hadn't wanted it. Whatever her reasons, her intentions had been plain on her face. She'd been in a bind, but she'd been looking for a way out.

All of a sudden, I needed to know if she'd found one.

What if Gordain was right, and my stubbornness and wounded pride meant a wasted chance? I dropped onto my bed and scooped up my battered old laptop from the rug.

Mathilda had told me where she worked—an international events company I'd not forgotten the name of —so I'd find her email and drop her a line. If she never answered, then case closed. In time, the hurt would go. I'd weathered worse.

I keyed in the search terms. Then lines of text—staff bios —appeared against the colourful backdrop. Huh. The company website had no record for a Mathilda Jones.

But there was a listing for a Mattie Storm.

I clicked on the link and stared, a sense of discomfort forming. It was her picture. Her beautiful face with golden curls spiralling around. I'd found the woman.

Her surname was Storm? Why would she lie?

A quick search of the other Storm I knew, Maximus, gave me his bio: a wife, Fi, and two daughters, Mathilda and Scarlet.

No way.

I leapt from the bed.

Well, fuck. This was no misunderstanding, like Gordain had suggested, but a bloody great obstacle that I'd slammed in her path as we'd said goodbye. I thought I'd seen something odd in her eyes, but I'd figured it was me getting heated up by telling her about the man I was there to see. Her father.

Oh Christ. I sat back down in a heavy slump, slammed the laptop lid closed, and fell onto my back. How was it even possible? Was it fate or luck, good or bad?

Then my resolve, reliable, stubborn as it was, came around. Mathilda hadn't rejected me, she'd pulled away because of the problem between her father and me. That was at least worth a conversation.

I had just the way of inviting it.

7

COME, WOMAN, GET ON A PLANE
WITH ME

M athilda

Monday morning marked the eleventh month of me being an event manager. I'd joined Halcyon Days in their marketing department straight after I'd finished my degree, but pitching concepts and drumming up business left me cold. My bosses liked me because I was diplomatic and calm, but that was only on the surface. Inside, I yearned for the buzz and pressure of the events side of the business, and when a year's promotion opportunity came up, I'd leapt on it.

The only tiny complaint I had was the work of swanky corporate dinners and presentation days had become repetitive and underwhelming. The large companies that employed us generally had a reasonable budget and didn't bring any drama.

I wanted more. I wanted my work to matter.

Over the next month, I needed to decide where to take my career. The promotion was coming to an end, but going back to my old job wasn't an option. I had another idea in mind, one that had my heart racing with excitement.

One weekend, I'd gone out with a former colleague who ran a wedding planning business—my dream career. Caitlin knew I had an interest in the field and invited me to shadow her preparations, including meeting the bride and groom and helping out at the rehearsal dinner. The day had been a joy, and I'd ended up volunteering to help at the wedding itself, too. I loved meeting a demanding person's needs. To see them happy with what I'd achieved, and to feel appreciated, like I'd delivered something of real value.

It's what had attracted me to Callum McRae, the man who'd kept on asking, who'd been all bark and no bite, and who I hadn't stopped thinking about in a month. His card was pinned to the notice board in my kitchen, his undialed number saved in my phone.

To make matters worse, last night, Beth and I had watched *Seven Brides for Seven Brothers* again, and midway through the opening scenes, my friend had had an epiphany.

"That big Scottish guy is your Adam!" She'd named the main character in the musical as she'd leapt up from the other end of the gold couch. Beth seldom sat still long enough to watch a whole film anyway, so I was used to pausing whatever we watched until she settled again.

"What are you talking about?"

"An oversized mountain man with a family of brothers living in the back of beyond. Callum is an Adam. You found your fantasy man!" She'd crowed in delight. "Did he have rough manners and offer to whisk you away to his castle? Wait, did he propose within ten minutes of knowing you?"

"Adam didn't have a castle." I'd rolled my eyes, wondering exactly how open I'd been with my innermost thoughts. "Besides, Callum isn't rough." He swore frequently and his hands had been like sandpaper from hard work, but other than that he'd been a gentleman.

"But the parallels are there. Hey, can we role reverse this

and go steal the men away in the middle of the night? I'd like to take his jumpy friend for a ride. Work out what his problem is with my driving."

Handsome men aside, it wouldn't be easy to change my job, but I had to try.

While I waited for my weekend's worth of email to open on my computer, my first coffee of the day sending up tendrils of steam, Beth's joke haunted me. Because she was right. Adam from the outdated movie wasn't exactly my fantasy man, but Callum McRae had been. At least he looked like he could've been. And I'd walked away without trying to work around the problem.

Dominic Hanswick had given me a date by which to accept his proposal. He needed to be married by the annual shareholder's ball in May as, after this, he'd be requesting further investment. The timing was optimal.

He assumed I'd say yes.

It was nearing the end of March now, and I knew from Dad that Dominic was still losing investments. But all I'd had from him was an email containing his terms and conditions, his available dates for the ceremony. I hadn't replied.

Things with my sister had calmed—she was still in school, hadn't been arrested, and her messages sounded upbeat—so deciding had gone by the wayside with work and life in general.

I had done one thing. I'd looked up the politician with whom Dominic had the affair. She was the mother of two small children. A boy and a girl. But her husband had forgiven her for the sake of the family, and her career had recovered. Reading the article left a sour taste in my mouth, and I only hoped they were healing as a family.

"Mattie?" Charlie, the office PA, stuck his head around the door, neatly missing the large fern installed by the office's previous occupant. Traffic sounds and roadworks rumbled behind him, care of the busy city centre road outside. I never opened the windows because of the noise and the pollution. "Your first appointment is here. Can I send him in?"

Shoot. It was only 8A.M., and I hadn't checked my diary yet, let alone absorbed my much-needed caffeine. My day had been clear, last I'd checked on Friday. "I didn't know I was expecting anyone."

I swigged from my mug, burning my tongue as I cast around for my pen and my journal. Longhand was my preference for taking notes, rather than tapping at a device. It meant my attention was in the right place—on the person in front of me.

"You're booked out all day. It's a first-time consultation and site visit for a potential new client. To be honest," Charlie leaned a little farther around the door, "he's scaring half the guys and making the ladies sweat—the guy is flipping huge. He's like a big tree. Can I hurry him in here? I want to take an early lunch, and that will never happen if an outbreak of gossip puts everyone behind."

A huge guy… I swallowed and I was right back in make-believe land. If only that could be Callum, and he'd be my boyfriend coming to pick me up. Maybe it would be a Friday evening, and we'd be travelling to Scotland for the weekend. I'd have a bag packed, he'd take my hand in his giant paw, pull me from my chair. No, lift me right out of it…

Whew. Calm, Mathilda.

I waved, glad after all to have a busy day ahead. It would take my mind off the constant, and frankly tiring, fantasising I'd been doing. Charlie's neat coiffure disappeared and, three long swigs of double-shot latte later, heavy footsteps sounded in the hall.

Then a low Scottish voice thanked the PA, and I nearly

dropped my mug as Callum McRae entered my office and closed the door firmly behind him.

* * *

For a long moment, time stopped, and a delicious pressure reigned, a tension, as thick and heavy as a city night in summer. Callum stared at me with an expression both cautious and determined, like he'd overstepped the mark and he didn't care. Then he squared his shoulders, advanced forward, and took the visitor seat, stretching out his jean-clad legs.

Callum blew out a breath and with no attempt at subtlety, carried out a quick scan of my hands. "No ring. You're nae married?"

"Callum, you… How…? No, no wedding. I still haven't decided." I stopped my babbling. My memory didn't do him justice. Too big for my visitor's chair, his long body took up more space than was his right. "You booked an appointment with me?"

"That I did." Callum's lips curled, a small gesture, but it lightened the atmosphere. "When we met, you talked about your work, and I have need of someone who can look at my wee house and give me an opinion."

"An opinion?" He'd travelled all this way for a real appointment? Disappointment sunk my bubbling joy. What had I thought when he'd walked in? That he was here to whisk me off my feet?

I absolutely had.

"Aye." He glanced to the window and I ran my gaze over his features. Then he huffed and abruptly jerked forward, fixing me with a stare. "I'd intended to play this cool, but I'm no good at it. You're a sight for sore eyes, Mathilda. My memory must have been trying to protect me, because God, woman, your face knocks me out. I can't even make a sentence."

"It's not so bad seeing your face, either." I pressed my lips together, fighting a grin. "Did you really come here for a consultation?"

"Yes and no. Do I want to take you home with me today, show you the place, and have you stretch your expert mind around it? Aye. Did I come here just for that? Not one bit."

Spring had been slow in arriving in Bristol, but it must have gotten warmer today. My skin flushed hot.

Callum's gaze intensified. "Whatever else there is to talk about, come, woman, get on a plane with me. It's a little over an hour to Inverness, and I've a car waiting at the airport. There's a return flight at four, and you'll be on it. If we go now, you can spend the day with me on my estate. The question is, do you want that? Tell me no, and I'll go without question. I'm not here to force an unwilling woman to heed me."

I opened and closed my mouth. The option of a glorious day spread out in front of me. The man I'd thought about obsessively over the past month had come to my office, on a Monday morning—team meeting day—and was offering me my fantasy on a plate.

I'd searched for him online. Found a website for his sprawling castle that left me desperate to see it in real life. It would be a fun day, for sure. I'd just have to convince my mind to check out and let the rest of me enjoy it. Not think about the reasons why I should be keeping the hundreds of miles of distance and focusing on issues closer to home.

Callum shifted, the silence drawing out. "Right. I'm sorry. The last thing I wanted—"

"I'll come," I interrupted as I stood, brushing my hands over my figure-hugging plum dress—a smarter choice than usual and worn to chase away the Monday blues. My dove-grey Manolo Blahnik mules were not the thing for a site visit, but they'd have to do. "I'd love to. Just one thing."

The big man unfolded from the chair. His posture changed from being restrained and tense to practically vibrating with energy. "Anything."

"You said you intended to play it cool. Try, will you?" My head was turned, but we still needed to take this slow.

The grin on his face turned dangerous. Thrilling. "I fly hundreds of miles to impress a lass, and she wants me to relax. I can try. But I can't say the same for all other things McRae. Be prepared to be impressed. That's as much as I can do."

* * *

Two hours later, we rolled through a pair of tall stone pillars which marked an entrance to the McRae estate. The actual land border lay miles behind us as the place was vast and partially situated in the Cairngorms National Park. Callum had taken a turning off the main road, and I'd wanted to open the window and taste the air. It was *so* pretty. Sweeping dark landscapes held mountains at bay. Wild, open nature abounded. Melting snow drifts lined the side of the road—the last of the season, Callum hoped.

It was so peaceful I could cry.

He lived here. I could barely comprehend it.

The road took us around a stand of soaring pine trees, Callum pulled over and killed the engine, the quiet sudden and complete. Below us, a loch sprawled, glistening in the pale sun. To the left of it, with a snow-topped mountain rising behind, lay his home. Castle McRae.

His wee house, as he'd called it.

I gravitated forward in my seat and stared. It was the first moment of silence since we'd met, the short plane journey being filled with conversation like we'd known each other for years. Callum was easy to talk to, but we'd avoided any difficult topics, and he'd gone to some effort to put me at ease.

He brought his arms forward, copying my pose as he rested on the steering wheel. "Home. Impressed yet?"

Imposing and grand, Castle McRae sat in the most picture-perfect setting. A mishmash of three individual structures—a big stone hall with a medieval round tower to one side and a large Tudor block to the other—it somehow worked beautifully as a whole. I wanted to explore every inch from the windows above the hall to the little boat house on the loch.

And then I'd climb the mountain, because my imagination had made me into an outdoorswoman. Who knew?

I managed a faint, "Yes," and Callum dipped his head and let out a short breath, like my approval meant something to him. He ran a hand over his blond hair then flexed his fingers over the steering wheel again.

"I've never looked at this place as... What would ye call it, an asset? It's just home, though we throw the doors open to the public now and then. I meant it when I said I could use your expertise. There's a lot on the estate that could generate the income we need to survive. A salmon farm that's not been touched in years. Cattle farming where we've recently installed new tenants, but which could be two or three times larger. But the time it takes to get them up and running is significant. I've only so many hours in the day, and getting my head around tourism is a step too far. We considered Land Rover tours and tastings at the distillery—"

He stopped talking, and I drew in a breath, because we had to discuss this. The elephant in the room. Callum had booked an appointment with me online, which meant he'd seen my real name. Of course he'd have made the connection to Dad, but being the perfect gentleman, he hadn't said a word.

An internal battle played out in the tick of his jaw.

I took the initiative, as it was my problem, not his. "Do you understand why I didn't call you?"

"No. Maybe."

"My father…" I stopped, because this wasn't about Dad, it was more about me and what I wanted. Dad was an element of that which needed to be handled. I pushed a lock of hair behind my ear and started again. "I liked you, when we met, but I need my father to be on my side for something specific I have planned, and—"

"And if you were dating me, not his favourite person, he'd be in a spin. Refuse you what you wanted?"

I twisted in my seat, my dress creeping up my leg. "Since when were we talking about dating?"

Callum shifted his massive shoulders so we were facing one another. Inside the car, he seemed to take up even more space, and a shiver ran through me. Of delight, and of absolute attraction. I could smell him, over the pine trees and clean air. Woodsmoke, aftershave, and clean man. He made my mouth water.

In a flash, I pictured him over me. Bare chested and waiting on my word. *Holy hell.*

Like he knew my thoughts, Callum's lips drew into a contented smirk. "You're trembling. Do I make you nervous?"

My mouth dropped open, and he grinned wider. The cheek of him. I couldn't help my physical reaction, but nervous? No. Magnetically lured into submission, yes.

If anyone, he ought to be nervous of me. In fact…

Reaching out a hand, I touched him gently on the shoulder—the first physical contact between us today. As we'd waited in the airport, and when our arms had neared each other's on the plane, Callum had anticipated me, respecting my personal space. He'd moved when I had, as if we were somehow connected. I was the last person on Earth to play the seducer, but I could make a point. However well he thought he knew me, I had a read on him, too.

Under my fingertips, his shoulder was hard, the muscle large and rigid despite the thickness of his sweater. Heck... *No, focus!*

"Perhaps. Does that work for you?" I trailed my hand down his chest. Purposeful. Adding pressure. "But maybe I make you nervous, too."

Callum held very still and, slowly, red flushed up his neck. "Christ, lass," he began, his eyes wide, his gaze held hostage by mine.

The pressure was too much. I drew back my hand and burst out laughing. "Now who's the nervous one?"

Callum dropped back into his seat and clapped his hands to his thighs in a dramatic fashion. Then he grinned, and the effect was infectious. We smirked at each other like we couldn't stop.

He raised his eyes and spoke to the roof of the car. "One look from her, one touch of her hand, and I'm toast. Done for." Heat and humour lit his gaze as it came back on me. "You had me forgetting what I was talking about."

"That was my intention."

"Cheeky wench. Oh, dating. I was only being honest. It's not like you were planning to take me around to your parents' house for tea as your new best friend." He drew his thumb over his bottom lip, his eyebrows raised. I had two additional inches of thigh showing, but Callum was doing a magnificent job of keeping his eyes on mine. "I'd say more, but a certain lass tells me I'm supposed to be playing it cool. The temperature in this car is already high enough to melt the snow."

My body warmed even more. He was right. I wasn't in this car today because I thought Callum would be a friend. "I still don't know you," I whispered.

He restarted the engine with a loud rumble. "Aye, you do. I've no hidden depths and I wear my heart on my sleeve. I've got the day to start you on the rest, so why don't we get going?"

8

HIS EX

Mathilda

We spent two hours touring the estate, saving the castle—which I was dying to see—for the afternoon. As we circled the length of the loch, and I made notes in my journal, Callum beamed, pride in his land infusing us both. He introduced me to everyone we came across—and, as he owned land as far as the eye could see, most were his tenants or employees.

One man, who'd been unemployed for six years following a breakdown, ran a dairy farm with his wife and stepchildren. An elderly couple did much of Callum's accounting in exchange for a cosy cottage. For which he could have charged a much higher rent.

Laird McRae cared for his people. I adored that.

We also stopped at the distillery.

Outside, the water of the loch lapped gently against the white painted walls. Inside, newly installed shiny facilities juxtaposed with the old, tall-chimneyed building. Exactly the sort of impressive image and pedigree Storm Force—Dad's line of spirits—would be sold on.

It was clear the investment Callum had poured into the place, and I bet it had been on the back of the conglomerate's order.

The thought knocked the stuffing out of me.

Crates of whisky labelled for Storm Force lay stacked on pallets in the warehouse. There was no mention of this being an unsold stockpile, or of debts owed. But it was a reminder too far of what my father and Dominic had done, and I wanted to talk about it, enough so I understood what it meant to Callum.

To gauge what he would make of the bigger picture, if he knew.

Callum had no idea that the man who'd proposed to me was also the one who had committed adultery, lost his income, and caused the Storm Force contract values to be halved. I also knew from Dad, amongst rants about Dominic's behaviour, the label itself was in jeopardy.

Storm Force could be scrapped altogether.

I stood, uncomfortable in my skin as I tried to find a way to talk about it, but Callum placed a gentle hand on my shoulder and steered me back to the car. "This is only part of the tour. Nothing meant by the visit other than showing you the place. Now I've seen that look on your face, I think I'm an idiot for bringing you here." His big brow furrowed. "The subject is banned, at least for the now."

We drove away, and a tension held between us. From the moment he'd shown up in my office this morning, I felt him like kinetic electricity over my skin, but there was an additional pressure. Of all we weren't saying and of the weight of my concealment.

Then it got even heavier.

As we travelled along the loch, heading to the nearest village for lunch, we passed a side road made of dirt and gravel.

"Where does that lead?"

"It's the route to a disused quarry." He didn't elaborate further, nor did his tone alter or his focus from the road, but I knew, somehow, that there was something about the place that bothered him. He rolled his shoulders and changed the subject, but I saw a tiny insight into the burdens Callum McRae carried. He wore his heart on his sleeve, sure, but he had closely held secrets, too.

Good. No one should be so obviously perfect.

We found our way to a café in the whitewashed village, the strange tension persisting over lunch but finally breaking when Callum jumped up from his seat and hollered at a woman coming in the door.

"My ex-girlfriend. Here for you to interview," he announced, and sat back with his hands behind his head.

This guy.

Two excitable children and their mother, Una, joined our table.

Callum's ex.

I regarded her with curiosity. Una was attractive and a couple of years older than me. She had the weary look of a woman used to chasing children around, but I immediately liked her brisk movements and confidence. But his *ex*?

The woman settled into a seat, her pretty children scattering to a play area in the corner of the café.

"Ah, I see what all the fash is about. I mean a fuss." Una raised a nicely shaped eyebrow before she twisted in her seat and pointed at Callum. "Laird McRae, a tea, here, if ye will."

Callum hesitated, and the woman huffed a breath. "What are you sitting there for, man? You demand I come down here when I'm up to my ears in things to do. What good is it to me if I dinna get to talk about you behind your back?"

"You demanded she come here? To speak to me?" I switched my stare to Callum.

He lifted his chin. "As a reference. It's no good me telling you how great I am all day. You'd believe it better coming from someone else."

I pinched my thumb and forefinger over the bridge of my nose. "Is this how you define playing it cool?"

He gave me a wolfish grin. It went straight down the centre of my body, my belly aching with a hunger my meal couldn't satisfy. Today was doing a number on me.

"It's how I ensure I've done all I can. I've three hours left. Wait to see what I have planned for you this afternoon." His voice dipped, and his gaze was resolute, and this time I shivered. *Wow.*

Across from us, Una heaved a sigh. "Children present. Go away, Callum."

With a smirk, he left, taking our empty lunch plates with him to the counter. I watched him go, bemused but intrigued by whatever trick he was pulling.

Una steepled her hands. "Aye, you suit him well. You're not afraid of him and you've the stature for the role of Lady. I always wondered what kind of lass he'd fall for. Not that I coveted the job myself, but Callum is a dear friend to both my husband and me. All the man does is work his fingers to the bone. He needs balance. Getting some down time with someone he cares about will do him good."

"You mentioned a fuss?" I asked, not wanting to embarrass Callum by correcting his friend on her mistake. We weren't a couple, and I wasn't being lined up for the role of lady of the castle. *Jesus. Lady Mathilda.* Inside, I was six years old and giggling with glee.

"Callum's brothers, the youngest two, are friends with my nephew, Sawney. According to him, the laird has been stomping about that castle for a month, yelling and bawling like he'd a permanent headache. My husband said it was a woman, and it looks like he was right."

She sat back, smug.

I blinked. "I'm sure it can't have been about me." Could it? Shoot.

"His message to me earlier today said, and I quote: I've a woman I want to impress. Will ye tell her how canny a boyfriend I was? I'm not sure she thinks all that much of me."

"He was serious about you being here as a reference?" I replied, my stomach flipping at the last sentence. Spending the past several hours with Callum at my side, hearing him explain how his world worked and him being genuinely interested in my opinions, I...thought a lot of him. To put it mildly.

Una threw her hands up. "We dated when we were seventeen! I'm more than happy to bore you on how he took me to the cinema in Inverness, or how he always walked me home from school, keeping his hands to himself. He was a little prettier then, aye? But he's still a lovely man, cares for everyone, and is always the first to offer help. But..." Una's cheerfulness left her, and she paused as I bristled over the fact she didn't think Callum attractive now. He was. Very much so.

Una's hand went to a rope of green beads around her neck, and she rolled the largest around. "That's not what you'd be asking, should you want to know him better."

This was a drift I could catch. I glided an inch in her direction. "What should I be asking?"

"About his da."

A shadow fell over the table, and Callum delivered Una's tea. We both winced at the timing. Callum gave me a soft look, but his forehead creased into deep lines as he turned to Una. "Go ahead and tell Mathilda whatever you see fit. She'll hear all kinds of chat at some point, so it may as well be sooner than later. I'll be outside, Mathilda. Come find me when you're done, and we'll go home."

His long legs carried him away, and Una dropped her

beads. Being blindsided by an ex-girlfriend was one thing, but whatever was coming about his father couldn't be good.

She opened her mouth. "You're aware Callum's father died several years ago?"

I nodded. When we'd shared breakfast in London, he'd mentioned that neither of his parents were living.

"The old man couldnae be more different from the son. Hamish, that was his da, had problems with his drink. That's what you'll hear around the place because people here are terrible gossips. The man's exploits were legendary, and the son has to live with that."

This didn't seem the sort of thing I should hear from a stranger. "Maybe I'll talk to Callum…" I started and glanced out of the window to where the man stood by his big car. His gaze sought mine in return, but it was guarded. Defensive now.

I had enough father issues to write the book, but Callum's intrigued me all the more for him being such a solid man. I couldn't imagine anything, or anyone, undermining his strength.

"Aye, do that. He won't hold back. I only thought to mention it so you weren't surprised if someone blurted out how Callum was arrested and all."

"Arrested?" As I swung my gaze back to Una, one of her little girls danced over and draped herself over her shoulder.

The woman reached in her bag for her purse, handing the adorable blonde moppet a toy. She patted her on the backside, and the girl scampered away, waving her treasure in the air. Una watched her children play and took a sip of her tea before she dropped her bomb.

"For killing his father. Did he nae mention it at all?"

* * *

Outside the café, Callum popped the Land Rover's passenger-side door open, handing me inside with a small, worried smile. After he'd reclaimed the driver's seat, he paused before starting the engine. "I'm sorry if you found that strange. Una is a lovely person, but she's also the queen of gossip in these parts. I wanted you to know what people were saying about me. I don't listen to it myself, but I didn't want…"

He stared at his hands, worrying the steering wheel's leather cover with a nail. There was something so open, so vulnerable about the confident man in that second, I wanted to lean in and kiss him. Just to make him feel better.

"She told me you were arrested. Is that what you didn't want me to hear later?"

He inclined his head. "I want there to be a later, so whatever she had to say would either send you running or have you ask me. Get it out of the way."

I wanted to say he could have just told me himself, but I sort of understood. Callum had expected someone to gossip about him, and for me to run away with that information and never call him again. It had bothered him enough that he'd arranged for me to hear it from a third party who I could question freely.

It seemed impossible that this gentle, brusque man could be dangerous—the idea so out there I wanted to laugh—yet at the same time there must be a truth here. Something he was obviously uncomfortable talking about.

"Why don't you drive me to your castle and we can sort the gossip from the facts?"

With the engine purring, Callum navigated left out of the loch-side village. Ahead, the sprawl of Castle McRae sat on the shore, its edges lit bright gold by a ray of sunshine. I could picture so many uses for the place already. As a backdrop for filming, though that could be disruptive for the family, as a corporate retreat, though nobody wanted a bunch of braying asshats hanging around for a weekend. Destination weddings would be perfect, depending on whether the castle had the right setup. But if it was plain inside or, worse, modernised, that might not fly.

But first... "Tell me why you think gossip would bother me."

Callum gave a huff. "That particular tale should bother anyone." He slowed the car on the empty road, glancing at me. "I didnae end my father's life, but I did report him missing. I was arrested after his body was found."

"At that old quarry we passed earlier?"

"Christ, woman." His cheeks paled.

"You were released without charge?"

"Aye. How did you...never mind. I wanted you to go home without any unanswered questions hovering over you. No more secrets or misunderstandings."

We were in danger of sharing too much, too soon, but the man was so upfront he was an open book. A good person, honest and true.

I wasn't prepared yet to be so transparent. It wasn't in me to do so.

I had a history of concealing my feelings and pretending everything was okay. I'd put a brave face on more times than I could count, and it was second nature to shut down any emotions that could harm me. Even with Beth, my best friend, I kept significant parts of myself closed off.

Callum and I were so different.

"How did your father die?" I blurted. Where on Earth had those words come from?

"He got drunk, drove out into the hills, and stumbled over the quarry edge."

"Why were you arrested?" I couldn't stop my mouth.

"I'd smacked him in the face before he left. Broke his nose." The car sped up, and Callum gripped the wheel.

"Did he deserve it?"

"Aye. I admitted the same to the police when they came knocking. I didnae blame them because it looked shady as anything. There were too many coincidences. Too much gossip. I'd just turned eighteen so could take control of the estate, my father had a reputation, and I'd publicly called him out. He had a problem with my brother…"

I stiffened, the parallels with my own life too close.

Callum drew a heavy breath, and we pulled off the loch road, taking an open path over a bridge. The tyres crunched over gravel-filled potholes in a carpark on the other side, and we were there. Castle McRae.

The laird took the keys from the ignition and rolled his shoulders before bringing a heavy gaze on me. "Story for another time. I'm about as good at playing it cool as I am holding my tongue when I see a wrong. It was the one thing you could ask of me I'd find hardest to deliver. So, I apologise. You…shake me up. You did from the moment I saw you. I won't pretend otherwise, not when I'm about to show you my home and want you to visit again. To call me sometime or answer when I call you."

"I'm sorry you waited for me to call." He'd waited on me, and I hadn't contacted him. Well, effing hell. My chest gave a little pang of hurt on his behalf.

Callum reached out and took my hand. We linked fingers, and warmth ran up my arm.

"To finish my story, I'd do anything for those I love. Kicking my father out of his home and raising my brothers without fear of violence had been my plan since I was fifteen. Younger. I'd never been quiet about it. My arrest was a natural outcome. He hit my brother, I defended my family. He drove out, and we never saw him again. Except

71

in the morgue. The fallout from that was shite but expected."

Yikes. I squeezed his hand. Did I think I had it rough with a difficult parent? "I'm sorry for your trauma, and for your loss."

A new beam of sunlight broke through the clouds, highlighting Callum's furrowed brow. "People dinna normally see it that way. They say good riddance."

"He was still your dad. I'm sorry for you losing what he should have been."

We sat in silence, the weight of the moment needing to dissipate. Maybe Callum was no longer such a stranger now I had an insight into his life, but this was still a two-way street. I'd shared nothing.

"Right. Enough of the heavy or you'll think I'm all up in my drama." Callum unclipped both our seatbelts and leapt out of the car, jogging around to my side. He opened my door and offered a hand, keeping mine on the approach to a huge wooden door, studded with iron and solid.

Open, like it's master.

"Now, tell me what you make of my place. Then let me make up reasons for you to return."

I already wanted to. In the moments between conversations, I'd run over my diary, considered the travel time and thought about my holiday because, and as strange as it was, I knew I wasn't walking away. Whatever else might come.

Callum McRae, with his honour, big heart, and even bigger frame, was far too addictive for just one day.

9

UNLESS I KISS YOU FIRST

C allum

Every little noise of delight Mathilda made on the castle tour had my pulse spiking. Each time she squeezed my fingers it was like she had a hold of my heart and was plucking the strings.

I walked her to the west entrance first, showing her the big dining room with its heavy, scarred wooden furniture, the den with battered green sofas abused by the twins, and then the kitchens. We climbed the first set of steps in the tower to see the gym, not going up farther as those were Gordain's rooms. Every time we passed the great hall, Mathilda's eyes were agog.

But I wanted to save that for the end.

Outside, I showed her the various repair work we'd done or had planned, and the vision I had to add a glassed-in atrium on the south side. In winter, daylight was rare. The five of us men were used to the gloom, but an outsider might not be. A woman from the south of England, say.

We returned to the big front door opening into the great hall.

"This is the perfect backdrop for wedding photos," Mathilda breathed. She climbed the deep stone steps and placed a hand on the door.

I swallowed, loving the sight of her about to enter the heart of my home. I bounded up to stand beside her, an idea catching me. "Weddings, aye? Indulge me?"

She regarded me, her perfectly applied makeup showing off her gorgeous eyes. "Okay. With what?"

I swooped, catching her up in my arms, then I shoved the door fully open and strode through.

"Callum!" Mathilda shrieked, but she clung onto my neck as I advanced farther into the interior. I placed her down carefully before stepping back.

Holding her was nice. Very nice.

"Worth it." I grinned, though my heart raced.

She stared at me, her hands smoothing over her skirt. The skirt which had been sliding up her thighs all day and driving me wild. "I can't even remember the last time someone picked me up. I'm not the smallest of women."

"You're perfect." I was far from being a small man, and her height was part of the attraction. I wouldn't have to stoop so far to kiss her red lips. Mathilda pursed the lips in question as if she knew where my mind had gone, but I couldn't drag my eyes off them.

I'd had more than one dream involving Mathilda Storm. Not all of them hot and heavy. In the one last night, before I took the 5A.M. flight to fetch her, she'd been standing in the hall directing some of my estate staff. Overseeing a busy morning, confident and in control. She'd been at home, and my chest had ached something fierce when I'd woken.

I knew I'd projected too much on a woman I'd met for a single night and morning a month ago. Except spending today with her, and the way she'd handled the surprise confession I'd choked out in the car, told me how bang on my instincts were.

Mathilda was beautiful, strong, far smarter than me, and calm where I was heat and instinct. I hadn't a hope of keeping cool like she'd asked. Impossible, when all I wanted was to push her back against one of the pillars that lined the east wall and kiss the living daylights out of her.

I drew a breath, watching as Mathilda turned full circle on the flagstones, taking in the hall. "This place is amazing. Everything I hoped it would be. I'd tried to guess from the pictures online but I didn't even come close."

"You looked me up? And you had hopes?" I blinked, and she threw me an amused glance.

"For you to hold weddings here. Target the American market. It's perfect in every way."

Hmm. "We've had a couple of people wed here, but we didnae charge much. Not for locals. Would it bring in enough to make it worth the effort?"

"Do you know what a venue can charge for a three-night event?" She gave me a figure, and my eyes widened.

I mean, damn.

"How is that possible?"

"You offer a full package. Accommodation, transport, privacy, so no other guests like a hotel would have. Entertainment, such as walks up the mountain, drives to see the deer, or boat trips on the loch. You haven't shown me the bedrooms yet." Her gaze flitted to mine and away as she tapped her fingers against each of her points. "But as long as you have somewhere beautiful for the bride and groom, the rest of the guests can stay in the hotel in the village. Or if you converted some of those cottages we passed back near the gates, you'd get even more income. You have no idea how close you are to being able to do this."

She gestured with her hand, stepping closer to me. I

mirrored the position of her body. "A few lights and chairs, and you don't have to do anything else to this room. It's already so picturesque. That fireplace with the carved chimney breast is incredible. I love it. And you have ancient swords up the wall. It couldn't be more perfect."

"Gordain put those up. We found them in the cellars." It had been my idea, too, along with the tattoos my brother and I had gotten, but Mathilda's enthusiasm was having a strange effect on me, and I had to keep talking to hide my reeling senses. This, her being here, was so *right*. "What about food and waiting staff?"

"A catering company can provide that. They can even bring the chairs and tables with all the fancy settings. Give them access to your kitchens and sit back and watch the money roll in. There's enough of you to mean you don't need to hire that many extra people. You'd need a coordinator to make it all happen, if you can't spare the time yourself. But seriously, Callum, you only need to book in five to ten of these between May and September and you'll be laughing."

A buzz of excitement filled the air around her as she talked. It was catching, and I found myself considering how we could do it. The profit was attractive, and running around after a wedding party would be no issue. On my land, the boys could drive legally, and they loved to chat. They'd enjoy being put to task. Plenty of local folk needed work, too, and would be willing.

"Of everything I've seen today, this is the easiest to set up and run with," Mathilda concluded. "It doesn't mean it's simple, but it's high profit for what you'd need to spend. And just look." She drew a breath, exhaling in glee. "What would it be like to be married here? Even I couldn't have imagined somewhere so romantic."

"You've imagined your own wedding?"

"Who hasn't?"

I snorted, but she had me. I'd imagined mine. Right here, in the great hall. My brothers as groomsmen and half the village as my guests.

The bubble around us tightened a notch, and Mathilda's gaze fell from the carved stonework that ran from the fire to the blackened rafters. "Right now, I'd trade everything I'd dreamed to marry someone I loved."

I'd avoided thinking about the fact she was considering another man's proposal, but now an uncomfortable jealousy crept into my chest.

We were standing very close. It wasn't close enough.

The expression she'd been wearing dropped, and Mathilda's brown eyes widened. "You look like you're about to kiss me."

"I was thinking about it."

Her mouth opened, but no words came out.

So I took the lead. "I've thought about you. About whether I'd made up how attractive you are or how much I admired you. I know you said you had complications"—I advanced an inch—"but you wouldnae be here today if you had no interest in me. You're hard to work out, but that alone gives this man a shred of hope."

I took one of her spiral curls then rolled the soft hair between my fingers. Mathilda leaned into my hand, her gaze on me, her eyes both cautious and bright with anticipation. The pink on her cheeks deepened.

"Everything you've described, the weddings and all, I'll willingly consider," I said, "but right now, my home and my problems have all taken a back seat inside my brain."

An echo sounded in the hall, boot steps in one of the passages. I blocked it out.

"Because you want to kiss me." She smiled, and my blood ran hot.

"No. I want you to kiss me. I'll chase ye to the ends of the earth but only if I know you want it."

In a move that I think surprised us both, Mathilda placed her hand on my chest, her touch gentle. She brought her other hand to join it, and I took her arm, anticipation growing as we moved in closer, her feet between mine and our bodies aligned.

"You won't kiss me unless I kiss you first?" she asked, her gaze on her fingertips, slowly moving them north.

Christ, she was feeling me up. Just like in the car when she nearly gave me a heart attack.

"I never said that." I left alone the soft curls I was rapidly becoming obsessed with and tipped her chin up. Just beyond mine, her lips parted. I drew in a breath and leaned forward.

"Callum? Is Mathilda still... Oh! I'm sorry," James's voice boomed from the top of the stairs.

I screwed my eyes tight shut. This wasn't happening.

"I didn't... I'm going to go." He chuckled.

Mathilda huffed an embarrassed laugh and stepped back from my arms. Fuck. Why was he living with me again? I was going to kill the bastard.

She cleared her throat. "Did you want to see me, James?"

At the start of the castle tour, I'd had my friend—my now ex-friend—come greet Mathilda. He was the only one home with the twins being at school and Gordain still away. We didn't have long before I had to drive her back to the airport.

"I wrote a note," James said. "For Beth."

Beth? Ah, right. I called to mind Mathilda's friend. Looked like the lass made an impact with her dramatic car stunt.

He ran a hand through his hair, rumpling it. "Would you be so kind as to pass it on to her?"

Mathilda cocked her head. I couldn't move as all my blood had rushed elsewhere in my body. "I forgot you'd even met her," she replied. "If you want, I can text her and ask if she doesn't mind me passing on her number? You could talk to her on the phone."

Finally, I regained control enough to look at my friend properly. His ears were red—a sure sign he was in over his head in whatever he was doing. Good. He needed the push.

"I… No, this is fine."

Mathilda held out a hand, and James descended the steps and handed the small, white envelope over. He hesitated.

"Go?" I suggested.

He pulled an apologetic grimace then went back the way he'd come, leaving us alone.

Mathilda tucked the envelope inside the notebook she'd been writing in all day, then turned her heated gaze on me. I liked knowing I'd put that blush on her cheeks.

She collected her bag from where she'd dropped it on the floor. "On that note, we should get going."

I sighed, trailing after her, wanting more than ever for her to return to my home.

* * *

The forty-minute run to the airport went by in a flash. A gale splattered rain on the Land Rover's windscreen, and I had to concentrate on the road, rather than think of ways to get Mathilda back into my arms.

"What do you think James wants with Beth?" she mused, tapping her bottom lip as we drove.

"No idea," I grumbled, feeling too big in my seat and too big for my skin.

"Is he seeing anyone?"

A snort this time. "No. James has lived a strange life. He's a canny lad, but his social skills are dented. Better, since he came to us, but he's quiet and he doesn't share much. He's never even looked at a woman, or a man for that matter, in a romantic sort of way. Not that I've seen."

"What sort of life?"

"One where he was kept away from other influences by his uncle. Restricted, you might say." Or controlled.

She twisted in her seat, that taunting skirt slipping up her thighs again. "And you just collected him and took him home? Is there anyone you don't help?"

A smile pulled at my lips, and I flicked the windscreen wipers on faster, the rain thundering down. "You think I'm a collector of lame ducks? I'm paid to mentor him. James is learning estate management from me."

"Would you have done it for free?"

I opened my mouth, but nothing came out. I would've. James was another brother to me. As honest and loyal as any of my kin. He had a quick mind, and I thrived on his changing opinions.

"Just as I thought." Mathilda dusted off her hands like she'd claimed a victory. "You are kindness through and through. I have your number, Callum McRae."

Hah. "Aye, ye do. Make sure you use it this time."

She chuckled, and the car sped on through the rain.

After cruising into the drop-off point at the airport, a sort of desperation came over me, and I pulled the car over, wracking my brain for a way to end this well. Mathilda hopped out before I managed a word, and I sped around to her side.

"Thank you for today. I can email you an outline for the weddings plan—" she started, brushing her hair from her eyes.

The rain fell on us in fat drops.

"Come back. Come and see me again," I uttered, moving in close but not touching her. Cold water ran down my neck. The next couple of weeks were manic with work, and I couldn't even think of a night I could get away to Bristol. Then a solution came to me.

"In a fortnight, it's the long weekend. Are you working?"

Mathilda inched closer as she considered the question. "No. Unusually, I'm not."

"There's a party on the next estate. A birthday. Highland games, the whole shebang. Come with me. As my date. Stay the weekend." Despite the chill, I was sweating.

"Maybe," she replied softly.

"One of my relatives is a miserly old arse who hates my branch of the family, so it will be fun to watch if he and I get into a row." I'd changed my mind about the party as soon as I'd decided I needed an incentive for Mathilda to return. Something more than just me alone. The twins would be delighted when I told them. Both wanted to compete in Lachlan's games.

"I can't promise you I'll come, even for that. Callum... I told you I don't want to lead you on."

Her honesty hurt, but there was no other way of getting her to fall for me if we were a country apart. *Fuck*. I was hurtling headlong into this. No brakes and no desire to stop.

A long moment drew out between us, and emotions played out over Mathilda's face, a torment to watch without knowing her mind. All I knew was the sheer magnetism pulling me to her.

Nae. She was hurting, too. She felt this.

I raised a finger and tilted her chin. "What if I don't care?"

"What if I do?" she replied. Then to my utter surprise and intense happiness, she gave an exasperated gasp, leaned in, and pressed her lips to mine. Her kiss was hesitant, then her arms came around my neck and she closed the distance between us.

Somewhere, a firework factory exploded.

"Mathilda," I breathed, my mind reeling, then I crushed

her to me and kissed the hell out of her beautiful mouth. If this was the only chance I had to impress her, I was going to make it count.

She didn't pull away, and rain coated our faces, puddles forming around us on the carpark's tarmac.

She tasted sweet, addictive. Just like in my dreams.

With a careful touch, I held her head and controlled the kiss, meeting her soft lips with my more insistent ones. Demanding entry and gaining it as her mouth opened under mine. Mathilda moulded her body to my form.

Lust surged through my muscles. Our tongues met, sliding together in a perfect dance that almost had me on my knees. I knew she felt it too by her rush of breath as she finally pulled away.

"I really have to go," she managed, and I blinked open my eyes.

Around us, other drivers and passengers gawped openly. Mathilda blushed, hiding her face in my shirt. I tucked my head down over hers, my arms a protective barrier.

"Just come back to me," I murmured. "Dinna marry someone else in the meantime."

Mathilda Storm pressed her lips to mine one last time and dashed off through the drenching Highlands rain.

10

BEAUTY BEFORE THE BEAST

*C*allum

For two days, I jumped like a startled stag every time my phone made a peep. Then, finally, the message I'd been waiting for appeared, just as I returned from taking the boys to school.

I'm volunteering to work with a wedding coordinator this week. It will help me make sure my ideas for your venture are strong. Pay back for our day out :)

I frowned at the screen of my phone. Aside from replying that she was home safe, as I'd asked her to, this was all Mathilda had to say? After that kiss? Slamming my Land Rover door shut, I glared at the castle and the hundred and one jobs it contained. I needed a moment. Instead of going in, I set out on the path around the Tudor block then across to the start of the foothills, treading onto soft beds of pine needles.

To my left, the sprawl of two new farms began, the result of hard work in applying for government funding. A success, though more for the locals who had work than bringing any profit to me.

As I walked in the cool, clean air of my woods, I typed.

Then you'll come back. To tell me how it went.

Thinking fast, I paused and snapped a picture of the ancient Scots Pine forest around me, then another of the view back down to the castle, the loch shining behind. With a few clicks, I sent them to Mathilda with the caption 'Wish you were here'. If she was sitting in her office, this would look like a slice of Scottish Heaven.

Her reply took a minute, and in that time, I'd ascended the first slope and emerged into a sunny clearing, spring melting the last of the snow and warming the air. I'd started to sweat, a trickle running down the sword tattoo at my back, so I stripped off my hoodie and shirt, finding a flat rock to take the weight off my feet. The foothill behind the castle led straight up Mhic Raith, our mountain, and I'd climbed it any number of times both alone or with my brothers.

You make a compelling argument...that is utterly beautiful.

There was a pause as she wrote another message.

Flip the camera and send me one of you.

My heart boomed. The woman had dominated my thoughts ever since she'd left, but I still had no idea where her mind was at. But she wanted a picture of me, and she'd kissed me first. I'd never forget that. I tapped out my reply.

You first. Beauty before the beast.

At my feet, a scattering of pinecones took the brunt of my stress as I punted them one by one down the hillside while I waited. Each one scattered pine needles from the branches they hit on the slope below. Then a message appeared. A picture.

Mathilda's beautiful face smiled cautiously at me. Her hair was up and her head tilted a little to the side. For a moment, I felt dizzy.

Then I read the caption.

I think you're beautiful, too.

My 'beast' comment was only half a joke—with my height, weight, and rough features, I didn't expect anyone to find me pretty. Some lasses didn't seem to mind, and I'd assumed they were attracted to the brutish look of me. Maybe had an idea I'd be an animal when we were behind closed doors.

Nobody, ever, had called me beautiful.

It took a while for me to gather my wits as I stared at the picture and the comment, and my resolve took another sharp turn. I had to win her. She liked me, but it twisted my stomach to think of her other choices.

Nae. When had I ever been daunted by a challenge? Even if the thought made me sweat more than the climb had.

A new message dinged.

So...I showed you mine...

Impatient, I liked that. I grinned and took a snap, then sent it without looking too closely at my brawny shoulders. I followed with:

I'll send more pictures. Of the estate. If it makes you happy.

fans self Put yourself naked in them and I'll be very happy. Wow, Callum. Just wow

I burst out laughing, scaring a pair of birds from a tree.

Aye, maybe I will.

All the way back down the slope to the castle, my cheeks ached from smiling.

Until I saw the expensive city car pulled up in my carpark. Two shark-faced land agents climbed out and strolled their shiny shoes to my door. I pulled my shirt back over my head and lost whatever joy I'd carried.

They'd been here once before, and I'd be damned if I was letting them over my threshold again.

* * *

"*M*r McRae," land agent number one said as I approached.

"I'm not interested. And it's Laird to you." I bore down on them, splitting them up where I took the steps in one long stride.

I turned back and folded my arms. The men paused and glanced at one another.

Inside the castle, a pile of letters—red bills—sat on Da's desk. In the very office he'd laid his fists into a wee boy. The place where I'd lost control and broken his bones.

My finances had gone beyond worrying, and I'd been forced to ask the bank for a loan extension and the ability to consolidate my debts. No answer had come yet, but it wasn't my only option. I had another path I'd take if things got desperate. It meant sucking up my pride and would be harder than keeping my cool around Mathilda—a near impossibility.

The men's fake smiles now could promise me the world, but I'd die before I took their offer. Selling Castle McRae would be the end of me. Seeing any of the land around here turned into a Highlands theme park, with no respect for history or clan, would kill.

I was more than happy to let them know.

11

MY LITTLE SISTER

*M*athilda

The morning sunlight gleamed on my collection of yellow bowls and vases, set high on the kitchen shelf. They were all new, no history to them. None had ever belonged to a person with a title, and at least two had IKEA stamped on the base.

Not that there was anything wrong with IKEA, but having seen the antiquities scattered around Callum's home, my trinkets felt meaningless. In his big central kitchen, a battered metal helmet had held cutlery. When I'd queried it, he'd waved a hand and mentioned some local skirmish where it had been worn by his ancestor. A ding in the base showed how it had protected the man from a sword blow to the head.

Lifesaving spoon holders. Nothing I owned could compete with that.

Propping my elbows on my square dining table, I ran my critical gaze over the rest of the kitchen in the house my dad had bought when I'd started at Bristol University. Was that doorframe always so narrow? Such low headroom. If I had my hair in a top knot, it skimmed the frame. Someone of Callum's height would be at risk of a dented forehead if they happened to forget the low lintel say, in the middle of the night.

He'd have to wear his helmet to be safe.

"Why are you chuckling at the doorway? What did it ever do to you?" Beth strolled in, carrying a breakfast bowl.

"It's too small for a tall man, if I happened to have one as a visitor."

It had been nearly a week since I'd seen Callum, and Beth and I had been ships that passed in the night. The ridiculous hours she worked meant we often went days without seeing one another. Now we were both home—I was working an evening event tonight but had the rest of the day off—I wanted to talk to her. I needed to share the confusion in my mind with one other person before I got on a train to London for lunch with my mother and sister.

A meeting that I set up in order to talk about Callum.

My need for moral support had never been greater.

Beth clattered about, shoving her bowl and spoon in the dishwasher. Then she took the seat next to mine. "You're talking about having the giant Scot over to stay. Go you! When, and do we need a special sign so I know to stay out of the house?"

Beth knew Callum had come to my office and whisked me away and, mostly through text messages, I'd recounted meeting his ex, and kissing him in the rain in the airport.

That kiss... It fried my brain whenever I thought of it. Cool rain on my skin, his hot lips on mine. The intoxicating taste of him on my tongue. Which was why my next sentence sounded so wrong. "I'm not sure if I should see him again."

Beth stared, agog. "Why? Is it because of Stephen?"

"Yuck," we said in unison, as we always did at my ex's name.

Stephen and I had only dated for a couple of months half a year ago, but he'd been all things charming. As well as an unapologetic cheat. When I'd walked into his office and found him entangled with another woman, he'd had the nerve to laugh it off and invite me to join in. Then he'd called me a prude for my outrage. Like exclusivity was suddenly old-fashioned.

My ex boyfriend's betrayal had formed part of my reasoning for even hearing Dominic's marriage offer. At the point he'd offered, my mind had been in a dark place. What difference did it make marrying for love when the relationships I'd seen sucked?

The crash course of my all-day date with Callum had shifted something in my perception. I hadn't asked him how he viewed monogamy, but I knew what his answer would be. He'd frown then cluck his tongue, maybe even swear as he gave me his opinion on cheats.

With the sands shifting around me, I needed another perspective. Watching Beth for her reaction, I shared my inner thoughts. "A little over a month ago, a man proposed to me, and I haven't told him no."

Silence. Then, "What man?"

"A colleague of my dad's."

"Someone you dated? Doesn't your dad work with a load of crusty old dudes?"

"He does, and no. I've barely spoken to this guy beyond polite chat."

"Then…why did he ask you?"

"He needs a wife for appearance reasons, and I fit the bill. Unmarried, discreet, and I've been seen in company with him enough to make a surprise engagement feasible."

"But you want babies. You told me you always did."

I raised one shoulder because I couldn't bring myself to say I didn't care. I'd be postponing having my own family for a few years. That hurt, but it was a price I'd be willing to pay to safeguard Scarlet.

My friend pursed her lips. "Without wanting to seem judge-y, what the hell?"

I exhaled and sat back in my chair. "I'm aware what it sounds like. But being married and settled will mean Dad will let Scarlet come live with me. Dominic knows this, and it's the only reason I heard him out."

There it was, the cold-hearted fact exposed. Beth and I had lived together for a year after she'd answered my room-mate-wanted ad, and she'd met my family several times. She knew I worried for Scarlet, but she hadn't heard the bitter comments from my father or seen the evidence of my sister's problems. Or Mom's. She had witnessed my family's divide, but we'd never discussed the reason for it, nor the damage that Scarlet was taking on.

I loved my friend, though we were chalk and cheese in almost every way. She was easygoing where I planned and replanned. I loved matching underwear—nice, silky pieces that made me feel secretly sexy. If Beth remembered to wear a bra, she wouldn't have a hope of matching it to anything. We both had goals, and that was why we got along.

More than once, we'd sat and strategized over how to cope in our busy lives. I cared about her as much as I did about my family, and right now, I just needed her to know my dilemma. To accept that I was in a bad situation and trying to make it good.

As I looked at her, she had her intense thinking face on. There was no true judgment there. She rocked back an inch. "How about this: if you want Scarlet to come live with us, let's just go and get her. I'll drive. I can be a couple of hours late for my first shift without getting fired."

A laugh erupted from me, a weight lifted from sharing my problems. "Dad would make her go back. He'd never tolerate it. But thank you."

"Ask him." Beth placed the words so simply, like I hadn't tried that already. She rolled her eyes. "Ask him again! You never know. Wait, is the proposal guy blackmailing you?" I shook my head. "Then tell him where to shove his plan, or as your best friend, I will protest the shit out of that wedding. Like in *The Graduate*? I would bang those windows until they fell in. Because no way am I ever letting you marry for anything other than a fine Scottish castle." My friend paused and threw me a wink. "I mean for love."

She left her chair. Then, almost at the door, she stopped. "Oh! I meant to say. James, the guy who gave me the note?"

My ears pricked up. I'd been dying to find out what was in that letter.

"We've been talking about…stuff, and he asked if I would come with you on your next visit. To see him."

"Right! Callum sent a message earlier this morning that alluded to you coming. Now it makes sense." Every time my phone vibrated, my heart sang, because we'd been texting every day. And every day he sent another teaser for the weekend. A photo of a magnificent red stag on a hill line. One of Callum in an apron, cooking, though sadly fully dressed. Even a video from his younger brothers, begging me to save them from his miserable face. I adored every message.

"He asked if I wanted to bring you. I thought he meant for moral support." It would be nice, having Beth there. Callum was surrounded by family, and I wouldn't feel so much like the outsider.

"It's a big place?" Beth asked. "They'd have space for me?"

"It's a castle. You're not going to be putting someone out of their bed."

"Chance would be a fine thing," she muttered. "I can come. But not for three days. Maybe a day and a night? But then I'll need to get back to work." My friend paused, her finger at her lip. "If you go, and you really like this Callum after the weekend, what then?"

What indeed. I needed to define that line clearly as my integrity was at stake.

"I'll make that decision before I go."

* * *

*M*om and Scarlet were already seated at Marylebone's Blue Rose restaurant when I arrived from the train station. My sister leapt to her feet and hugged me, not letting go until I nearly fell into the chair next to hers.

"Dad's joining us for lunch," she said, her kohl-lined eyes widening and her tone a warning.

"Oh?" My appetite evaporated, and I leaned over and gave my mother a polite one-sided hug. "That's unexpected."

Handling Dad wasn't on my agenda. During my train journey, I'd been preoccupied thinking about Callum, alongside working on the proposal for him, researching catering companies in Inverness and looking into other costs. I'd spent every bit of my spare time this week on the wedding topic, and it was a no-brainer.

Similar venues in the area were booked out for two years in advance, and I knew with clever marketing I could get Castle McRae into the high-end market. He'd already had happy customers—the two couples who'd married there had posted some great photos online. We could use them as testimonials.

But there was a list of changes he'd need to consider first, potentially expensive ones if there was money to invest, and I'd only had a small glimpse of what he had to offer.

My fingers itched to get back to my laptop and continue work. Lunch with Mom and my sister would've given me an outlet to talk some of it through. Except now, I'd have to sit through a meal with my whole family. My plan fell to pieces.

My pink lemonade arrived just as my father walked in the door. His height, though not matching Callum's, drew the eyes of the other diners, and it took me a second to notice the other man behind him. Suited and booted and heading right for me.

I nearly choked on my drink.

Dad had brought Dominic Hanswick. I eyed the exits and cursed inwardly.

On the train, I'd made a deal with myself. If Scarlet seemed herself today and didn't give me cause to worry, I would call Dominic and refuse his offer. The deal might have been perfectly logical, providing me with a solution to my closest-held desire, but doubt had set in.

A sizable, Callum-shaped doubt.

He made my toes curl and my heart burst with life, and kissing him changed everything I knew. I couldn't ignore the possibility of true happiness and I had the notion that, just maybe, I could marry for love and get my sister. An outside possibility, considering the problem with Dad, but there all the same.

I'd decided to work on convincing Dad first. I just needed to find the right lever to pull to make him listen. After all, I'd got my logical mind from him. Only mine wasn't tainted by the experiences he'd had. Didn't suffer the fears that made him the man he was, for better or worse.

At my side, Scarlet heaved a dramatic teenage sigh, her gaze flitting from Dad to Dominic. "Isn't that the guy who screwed around? Why did Dad bring him?"

Mom started, her hand rushing to her chest like her mind had been elsewhere. She rose, brushing her skirt out, and plastering a pleasant expression on her face. She wore vintage Dior—an off-the-shoulder satin dress with a cinched waist. A former model from Los Angeles, Mom had more designer gowns than an Italian countess, and I'd inherited her taste for style. We shared the same bone structure, though she was a natural blonde and several inches shorter than me, and I'd stopped being able to borrow her clothes years ago.

"Shoulders, Mathilda," Mom murmured with a glance to my posture. She never used to care for things like that. She used to be fun.

Scarlet silently mocked her as Mom kissed my father's cheek then turned to greet Dominic, and I held in a sigh. This was going to be a far worse lunch than I'd prepared for.

* * *

Over the first two courses, Dad kept the business talk to a minimum. Dominic made polite conversation, mostly with my mother, and I avoided his meaningful looks, trying to talk to Scarlet.

Named for her gorgeous, if treacherous red hair, my little sister was one of my favourite people in the world. From the moment I met her as a newborn in the hospital, I'd adored her, and being a decade older, I was almost a third parent to her.

Much the same as Callum was to his twin brothers.

He demonstrated the precise relationship I wanted with my sister. And I was sure she wanted it, too. Scarlet had overheard Mom and Dad discussing my offer the first time I'd made it. Mom had cautiously encouraged the move before Dad had blown up, and Scarlet's eyes had welled when she'd recounted the story to me over a video call. Scarlet cried about as often as I did. It nearly broke me to witness her pain. To have one parent reject her had been hard, though she'd grown up with Dad's behaviour, and the effects had been slow and incremental. But to have her own mother do the same, no matter the intention—that was cruel.

Living with Dad and our mother affected her every day. One glance at our table would tell any passerby why.

Scarlet, with her glorious auburn waves, was clearly not my father's genetic child.

And where he had a permanent dark tan, and I a medium olive skin, Scarlet was pale. More so than even Mom's fair complexion.

Freckles sprinkled wilfully over her upturned nose and cheeks, her limbs were long and colt-like, and our mother's high cheekbones stood out prominently, giving her a gamine look. At fourteen, she drew attention and could pass for years older—a fact she'd started to realise.

My father's unknown roots—likely Middle Eastern or Mediterranean, though his background was a complete mystery, even to him—did not exist in her DNA, a fact that had been scientifically proven a few weeks after her birth. Though that only confirmed what everybody knew.

Near the end of her pregnancy, Mom had confessed to falling in love with a teacher at my private school. When challenged, the man had acknowledged Scarlet was his child, then promptly ran for his life, never to be heard of again. Mom had been devastated.

Dad had been deeply hurt, but he'd eventually forgiven his wife. The crying and wriggling evidence of her deceit? Not so much.

I shifted my chair toward Scarlet's, and my life-toughened sister smiled prettily at me. "How are things?" I enquired.

Scarlet rolled her eyes as I cast a meaningful look at Dad, who was pointing out something on the menu to a waiter. The noise of the restaurant concealed our conversation, even if he had been paying attention.

"I quit ballet," Scarlet drawled.

"Why?"

"Parent expo. Neither of them came. I lost it and threw up. It's not worth the stress."

Effing hell. "But you loved that."

She shrugged a shoulder, then from the hook under the table, collected a small handbag. From inside, she took a lip gloss and unscrewed the lid. My sister applied the brilliant red shade at the table using her butter knife as a mirror—a poor display of manners primed to wind Dad up. I eyed her new bag, my stomach shrinking.

It was a very expensive couture wallet. Chanel, with a gold chain, the entwined letters of the logo glinting under the restaurant's bright lights.

The bag was not one of Mom's.

She was stealing again?

I glanced at Mom. Under the cover of the table, she cracked a pill packet, swallowing a little white tablet down with water. *What the heck?*

With my thumb and forefinger, I pinched the area between my eyes. "Lottie, the bag?"

Despite my using her nickname, the one only I used, my sister kept her fierce blue eyes on Dad. She snapped the lip gloss lid into place and said loudly, "Do you like it? I'll get you one, if you want."

Across the table, the source of her worst view of herself, the motivation behind her every negative thought, raised his head. Dad paused in his conversation, switching his gaze to her. A moment passed where my little sister froze under his scrutiny, her spine straight and her proud chin tipped up in defiance, then Dad spoke and I watched her crumple.

"Mathilda, I'd like to bring you up to speed with Storm Force. You're practically a stranger to my office these days." His attention settled on me, and a fond smile broached his lips.

He'd dismissed my sister without even saying a word to her, just the same as how he'd spoken over her when she'd provoked Dominic about his politician lover and ignored her multiple attempts to bait his temper. Ordering ketchup to go with her salad. Applauding as a diner mistimed their stand and hit a passing waiter, sending a tray of drinks flying.

Attention-seeking behaviour at its finest, and worse than she'd ever been before. My hopes for a happier situation slowly ground into dust.

My sister's eyes filled with tears, then she leapt to her feet, knocking her chair over in her haste to flee the table. In a flash, she'd punched open the restaurant's exit and vanished.

A hushed silence fell, the attention of the restaurant on our group.

"Excuse me." I stood, needing to go after Scarlet.

"Stay," Dad ordered. "We don't indulge tantrums." He said it in the way presidents say they don't negotiate with terrorists.

I sent a pleading gaze to Mom, but she dabbed her mouth with a serviette and remained in her seat, not meeting my eye.

"Yes, stay," echoed Dominic, his voice as smooth as honey. "You need to hear about this ass—pardon me, this guy, who thinks he can sue us because he can't read small print. Isn't that right, Maximus?"

Dominic slapped a hand on the table, garbling something

about ungrateful Scots, and I slowed, collecting my bag and jacket, my brain catching up.

Dad was being sued over Storm Force? It couldn't be.

No, Callum would have said.

In that second, I was utterly torn. I needed to go after my sister. I had to hear what Callum had done.

"Laird Callum McRae," Dominic pronounced, looking directly at me. "Tell me that meathead of a guy needs the cash? Google him. He's old money. Rich as Croesus. You can practically smell the privilege."

Dad's gaze turned black, and my heart froze as I paused at the corner of the table, waiting for my mother to move out of my way. Mom fussed over keeping her dress from touching the table, and the pressure had me dying inside.

No, no, no, this couldn't be true.

"What are you talking about?" I didn't need to ask—I hadn't misheard Dominic abuse Callum's name. I just wished I had.

"Some jumped-up Scot thinks he can take me to court." Dad's cheeks flushed, and he clutched the stem of his wine-glass, the red liquid slopping. "Because he has a title and land that his ancestors plundered."

Zoning out, I slipped past Mom, nudging her elbow and muttering an apology. I knew how Dad's rant would go. He despised landed gentry, anyone who wasn't a self-made man like him. Dominic was playing to that, talking about privilege when he himself was as upper-middle-class as it got.

But where Dad could ignore that in his business partner, would he do the same with a guy like Callum? No. He wouldn't. My chance of bringing his name into the conversation vanished.

Even so, I couldn't let it go. Loyalty to Callum surged, dislodging my usual calm.

At the end of the table, I paused. "Maybe if we acted with

integrity we could be fair in paying our contracts," I snapped, then I gave a meaningful look to Dominic before swinging my gaze back to my mother. "Mom, I'm going after Scarlet."

"There really is no need. She does this all the time," Mom finally spoke, her accent soft but distinctly Californian. She regained her seat and smoothed her dress out. "We're only ten minutes from home. Or if she hasn't gone there, then she'll be in Regent's Park—she goes to the boating lake with her friends after school. Just like you did at that age, though you never behaved like she does. Now, darling, your father wants you to finish your conversation. Surely you don't want to upset him further?"

On my mother's striking face, I searched for any kind of masked worry. For years, she'd carried herself in a sort of bubble, with blithe smiles and a placid air, and I wanted to shake the emotion out of her. I searched hard to see in her the distance she and Dad had travelled, the pain she had gone through to have her lover run out on her, and her contrite behaviour to a husband she still loved. But all I saw was a flighty, overindulged star who'd made a huge mistake, damaged everyone around her, and ducked the consequences by zoning out.

Mom loved Scarlet, I was sure of that, but she ignored my father's behaviour and its effects, because facing it would mean tackling Dad. I knew why she didn't want to rake over that ground—Dad could be unbearable in one of his moods. But she'd never even tried. Neither had he.

I loved them both, but it didn't mean I could readily forgive either of them.

"Will you stay?" she asked, no true emotion in her eyes.

"No. Will you help me find her?" My reply was thin and small, and I cleared my throat. "Please."

Mom's pleasant expression faltered. "I... Your father is

still eating." Then she smiled like she'd had an epiphany. "I'll send Scarlet a message and tell her when we'll be home."

Right. "Dad, Mr Hanswick, please accept my apologies for leaving early. Mom, I'll call you next week." I pushed away from the table, about as angry as I allowed myself to get.

The click of my heels raced my heartbeats as I followed Scarlet's flight path to the restaurant exit, unsure of which I was more worried about: helping my sister or calling Callum.

12

I HAVE NEVER SAID THAT
OUT LOUD

*M*athilda

I reached to grab the restaurant's door handle but a manicured hand landed over mine, preventing me from exiting. Dominic spun me around.

"Hold up, Mathilda. I need a moment with you to discuss wedding planning. For starters, telling your parents we're dating. I intend to do it today, if you are in agreement?"

"What? No, I need to find Scarlet." I twisted away from his grip, but he didn't release the door. As I huffed in surprise, Dominic raised his dark eyebrows.

"Please. Your sister will be fine, and a few minutes is all I need. Over the next month, it would be prudent to start people talking about us before we announce the wedding. We should be seen together." He gestured to the restaurant as if to demonstrate why he was there. "I have a holiday booked with Abigail, but other than that single week, I'll make myself available."

"Dominic, not now. Didn't you see what just happened?" Had she gone left or right? I craned my neck, peering through the door glass. Weekend crowds filled the London street. Knowing my sister, she wouldn't hang around.

"She's a teenager, what do you expect?" He rolled his eyes, looking bored, then he shifted to a casual pose with his elbow holding the door closed. It would look to anyone watching like we were having a cosy conversation. I didn't want Dad coming over, so I lifted my chin and levelled my gaze at Dominic.

I was about to say something about expecting Scarlet to be cared for, when something stopped me.

"I have a holiday booked with Abigail."

Dominic's words repeated in my mind, and realisation dawned. He was still having the affair? My stomach dropped in disgust, and I reared back. Until that second, it hadn't occurred to me to ask. I'd assumed he was out of it. That the politician—Abigail—had put her family first following the humiliation they must have endured. But no. They were going on holiday together.

How could they?

I hadn't thought through Dominic's proposal, not with any real rigour beyond how it would benefit my sister. But it was easy to decide on it now.

"You're still seeing her," I said dully.

Dominic tilted his head, regarding me quizzically. "Yes. Why wouldn't I be? Is that a problem?"

Only a huge moral conflict of which I had no intention of getting in the middle.

I needed to find Scarlet. Dominic didn't deserve a second more of my time. I was done with him.

"I need to help my sister," I hissed. "I'm leaving. Please release the door."

"One question, before I let you go. That man, that Callum McRae, is his name familiar to you? I think it might be."

I stared at him. That sounded like a threat. "What business is that of yours?"

"It's very much my business. He's suing me." Dominic leaned closer, his features in a careful, flirtatious smile, but his tone dark. "If he's going to be your fuck buddy, I have something to say about that."

Seriously? "No, you really don't. Leave me alone, Dominic."

Dislodging his hand from the door, I twisted the handle and slipped outside, my sister the only thing on my mind.

"Look out for my email," Dominic called into the street. "This little display from your sister is all the more reason to get ahead of the game, don't you think?"

* * *

Following a fruitless search along Marylebone High Street, I headed in the direction of Regent's Park, trying Scarlet's number again and again. Nothing. After I crossed the busy roads leading to the York Bridge entrance, my phone rang in my hand, Callum's name bright on the screen.

I dragged in a breath. In my hunt for my sister, I'd cooled down over Callum's legal action against Dad. He had every right to go after his money; in fact, if it had been anyone else, I would have encouraged him to take the case to court.

But the reason I'd taken it so hard was because it wiped out any chance of Callum and me being a thing. Dad would never allow Scarlet to live with me if I became serious with someone he didn't approve of. Her behaviour had worsened, and I worried so much for her emotional health, let alone her petty thieving habits, so she needed my help. Now I'd discounted Dominic, my options were even more limited.

If I went to Scotland, I'd like Callum all too much. I'd

want to be his, and it would make things ten times harder with Dad. I'd be choosing Callum over Scarlet, and my sister needed to come first to someone.

That could only be me.

It was better that I didn't go at all and let the feelings I had for him die.

A fire inside me had gone out, and I answered the call, trudging through the ashes of might-have-beens.

In contrast, Callum's greeting was ember-warm. "I made up about six different reasons to call, but I'm nae good at that. I've been working my backside off all morning, and all I wanted, lass, was to hear your voice."

God darn it. "Tell me one of the reasons. Or two." I couldn't help myself. My heart hurt at his impossibly familiar voice.

"To remind you to bring something fancy to wear when you visit. For the party, ye ken."

"I hadn't forgotten. I went shopping," I replied as I scanned the park's expanse of green fields for Scarlet. The narrow neck of the boating lake wound its way to my left under the bridge, so I navigated past the tourists and headed for the footpath.

Callum made a sound of approval. "I'd ask you to describe your choice, but I want to be surprised."

I'd picked out a couple of options, but a liquid satin maxi dress in a silvery blue was my forerunner. It had a single shoulder strap of tiny silver flowers, and I'd fallen in love with it the moment I'd stepped into the store. Paired with a long, gauzy wrap and the sort of heels I could only wear with Callum, I couldn't wait to wow him.

Between sorting through my wardrobe options and working up the wedding proposal for his land and castle, I'd done little else but plan for seeing the man. I'd booked in to have my hair done, then a waxing. All to have him look at me with that intense stare. The one that made me feel beautiful.

The anticipation of kissing him again had the power to derail me from any coherent thought. I didn't want to cancel my weekend.

A sucker for punishment, I clutched the phone tighter and said, "Give me another reason."

"You can have my every thought, but...is something wrong?"

"I've just had lunch with my family." I stopped, unsure of how to proceed.

Callum huffed. "Did my name come up by any chance?"

"It did." At intervals along the edge of the path, benches perched in shaded positions, giving views to the Regency-style Georgian mansions on the other side of the water. Houses designed to be imposing—they had no effect on me, having been raised in the penthouse apartment of one.

Finding a vacant seat, I dropped into it. I could keep an eye on the open park at the same time as having a mini heartbreak for a man I was only just getting to know.

"Did it cause you a problem? I should have told you. I'm ready to cancel the paperwork if you say the word."

Of course he would. My stomach flipped. "Don't. Storm Enterprises owes you the money. I don't want you to change anything, but..." I picked at a thread on my tartan skirt. Strange that I'd picked Scottish tartan this morning. I hadn't even consciously noticed until now. I blew out a breath, trying to be brave despite my insides quaking. "Do you remember I said I needed my father on side for a reason? That reason is Scarlet, my sister. Dad upset her over lunch, and she ran off. I'm trying to find her so we can talk about her coming to live with me."

"And you need your father to agree to you taking

custody? Is that why you thought to get married? Would your mother agree to let her go?"

How effortlessly he accepted that.

"Under the right conditions, they'd release her. I hadn't thought about custody, just her living somewhere else so she wasn't under Dad's nose."

"They dinna get along," he stated. Then his tone changed. "Are you worried for the girl's safety?"

"No! It's not like that. Dad isn't a bad person." I hastened. To anyone else, he'd be an ogre, but not to me.

"Then she's not his, aye?"

"Jesus, Callum." My heart thundered. In our family, the subject had never, ever been raised. I'd heard gossip, of course, but I only knew the truth because Mom's best friend told me the full story several years ago. Her revelation had changed my childhood. It had made me realise just how not-normal we were.

"I looked you up, too. I saw there was a scandal and put two and two together. Ah, Mathilda, it's killing me here, knowing you're unhappy. I'm nae trying to tear open wounds. I want to help. I didnae mean to upset you."

The scandal had been an old modelling colleague of Mom's who'd written a memoir. In it, she'd made sensationalist claims against a number of other celebrities, including allegations about my mother's affair. Dad had managed to pay off the publisher to keep certain details out of the press —mainly around the dates, but the story had the gutter press's interest. In school, at my ladies' college, I had suffered whispers, and I hated that my sister had heard them, too.

"You didn't. But you're right. Scarlet isn't Dad's biological daughter, and I have never said that out loud."

"It's bad for a family to have secrets."

"Doesn't yours?" I asked gently. "Do you talk about your

father with your brothers?" I could only imagine the difficulty of rehashing those memories.

"Are ye kidding? For six months, it was all we spoke about. Ally and Wasp were eight years old and would sleep in my bed some nights, or in with Gordain. They'd have nightmares over imagining his death, sometimes in anger, wanting Da to suffer, and sometimes in sheer pain because they remembered the evenings when he'd be drunk and going after them in a rage. Their mother hated it, but we made her talk about him. It was the only thing that kept us sane. Someone that overbearing doesn't deserve to keep their control once they've gone. Secrets hold power. Talking about them stops that."

A long pause drew out as I processed his words. Down the path, an octogenarian man pushed an equally elderly woman in a wheelchair. She reached a hand back, and he stopped, squeezed her fingers, leaned forward, and kissed her hair. Then they carried along as if their tiny display of connection and affection hadn't broken something inside me.

Hot tears pricked my eyes.

I hadn't cried over anything in the longest time.

"Am I holding you up in your search? Because I have something to say before you go." Callum's words were careful, but his tone contained a new urgency. Like he could tell I was about to cancel our plans and retreat like I'd done before.

I didn't want to do that. It hurt to think about it, but what other choice did I have?

"I'm responsible for part of your worry, so I'm taking that on. I caused it, and it's my problem now, and I'm going to come up with a solution."

"No, you don't have to."

"I do. You should let me. Will you give me a chance to fix this?"

"I like you," I uttered. "So much. My family's troubles are nothing to do with you."

"But you are, and I've made life harder for you. Mathilda, I have not stopped thinking about you from the moment we met. Remembering your lips on mine has tormented me, and I want, nae, I *need* to see you again. Do ye want to know how many times I look at the pictures of your face? Dinna make me beg, lass. It'll dent my pride, and that's already as thick as my house's walls."

Torment was a good word. Since he'd walked into Storm Enterprise's event like he'd owned the place, I'd felt his pull like a magnet. Unwavering and strong and impossible to ignore. "I want to see you, too."

Over the water, a flash of red caught my eye. Scarlet! I jumped to my feet and waved. My sister hesitated on the opposite path, then waved back and pointed in the direction of the bridge. "I've spotted Scarlet."

"Go, get the lass, but I have the worst sense you're planning to call things off with me. So, let me say my piece before you do. Mathilda, you are extraordinary. There's a force about you that has laid me flat on my back, and I can't sleep for wanting you."

My heart sang as my feet flew. "How can you say things like that?"

"Because I am hanging out here trying to make you see how good we'd be together. At least we can try, aye? Give me the opportunity to fix the issue with your dad. We'll look at it together, plan for your sister, too. This is what I'm good at— making my clan strong. Let me."

At the end of the footpath, where it joined onto York Bridge, Scarlet darted around the corner. Her face lit up, and in a second, she was in my arms, squeezing the life out of me.

"Who are you talking to?" she whispered.

"A friend."

Though I wanted him to be so much more. He was throwing offers of help at me, but I hardly knew how to accept them. Too long, I'd made plans on my own, any occasional and desperate requests for help from my parents batted back. Like Mom, when I'd needed to find my sister.

Callum cared for so many people, his broad shoulders taking their strain. I'd planned to help him with my professional expertise—ease his burden, not add to it, though I got the distinct feeling he wouldn't see it that way.

"Friends who shared the best kiss of my life," Callum murmured in my ear. "Goodbye, and please to God let me see your face at the airport on Friday."

13

THE COMING STORM

*C*allum
My solar was in chaos, the main room turned upside down in an attempt to make it tidy. Piles of outdoor clothes, paperwork, and files that were going down to the office, mugs that needed to be returned to the kitchen. I didn't live like a slob, far from it, but the castle's highest rooms were my refuge, and no one came in here but my boys.

Mathilda had sent a message to expect her tomorrow, as planned. Something had changed after she'd spoken to her sister, and she hadn't ditched me as I'd expected.

My heart was in a vice, had been for days.

"Are you taking your girlfriend to Braithar for the party?" Ally asked from on top of my quilt, his sprawled frame making the room even more untidy. I wasn't expecting Mathilda to stay in my bed, but the chance was there, and I wasn't going to put her off with clutter.

"Aye."

"Did you change your mind about the raft race, yet?"

Him and that damn race. Lachlan's invitation to Castle

110

Braithar mentioned Highland games, including everything from caber tossing to a raft race across his river. The boys, of course, wanted to compete in the most dangerous part. It would be at night, in Spring, when rivers ran high.

"No."

"Why? Are you going to fight with Lachlan? Take him on head-to-head in wrestling? That would be epic."

"No." The man was fifty for Christ's sake.

My brother snorted. "Can you say anything other than one-word answers?" I gave him a look, and he rolled his eyes. "You're no fun."

Beyond other plans I had for Lachlan, I also wanted to reconcile with our relative. Lachlan was chief of the clan. I respected him and I was also the heir to his title. The head of the House of McRae. He had two daughters, neither of whom had any interest in the clan, or in Castle Braithar, their home. I didn't know what he had planned for Braithar, but the chieftaincy would pass to me.

The likelihood was we'd never reconcile to discuss it, and I only had myself, and my father before me, to blame. We'd both pissed the man off no end.

"What's it like being in love?" Ally rolled onto his back, rucking up my quilt further. He took his headphones from his neck and toggled the buttons. "Because it looks like an epic case of blue balls. You've gone from miserable to super-strength edgy in a week. I hope to God she puts you out of your misery and takes you to bed for the weekend."

So do I.

"Ye ken I dinna like you talking like that. Get away with ye," I muttered and dropped down the stack of invoices I'd been sorting through then pointed toward the door. Ally made a sport of baiting me, and I was close to the edge already. "Take that tray of mugs down. Then find Wasp and sweep out the great hall."

James knocked politely on the outer door at the top of the spiral steps—it could only be him as none of my brothers ever knocked.

"Come in," I yelled then turned back to Ally. He hadn't moved.

"You aren't too big for me to pick up and throw," I growled.

With a chuckle, Ally clambered up as James entered the room. My youngest brother flounced away, the tray left on the heavy wooden chest of drawers. "By the way," his voice came as his boots rapped down the stone stairwell, "I need a new laptop. Mine broke when my bike landed on it."

"Ally! For fuck's sake. How?" I threw up my arms, my exasperation spilling over. He'd had the laptop for his birthday, same as Wasp. Except he couldn't cope without his. How the hell was I going to afford a replacement?

The bank had refused to help with my debts. I'd had the letter yesterday. They were as fast to say no as they were to demand new payments, and I had fewer and fewer ideas on how to make them.

I parked the thought in my overflowing box of worries.

James gave me a small smile, his dark hair in disarray, telling me he'd been running his hands through it. Worrying, too, it seemed. "You wanted to see me?"

Despite my constant woman-shaped distraction, I still had a business to run, and younger men to keep in line. All week, James had been as preoccupied as I was. He'd been texting Beth, Mathilda's friend, after he'd written his note to her. They'd also been talking late into the night. Whatever conversation they'd had was affecting him, and I wanted to gauge where his mind was at.

My aim with him, in the months left before he returned to his arsehole of an uncle and his own responsibilities, was to change the mindset he'd been poisoned with for the past decade. Make him into the fair and equitable man I knew he could be.

"I've a tenant in the village who can't pay his rent. Tobias Sinclair. Talk me through how you'd handle it, then it's yours to go and settle."

James straightened his spine, and his gaze switched to the window. "My uncle would have an eviction notice drafted. How behind is your tenant? A month to repay is reasonable, but any more compromises your income."

My already raw temper simmered. He hadn't asked a single question about the circumstances. "The man works in quality control at the distillery. He has a new baby, a wife who is ill, and he's given up work to care for them both."

The younger man in front of me paused, and I prayed for a glimmer of insight to show my work with him had made a difference. Any little sign that my energies—already too thinly spread—were making an impact and denting his uncle's malevolent teachings.

"How do his personal issues affect you?"

That was it. My lid blew.

"For fuck's sake, James. Where would you send them? An ill woman, a tiny babe, and a desperate man? What good would it do the world to make that family homeless?"

His forehead furrowed, dark eyebrows slanting down, but my rant escalated, and my breathing sped up. All the frustration in me spilled over. At the twins and not being able to give them all they needed. At Gordain and his career and wanting desperately for him to get his streaming. Over wanting Mathilda and having to control how I fought for her.

I advanced towards him, forgetting my size. How intimidating I could look.

"These are real people we're talking about. They've hit hard times, but that isn't their fault. You can't think like this when it's your own tenants who have issues." I chopped the side of my hand into the palm of the other. "Fine, if they abuse your properties or your goodwill, but you need to ask the question before you serve a judgement. Find out the details and help them. A payment plan, a six-month hold on their rent, a no-interest long-term debt, if needs be. Whatever works. Marie Sinclair is a chemical engineer, so when in time she goes back to work they could clear the debt, no trouble. James, get it into your skull that people come first, every time. Kindness above money. That is your responsibility when you're as blessed as we are. What the hell have I done wrong to make you think you can just take a home away like that?"

I glared then pulled back an inch, seeing his paled expression.

Oh no.

James had frozen, locked himself down, his expression and his features held neutral. Just like he'd been when he'd moved in.

My brothers understood my bluster. I could storm about the place, ranting, and none of them would bat an eyelid. Or they'd even laugh and bait me all the more. James didn't have the same resilience. I normally—mostly—had better control, and guilt ate at me from how I'd lost it.

I took him by the shoulder. Squeezed. "Christ, man. Come back. I'm sorry for yelling. If I shout, shout back. Explain your thinking or ask me to explain mine. Don't shut down on me."

His jaw ticked. The neutral expression left his eyes, and his gaze flew to mine. Panicked. Alive. "I know. I know! On one hand I have my uncle telling me to underline profit and protect the estate, and on the other I have you, my childhood memory of my parents, and my own reason telling me the opposite. I don't know how to rationalise it. Any of it. Tenants, compassion, making the right decision."

"Aye, you do—" I began, but he hadn't finished.

"Relationships. Women."

The words hung in the air. I drew my head back. Okay, this was more than I'd expected. But it was good. Very good. I gave him a shake. "Sit down, will ye?"

We moved to a pair of armchairs placed under the main window at the front of the castle. The blue-grey loch and rich colours of the estate were as familiar to me as my own hand. James and his thinking, however, were entirely alien. My burst of temper evaporated as quickly as it had arrived. I trod carefully.

"I yelled out a number of options for Sinclair. I trust you to help them choose the best one, but I'm right here if you want to talk through any part of it." James nodded, and I took a breath. "Now, tell me about Beth. You two have been talking? I take it she's the woman you mean."

He dipped his head, his gaze keen. "We've spoken every day."

Every day? My jaw ached to drop, but I controlled my reaction. "Aye, it has been something like that between Mathilda and me. Are you...courting her?"

He let out a short laugh. "I hardly know."

"But you have no choice?"

My mentee, James, tenth earl Fitzroy, and twenty-year-old heir of Belvedere, one of the grandest homes and estates in England, placed his palms on his knees like he was trying to ground himself in the middle of a tempest. "That's a good way to put it."

"What's another way?"

"That I want to. Consciously, despite knowing all the problems it will bring. Callum, she's more alive than anyone

I've ever met. But I'm failing before I even start. I don't even have the first clue how to impress her."

I pursed my lips. I'd long suspected that James had little experience with relationships. He'd barely known how to fit in with me and my boys when he'd moved in, though that had slowly changed. He was bursting with energy, he worked as hard as any of us, but his emotional development still had far to go. Better to lay out the basics and show him how my approach with Mathilda had beaten hurdle after hurdle thrown in our path. "Beth likes you in that way?"

He swallowed. "I don't know. How can I tell?"

"She asks you questions, answers what you put to her, seeks you out for no real reason." I swallowed now. "Calls you back." At least I'd solved that problem in my own area. Mathilda used my number now, though we hadn't spoken since she'd been with her sister.

"She does those things," he said simply, his cheeks reddening under the black stubble he didn't usually wear.

"Then I can only tell you what worked for me. Being so... moved by another person is rare. Rarer still if they return the opinion. Find a way to make it work, wee steps to get to know one another, and dinna let go unless she says so."

He huffed, his gaze drifting to my bookcase, the titles a mix of leather-bound estate ledgers and paperback crime procedurals. "Maybe it's easier for you with Mathilda. You don't have the same barriers I do."

A laugh erupted from me, and my mood lifted. "Aside from me suing her father?"

James's eyes widened. I had an idea on how to tackle Mathilda's father, but I wasn't sure she'd agree to it. The woman I was falling for had caution and poise written through her bones. I was bullheaded if I didn't plan. And sometimes even if I did.

"I have such a weight of expectation and duty against me, Callum. I hardly know where to start changing that."

My mirth dried up. I wasn't sure what he meant, though I knew he had hoops to jump through in order to inherit later in the year, but James needed to become his own man and take his own path. My version of my duty—to my family, my name, and my clan—wouldn't be identical to his, and I didn't want to lead him.

"You shape what you can around what you want. Around what's right for you. It's your life, nobody else's. If you want the woman, ask her out."

James shook his head like nothing could be so simple, but he smiled, and for the first time today, I felt that I'd got something right. I leapt to my feet, renewed in my intentions and with a list of jobs needing doing before a certain pair of lasses showed up at Inverness airport tomorrow at lunchtime. "Now, help me straighten up this castle. You're as responsible as I am for the coming storm."

I had four days to make Mathilda Storm fall for me, and I intended to make every minute count.

14

SCOTTISH TARMAC

Mathilda

The wheels screeched, and the plane jumped as we touched down on Scottish tarmac. I'd gripped the armrest the entire flight, my emotions a precisely equal mix of nerves and anticipation. In minutes, we'd be off the plane and into the airport where Callum waited.

A shiver caught me. Undermined me.

I'd been attracted to men, content on dates, acquiescent to sex, but never…more. Never the incessant yearning I had to be near the big Scot. It might make things harder for me, but my decision was made.

My conversation with Scarlet, as I'd walked her home from Regent's Park last weekend, stayed my fears a little. Her worsening behaviour was a stunt. She'd planned it all to play Dad, winding him up to the point he'd send her away. And where? To the sister who kept asking to take her in.

That a fourteen-year-old had constructed such a plan hurt my heart, but I'd hugged her fiercely and promised her a happy home. I just had to find a way of making one.

Being closed off couldn't help her. I needed to stop trying

to cope on my own. It was a huge step but, if what I felt for Callum was real, I was going to let him in.

Beth fidgeted at my side, flicking her seatbelt fastener open then closed. Neither of us had been talkative during the flight, as though excitement had us strung out. When the plane taxied into its stand, I switched my phone back on, and my friend followed suit.

Both devices lit up with alerts.

Below a missed call and voicemail from my dad—yeah, I'd get right onto calling him back—was a picture message, Callum and James standing together, the sign for the departure lounge behind them.

"James is here, too," I uttered, though it was Callum's face that I got stuck on. How had I ever thought him not handsome? The man's face melted my bones.

Beth hugged her knees, her face concealed under a sheet of dark curls. "I feel sick. But I'm not nervous." She deliberately made her voice quiver.

"No, of course you aren't. Neither of us are shaking." I sent Callum a quick message to say we'd landed, and he replied with a heart. *A heart.*

I wanted to make like Beth and hide my face despite being minutes away from making a fool of myself. I couldn't run to him. It would be undignified to cry his name and jump into his arms, even if that was everything I desired to do.

"If this is just a hookup, why are you so freaked out?"

"I don't know," came the reply from under Beth's hair. "Maybe I'm just ill, there was a bug going around work. Or I might have a problem here. I've never taken the time to get to know a guy like this before. Been friends, first."

"It's good if you like someone like that." I'd always wanted Beth to have a boyfriend, someone to breach the walls she had around her, but maybe I understood her reticence. From what Callum had told me, James didn't seem all that available. They lived miles apart, and Beth's life was so busy.

The cabin's seatbelt light extinguished, and people stood, grabbing bags and sliding arms into jackets. My pulse stuttered. "We can't hide in here," I managed, but the control in my voice wavered.

Beth peeked out, sat upright, then threw an arm around me. "We are strong, independent women. They should be quaking in their boots at seeing us, not the other way around." She straightened, leapt on the seat to grab our bags from the overhead cabin, and hopped down again. "Come on, tiger, let's go get them."

Callum solved my dilemma about our method of greeting. As I rounded the corner, he started like he'd been shot, slapped his friend in the chest, then roared my name over the hubbub of the crowd.

His long strides ate the distance between us and, in seconds, I was crushed against his chest.

"Mathilda," he murmured into my hair. Still holding me, he backed us into a pillar, giving us a semblance of privacy in the open space. He dragged in a breath, like he was inhaling me. "Christ, woman, you're actually here."

"I should have known you didn't mind public displays of affection," I mumbled into his shirt, inhaling him right back, flooding my senses with outdoors and coffee, woodsmoke and musky aftershave. But my mountain man wasn't done. At my words, he rumbled in satisfaction, dipped his face to mine, and laid a sweet, gentle kiss on my lips. Brief but perfect.

I melted into him.

"You have no idea how good it is to do that." He inched his head back, and for a moment, he watched me.

A tremble began in my hands, because what I saw in his eyes scared the life out of me.

"If ye keep looking at me like that," Callum said, his hold on me so tight, "you're putting us in grave danger."

"Of what?"

With a nod, he indicated across the arrivals lounge to where two airport security guards stood, then widened his pale-blue eyes. "Taking this display of affection thing too far and getting us arrested for indecent exposure."

I burst out with a laugh, the intense spell between us broken. Callum was the last man on Earth who would engage in anything too risqué in public, same as I was the last woman.

Though the mere idea of being intimate with him took my stuttering pulse and sent it through the roof.

"Take me home, will you," I managed.

He threw me a smirk, grasping my hand in his as he led me to the exit. Ahead, Beth and James crossed the road, his gaze on her, their bodies close.

"Home. You've said it now. I can't unhear it. Those are the sweetest words to have come from your lips."

Then he ducked his head so his lips were next to my ear, and I burned at his next words.

"Until, lass, ye scream my name. Those words will be all the sweeter."

* * *

*A*t the castle, Callum introduced me to his twin brothers—an experience in itself as the pair didn't stop with their teasing and swiping at their brother—then showed me upstairs to my room. A bedroom just for me.

I paused at the door while he strode in then deposited my case and bag on a solid-looking dresser. As he turned back, I snapped my mouth closed. Disappointed.

"Do you like your room?" he asked.

"It's lovely." White plaster walls, exposed stone around the window seat, views over the loch. What wasn't to like? Except... My cheeks heated. "I thought I'd be sharing with you."

On the drive from the airport, Callum had held my hand clamped in his. He'd described the plans he'd made for us for the weekend, the sights he was going to show me, and the fun we were going to have.

He hadn't tried to kiss me again.

"Did ye now?" Callum retreated to the wall, his hands behind his back. He squared his shoulders, a wicked glint in his eyes. "You haven't even bought me dinner. Whatever made you think I was that kind of man?"

He joked, but the message was clear—he hadn't automatically assumed I'd share his bed. A little piece of my heart became his.

I took a step into the room. "Well, I brought you a wedding venue proposal, but I think you like me for more than my good ideas."

In my own way, I had the confidence to go after what I wanted. Except not always with a direct approach. With my career, I'd studied, taken a job in the industry I could easily find work in, rather than specialise with the one I loved. With my sister, I was working on options and moving carefully.

Callum took a more direct approach in life. There was a lot to be said for his way of thinking.

Dragging in a breath, I held his heavy gaze. Then I slid my coat from my shoulders and tossed it onto a chair. Beth, James, and the twins were downstairs, the hallway outside deserted.

I closed the door then stalked toward him.

"Mathilda," Callum warned.

"Callum."

Nerves gripped me, but I reached out and pulled his hands free, sliding my own up his arms until I'd circled his neck. He took hold of my waist, his gaze burning into mine.

For a glorious moment, we stared into the other's eyes, not doing anything more than holding each other. The intensity of it alarmed me. Excited me.

My knees trembled. I pushed up onto my tiptoes.

"Careful, lass," Callum murmured, but I didn't want to take care. I wanted him.

So I took a taste.

Inching forward until my lips met his, I pressed a kiss to the laird's mouth. Then another. Slow, sensitive movements. Chaste enough, but warming my blood.

Callum made a welcome, strained sound, and he brought a hand to my face and gripped my chin with his big fingers. "Fuck," he muttered, then his mouth slanted over mine as he surrendered his restraint and took my mouth in a single plundering kiss.

The taste of him... We'd barely started when Callum tore his lips from mine. He dragged in a breath and turned his face, pressing his temple to my cheek.

"What's wrong?" I breathed.

"We can't do this now."

"You're telling me. One kiss and I want to rip your clothes off."

"Christ," he muttered and brought his gaze to mine. "That's half the problem."

"You like your clothes? I don't have to tear them."

This restraint in him was unexpected. His fingers gripped me as if holding himself back rather than drawing me to him.

A thudding came at the door.

"Cal! G's home. He's just parked his bike outside. Leave that poor woman alone and get out here." It was Ally's voice.

Callum groaned then called out, "News?"

"Aye, but he won't say until you're downstairs."

"We'll be there," Callum replied.

His attention came back to me. Hot and heavy. "Gordain has been waiting on the result of his application. The next stage of his career. We haven't seen him in weeks."

"You've been worried?" I ran a finger over his furrowed brow.

"Aye."

"Then we should go down."

We stared a few moments longer, a tactical decision made —if we kissed again, if he allowed it, it would be too hard to stop. I already ached, a taut energy building in the centre of my body that needed a great deal more of Callum to ease.

Without any more words, we suspended the need, the burning desire to devour the other, and left the room.

15

MY HEART WAS TOO BIG

Callum

Mathilda and I reached the great hall's open staircase at the same moment Gordain closed the front door. He slung his RAF backpack to the floor, dropped his black motorbike helmet on top, and was immediately engulfed by the twins.

"What did he apply for?" Mathilda asked, her voice low and for me alone.

"Search and rescue pilot training. Helicopters. Very hard to get into."

She arched her eyebrows. "Fingers crossed."

I squeezed her hand and didn't let go, making my way to my brother. As with all my family, their successes were mine, their failures hurting me just as hard. I hadn't the heart to see Gordain disappointed and, over the previous weeks, my stomach had tied itself into a knot every time I'd imagined this scene. His disappointment or, please God, elation.

The surge of lust from Mathilda's kiss amplified my emotions until I practically vibrated. I owed her an explanation about the separate bedrooms, but it was all part of my plan, and it would wait.

Gordain emerged from his impromptu wrestle with the twins, hugged James who'd appeared from the back of the hall, greeted Beth, then turned to us.

His broad smile had infected everyone, though a sense of acute tension reigned. We stood in a ragged circle, all breathing suspended, all eyes on Gordain.

"You must be Mathilda," he introduced himself, his bright-eyed gaze resting on my woman.

"And you're Gordain." Mathilda shook his hand. "Please, don't stand on ceremony for me. I think everyone is about to pass out if you don't share your news."

Gordain settled his expression then pulled an envelope from inside his leathers. He ran it between his fingers then pursed his lips. "I'd just like to thank ye all, my family, and friends, for supporting me—"

He was killing me. "Fucking hell, man. Out with it," I croaked.

Fighting a grin, Gordain opened the envelope then shook the letter out. "Streamed to rotary," he said quietly, his attention on me. "I got in."

A roar ripped out of me, pure relief and joy surging. Slamming into him, I picked up my brother and thumped him on the back, crushing him. Around us, James and the twins bellowed their delight, two feminine voices adding to the happy sounds rising to the rafters.

"You clever fucker." I smacked Gordain on the cheek and dropped him down. He'd done it—achieved his dream. He beamed a lopsided grin at me, then spun around to hug it out with the rest of the family.

I took my first deep breath in weeks.

The weekend was perfect. I had Mathilda here, my family had received the best news in an era, and we were going to make the most of it. In preparation for Gordain's success, in whatever career he'd been assigned, we had a feast organised for tonight.

A hand snaked into mine. Mathilda's. "Congratulations," she whispered.

"For him." I nodded to where my brother showed James the letter. I was prouder than a parent, relieved to the moon and back.

"He handed the letter to you." Mathilda squeezed my fingers. "I don't know who's happier. You for hearing the news, or him for bringing it to you." Warmth spread through me, but she wasn't done. "You're an inspiration to me, do you know that? What you've made for your brothers, this is what I want for Scarlet. All of this."

"You'll have it," I vowed, instantly adding a space for Mathilda's wee sister in my planning. Because if she was to live with her, that could be here. I'd made a giant leap in my head, and it didn't faze me. My woman, on the other hand, would disappear down a rabbit hole if I told her too soon, but the idea was there, and now I could work on making it happen.

* * *

*H*ours later, my family slouched in seats in the great hall, full of chicken stew and warmed by our roaring fire, safe within Castle McRae's thick walls. The evening had been taken up with celebrations and eating, and now we needed either our beds or strong coffee.

My mind was on the first option.

Sitting back, I regarded my family. Three large men, a pair of oversized boys, and two women the centre of all of our attention. Mathilda being here was right. Everything about it. She'd owned the twins, not taking their shite and

127

giving back their teasing with smart quips that delighted them. I'd kept them around us until dinner and since, the temptation of being alone with her too much to bear.

Gordain and Beth chatted easily, laughing about something I hadn't paid attention to. Earlier, Gordain had taken the lass off-road driving, with James swallowing down whatever reaction he was having. She'd asked James to go with her first, but he'd refused point blank to get into the Land Rover if she was behind the wheel. When she and my brother arrived back, mud-splattered and laughing, James had left his post by the door and stalked off, his expression dark.

I'd flagged Gordain down as Beth danced across the carpark to Mathilda, hooting about her wild driving. If the woman had turned two heads, there could be trouble. Gordain enjoyed the company of women and had never suffered a lack of attention.

"Do ye think it worked?" Gordain had slid his aviator sunglasses into his shorn hair. "Fitz was watching for her safe return, aye?"

I'd cocked my head at him.

"He's interested in a woman for the first time ever," Gordain had explained. "Nothing wrong with giving him a little push. Fuck if he's going to get there on his own."

"You wound him up on purpose?"

"No, she wanted to go, and I offered because I knew he couldnae, ye ken. He's got to get over his issues, because the lass is fuming that he refused to get into the car with her behind the wheel."

So, Beth was into James, too. Good.

Gordain had switched his gaze to Mathilda. I'd watched her as well, a fitted woollen jacket protecting her from the breeze, my hopes and dreams in her pockets. "Speaking of lasses, what does Mathilda make of the place? It's a long way to relocate if she'd move in with you."

My laugh had been weak. "This is her second visit. What makes you think she'd even consider it?"

"Ah ha, you said 'she', telling me that for you this is already a done deal." He'd clapped my shoulder, and I'd frowned at him. "You don't have the luxury of moving, so whatever lass takes you seriously would already have done that thinking. I'd say that ship has sailed, no?"

He'd left me standing there, an unnerving sensation suspending me like I was balanced on a wire. With my worry for Gordain over, my whole attention could be given to whether or not Mathilda returned my feelings. Maybe he was right and this visit was a good sign.

Or maybe he was wrong, and my castle was yet another hurdle to add to my list.

The assumption people had of me was that I, the big laird, had no concerns. Brutal in my approach to life because I could walk right through anything that got in my way. Violent fathers, isolation, and a family in chaos. Nothing could be further from the truth. My heart was too big, too full of fear.

Even now, hours later, I brooded on the barriers I'd have to carve my way through.

Some arsehole had proposed to Mathilda. I needed to hear it from her lips that she'd turned him down before we took things any further. If she hadn't made up her mind, I was in trouble, as the way she'd been looking at me had my lust threatening to take over my thinking.

We couldn't sleep together until I knew she was mine. The McRaes might be hard to break, but this one didn't want to put it to the test. It would hurt too badly. But I already knew how my impulses overruled me.

If nothing had been resolved by tomorrow, I had a backup plan.

"Boys, a movie?" Gordain stretched, tattoos peeking from

under his shirt sleeves, the bottle of beer he'd brought from the dinner table in his outstretched hand.

"If I can choose." Ally slid his phone into his pocket, his permanently present headphones around his neck. Sometimes I hated that he needed them.

"You have the worst taste," drawled his twin, uncurling himself from an armchair he'd dragged out of the den. "Always superheroes."

"I'm sorry. I don't think I can watch *Casablanca* again without wanting to die. Ye ken there are other films out there—"

The boys argued as Gordain shepherded them into the passage leading to his tower, leaving Mathilda and me, plus James and Beth in the tall-backed chairs. James appeared to be sleeping—he hadn't eaten anything over dinner and had waved me off when I'd asked if he was sick. He could take care of himself. I had only one thing on my mind.

Mathilda looked up from where she'd leaned over to speak to Beth.

In the firelight, her eyes gleamed.

Aye, lass.

I stood and held out my hand, not trusting myself to speak. Mathilda whispered something else to Beth who raised a hand to say goodnight. I was being a shite host to Mathilda's friend, though I wasn't entirely sure whose guest she was.

Together, fingers entwined, Mathilda and I crossed the flagstone floor then mounted the stairs lining the wall.

Kiss her. Here. Now. In the shadows, against the wall.

My skin was too tight for my body. I weighed too much. My blood pumped around my veins too fast.

My resolve held.

"Today has been out of this world," Mathilda said, low and sweet. "I love your family."

"It's mutual." My voice was a grunt, but the sentiment real. I'd seen it in Gordain's interest in her as she'd asked him about training, in the twins showing off in front of her, seeking her approval.

"And you? Do you like having me here?"

I did. Too much and too fast.

"Tell me, Callum."

We rounded the corner to the hall, and I broke. With rough hands, I swung about and pulled Mathilda into my body. She gave a small gasp but just as quickly clutched my neck. Our lips met in heat, fast movements, and escalating pressure.

That resolve I'd built, layering reason on reason all afternoon long, crumbled under her touch. Mathilda tasted sweet as she opened her mouth under mine, and our kiss turned nuclear. Passionate and heady, an unleashing of pent-up need.

A dim light came from a lamp in Mathilda's bedroom two doors along. Beth had a room on this corridor, the twins and James around the corner. I silently thanked Gordain for taking the boys away so I had this kiss without an audience.

I tangled my hands in her soft curls, wedged my knee between her legs, and we crashed against the panelled wood of the hallway.

Mathilda's fingers found the buttons of my shirt, and she wrenched the first open.

I didn't stop her.

Instead, I slid a hand free from her hair and grasped at her waist.

"More," Mathilda spoke into our kiss.

Fuck. With my impulses out of control, I lifted her then pinned her to the wall, my hips to hers. Her legs encircled my back, and then somehow my hands were under her thighs. In touching distance of Heaven.

I grazed a line of lace with a fingertip.

Mathilda gave a gentle moan. Encouragement almost impossible to deny.

Except I could. I dropped my forehead to her shoulder and clamped down on the staggering lust.

"Why am I not sharing your bed?" Mathilda asked, her breathing heavy.

"Not tonight." The words scratched my throat. I was a fool. A hard-headed, soft-hearted idiot. Stubborn to a fault and about to kick my own ass all over my damn solar. "We have all weekend."

Raising my head, I kissed her again, lingering this time. Softer, to show that I could.

"I have a surprise for ye tomorrow," I murmured, laying a gentle kiss on her temple then placing her back on her feet. The scent of her drove me wild. "Pack an overnight bag. We're going somewhere after the party."

She hummed agreement, her cheek on my shoulder, and we stood for a moment longer, locked in each other's arms.

"Goodnight, Mathilda. Get some rest." I released her, needing to walk away before I begged her forgiveness for holding out on her and took her soft body against the very wall.

"Until tomorrow," she whispered back, then disappeared, leaving me cold.

16

YOU'RE NEVER LEAVING

*M*athilda
         Low-growing heather spread over the open slopes leading up Callum's mountain, springy under my feet as I navigated the overgrown track. Where Bristol was surrounded by green fields, the McRae Estate had an abundance of this tougher plant that would burst into colour—lilacs and purples—in a couple of months' time.

Hardy yet with hidden beauty. It reminded me of a certain laird I knew.

Ahead, farther up the slope, the twins disappeared into the tree line, their loud conversation easy to track. Callum and I followed hand in hand through the warm spring day.

I'd asked for a hike to see the land, and Callum had delivered. We drove to a wide glen then climbed the slopes into the foothills of the mountain. A wild and romantic place, deer herds thundering away at our approach, birds of prey soaring overhead. Perhaps being alone would've been better, but I enjoyed the company of the two boys and wanted to get to know them, too. They were such a big part of Callum's life it made them a package deal.

Though sixteen, his youngest brothers stood two inches taller than me but lean in the way of thoroughbred colts. Nothing of the muscle bulk their older brothers carried. Ally was also as enthusiastic as a puppy. Where his twin seemed more in Gordain's image, quieter and stoic, Ally came across as impulsive and a little wild. More like his oldest brother in being led by his heart.

There was something about him I couldn't put my finger on. A vulnerability. Maybe in the way his brothers seemed overprotective of him. Even Wasp who was identical in almost every way.

My repressed maternal instinct stirred.

"Come on!" came a shout from the trees, and I pressed on, supported by Callum, clambering uphill through the copse of spiny trees. We weren't even close to the top of the mountain but, as I emerged onto a plateau and looked back, the view took my breath away.

The McRae estate sprawled for miles. Open, rich with life, and glorious.

Callum strode over to stand on a ledge. *Whoa.* With his back to me and the castle and loch beyond, he stole my attention. No sight in the world could compete with the picture of my massive, powerful Highlander overseeing his land, heavy boots on the rocks where generations of lairds before him would've surveyed their property.

It wouldn't have surprised me if a kilted battalion marched over and reported to him for duty. His troops, awaiting his orders, off to fight some battle.

"Stunning," I mumbled at the sight.

"It's not bad." Ally scampered back to join me and laid his head on my shoulder like an affectionate pup. "If we climb to the top, ye can see all the way up the river to Braithar."

"Is that a town?"

"No. It's another McRae castle."

Reaching out, I tousled his silky hair. The brothers hugged one another all the time. They were a very physical family, bonding constantly with thumps to each other's shoulders when they passed or impromptu wrestling matches.

With Ally cuddling up, it was all too easy to see how I could find a place with them.

I'd grown up in a fractured home with an imbalance of power. Mom's over Dad, then vice versa. Everyone McRae had a role and knew what they were doing. All equally valued. Over dinner last night, Gordain had talked about his job in the military and his eventual plan to pilot for the local Highlands mountain rescue. The twins had school but both worked on the estate in their free time. I'd seen workers and locals pop by the castle with questions any of the brothers seemed able to answer, and it had made me appreciate just how much a way of life it was, living on the estate. The community living on Callum's fifty thousand acres was tight.

The strength to which I wanted to belong staggered me.

"The McRae's built more than one castle?"

"Aye," Ally replied. "Braithar is still owned by one of us. It's our relative's, but we've always thought of it as Gordain's. He wants to own it someday. Unless you fancy the climb now, you'll see it tonight."

"We're not climbing to the top." Callum turned to face us. His lips curved as he took in his brother and me.

"Wasp!" Ally suddenly blared, and I jumped. "Get over here."

His twin jogged over, leaping over a craggy rock. "What?"

"Get on Mattie's other side and cosy up. Woman sandwich." They'd heard Beth use my nickname and copied it.

Callum hadn't followed suit, and I was glad. The way he said my name in that soft lilting accent sent tingles up my spine.

"Why?" Wasp obliged regardless, and I laughed as the two young men linked arms around me, squishing me. Ally raised his phone and took a picture, all of us with big grins.

"Would ye look at Cal's face," Ally said, his voice a little lower. "That smile. He's happy." To me, he added with a blissed-out sigh, "You're never leaving."

The smile dropped, and Callum's grumpy frown returned. He gestured at the boys to go away, and they took off, chuckling. His tone with me, though, remained gentle. "I like seeing you with my brothers."

"Where did Wasp get his nickname?" I'd worked out 'Fitz' for James, as it was short for his surname, but nobody called William 'Will' like they abbreviated the other family names. These were the little details I wanted. Small insights so I didn't feel such an outsider.

Callum gestured for me to come to him. Like a gentleman, he slid his jacket from his shoulders and laid it on a damp rock. Then he put his arm around my waist and we sat. I leaned on his shoulder.

The fresh air had me giddy.

"I'd tell you it's because he was a pest, but that's not the truth. It's for a shite reason, and I've told you enough miserable tales."

"Don't hold back. I'd like to know everything about you."

He kissed my hair, and I sensed his pleasure in my words. A chill wind rose, and I huddled closer.

"I told you Da was violent, aye? He used to go after my brother."

"One of the twins?"

"No, Gordain."

I blinked, not expecting that answer.

"A story for another time, why Gordain was the target." Callum's hand found mine, and he linked our fingers over my stomach. "I'm only sorry I couldnae help him sooner than

I did. But the twins, I could. Ally is dyslexic, did anyone mention that?"

I shook my head, a number of things making sense. The headphones Ally always wore. The text-to-speech I thought I'd heard him listen to at the breakfast table. One of Beth's foster siblings was dyslexic, so I knew a little about the condition.

"He used to get the most shite reports from school before we realised. I'd hide them from Da and sign them off myself, but once, one somehow got into his hands. Da went on the warpath after Alasdair, saying he'd beat sense into him. He grabbed the wrong twin into his office as he was drunk, then whipped William with a cane. The 'Wasp' nickname is from the stripes he had across his back when Gordain and I treated him later that night."

My blood froze and, open-mouthed, I twisted around. Callum's expression was stoic, but his blue eyes were fathomless.

"First and last time Da hit either of the twins. That was the night he died," he said simply, and I shivered.

I pictured the scene, trying to work out what to say. An eighteen-year-old Callum finally losing it and punching his father, breaking the man's bones in order to protect his brothers. The boys would have been eight. So young.

"It was Wasp's choice to use the nickname. Something about being fierce. Maybe he and Ally found comfort in creating a positive from it all. Gordain has a tattoo to represent the night. I had one, too."

"You turned it around and created this incredible world," I managed, hurting for the way this family had. "I wish it hadn't been like that."

Callum smiled now, and I loved the change. The crinkling at his eyes and mouth, the way he glanced between my eyes and my lips like he wanted to kiss away my sadness at his

137

story. "Life is what you make it," he said. "We've made a good home. I've raised my brothers to be good men, and they have everything they need."

Callum had already told me his mother had died of cancer when he was six and Gordain a toddler. The resilience of the man astounded me. His size, the spread of his shoulders, held up a world. Alone.

In telling me his stories, he laid himself bare. Built up my trust so much I wanted to tell him more about myself. But the fragility of the moment scared me.

I blinked and looked away, scurrying for a subject change as I kicked at a stone with my shoe. "Does Ally get good support at his school?"

Callum huffed. "No. There's no need for them to know."

"They don't know he's dyslexic? Why not?"

"Because he'll be judged and labelled, and it's no one else's business. We've found ways for him to cope. We help him with homework."

This felt off. I knew Beth's foster sister had a support worker in lessons and was permitted extra time in exams. "What about in tests? How does he manage?"

Silence for a moment, then, "Alasdair and William dinna take the same courses. If needs be, William can sit in on exams. In contrast, he can learn anything in five minutes, so it's nae bother."

Jesus. "You mean he cheats for Ally?"

Callum sighed. "After Da's death, the boys were bullied. Kids can be wee arses, and they were already targets for who and what we are. Gordain got into a lot of fights trying to protect them, and it all became a mess. In the end, Patricia and I moved them to a new school, and I decided not to have Ally tested so that the bullying didnae start up again. It might not have been the best decision, but in a couple of years he'll come and work for me full time, so it doesn't matter. There's no problem with my thinking."

I bit my tongue because I didn't agree.

A weighty silence held the air. "If you have a different opinion, tell me."

"How does Ally feel about his condition?"

Callum shrugged. "He doesn't talk about it. Except to Wasp when they have arrangements to make."

"He's ashamed?"

"I wouldnae put it like that."

"Are you ashamed of him?" The words fell from my mouth, not sounding at all how I meant them.

"Christ, no."

"Does he know that?" Callum had told me the family discussed everything openly, but that relied on there being an audience. Carefully, I added, "If Ally feels his brothers don't want to talk about his dyslexia, he'll suppress it. That isn't healthy."

The moment strung out, and Callum tightened his arm around me. We'd been speaking to the open air, but a pang of guilt tripped me, and I glanced back at his face. How could an eighteen-year-old make all good decisions? And who the heck was I to judge him? The boys weren't mine, and it scared me to even think that they could be part of my life. "I'm sorry, I spoke out of turn. It's none of my business."

"Aye, maybe not, but I told you all the same, so you have a right to reply. Now I want to say I'm sorry because you've tensed up like I'm about to lose it. I dinna want you to be afraid of being honest with me. Actually, I'm thinking about what you said."

My shoulders sagged, but the strange state I'd got myself into persisted. Trusting someone was hard, but I'd pushed my opinion far past being diplomatic...and had been heard.

"What is it you need? What are you looking for in a girlfriend?" I straightened the sleeve of my light sweater then entwined my fingers. "Not the laird of all these people, the mentor, or the oldest brother. Just Callum."

"I need someone of my own. For me."

"But you aren't available. Whoever comes to you becomes part of a family. Of an estate as well. How do they fit in?" I was pushing and I wasn't sure why.

He frowned and pressed his lips together, maybe trying to stop certain words escaping. "You come to me as mine. I can't move house, but you can, and you bring a career with you. It's a perfect fit. Family...is more, aye? A different conversation for another time."

The fragile moment and Callum's openness pulled at my soul. He'd gone through hell and high water to safeguard all he loved, and the walls around that were steep. Sharing that meant letting go of some of his controls, and it made sense why he was holding back about his family.

He watched me, determination in his eyes, like he was testing me. "What's your plan? You want your girl, aye? How are we going to get her?"

I'd been prepared to enter a sham marriage for Scarlet, but that was so far from my radar now, I couldn't believe I'd considered it an option. "I'm going to find a way to talk to my dad."

"We'll go together and present a united front. Demand he release her into your care. Tell him how he's messing her up."

Shifting, I drew up my knees and hugged them. "Mom begged me not to. Last time I did, Dad became difficult for weeks. He's not aggressive but he does have problems and he can be hard to live with. Mom's already vacant half the time."

I took a deep breath, not wanting to paint Dad in a bad light. "It would hurt him, and when he's hurt he feels challenged and overreacts."

Then I went all in. "Dad never knew his parents. He was

an orphan, found in a group of migrants when he was a small boy. He doesn't even know his own birthday. Dad has no ties to anyone but us. Not one. I don't want you to judge him. He's so fiercely loyal but he's got demons, and letting Scarlet go means acknowledging what Mom did…"

I trailed off.

"He chose his own name, Callum. No one knew his. For a man like you, whose name and history is everything, try to imagine what that was like for Dad."

Callum blew out a breath. "And you mean to tackle it gently. What if it doesn't work? The direct approach breaks the bad situation enough that it can't go on."

I tried to picture challenging Dad directly, and my stomach shrank to a cold, hard ball. I couldn't answer.

"The last thing I want," Callum stood and pulled me with him, "is for you or your sister to suffer more. But your parents made their own decisions, and they can deal with the fallout. Either way, I'm here. I want you to let me help."

He dipped his head and laid a gentle kiss on my cheek, bringing a roar of mock-horror from the returning twins.

The morning had left me confused. Callum's world was almost all so perfect. But I wasn't sure he could help in the way I'd hoped. Callum's bullheaded, bone-breaking approach directly opposed what I knew my family needed.

In a decisive move, I changed the subject to new territory. Not about the unique, happy appeal of Callum's family group, or my own family plans where his idea couldn't work, but one where I at least had a head start.

"Let's talk through the wedding venue proposal."

Callum sighed and directed me back down the mountain. "Aye, lass. We'll do that."

TAKING RISKS

Mathilda

Four male faces regarded me from around the vast wooden dining table.

"Are ye serious with the money?" Ally asked. "People pay that?" He squinted at the blue folder of information in front of him and rubbed his eyes in an exaggerated style.

Over lunch, Callum and I had briefed his brothers on the wedding plan, and I'd gone into detail, talking them through how the events typically worked, how they could copy the format at Castle McRae, and what the pros and cons were.

So far, the main pro—the potential income—had made the biggest splash.

"Aye, Mathilda knows her stuff. Of all the ways we could use the estate to make money, this idea comes top of the list."

Callum echoed the words I'd said to him on our walk back down the mountain. As I'd explained my logic, he hadn't held back on questioning me, and his thoroughness made me feel all the better. He supported me completely, and…I loved the feeling.

Under the table, I found his hand and held it. For some

reason, it became of vital importance that his brothers liked my plan, too. Not because of my professional pride, but I wanted their backing.

Callum gave me a gentle smile, then continued to his brothers, "Though I'm head of the family, we all need to agree and commit to this if it will work. It means sharing our space and becoming hosts for a number of weekends per year. That's a big change, and it affects us all. I dinna want to force this on you, so give me your thoughts. Ally?" He looked across the table to the livelier of the twins.

"I don't mind the work, and the parties sound fun. Do I get a say in how we spend the money? It would be nice to have hot water in my bathroom again," Ally replied. He tossed a ball into the air. It looped neatly over a candelabra made of antlers.

"Seconded," his twin added, catching the ball on its descent. "I'd enjoy not freezing my backside off every time I wash."

Callum explained to me, "One of our boilers packed up last month. Your room is one of the few with a shower that isn't connected in to the heating system." He looked back to his brother. "We can write up a list of priorities, but the boiler will need fixing before we'd get any cash back on this venture. I'll get onto it this week myself. You can help."

To my right, Gordain blew out a breath. "The money is good, and I'm not here often enough to have an opinion on the disruption, but how are we going to afford to ready this place for it?" He slid the folder toward him across the gnarled table surface and scanned the list. "We'll need to redecorate rooms, buy in a coordinator ahead of any bookings—"

"A coordinator? That'd be Mattie's job. You'd be doing that, wouldn't you?" Ally looked to me, and a bloom of want rose in me. This plan was my baby, but I didn't live here so I had to hand it over.

The way Callum's hand tightened over mine contradicted that thought. Even thinking about working on this longer term with him had my heart racing.

"Whoever did it, we'd need to pay them," Gordain continued, saving me from having to answer. "On top of that, we'd need to pay deposits for contractors, get the right licences, have decent transport. The money comes from the luxury element, aye? We can't expect our ramshackle way of living to impress big money. Boat trips on the loch in our old tub? What if we sank with the bride and groom on board? There's charmingly rustic and then there's reckless."

One of the twins spluttered a laugh, but the mood dipped. I knew the family had tight finances—it was plain from how tirelessly Callum worked, but he'd never mentioned just how hard up they were. They had the bare bones they needed for this plan, but Gordain was right. At the bottom of the page was the amount they needed to get it going.

I wished I had the money myself. I'd lend it without question. Whether they wanted my involvement or not.

"That's been on my mind, too." Callum ran a hand through his hair, staring at the folder. "We'd need investment. A loan."

Again, my mind went to Storm Force and the cash they should have had, but then Callum and Gordain exchanged a grim look that I didn't understand, and I sensed something else was on their minds. Callum brought his hands to the table and pushed himself to standing. "Is investment the only concern anyone has?"

Collectively, his three brothers nodded or shrugged.

"Then leave that with me. Mathilda, I need to talk to you about something. We'll go to your room."

I took his offered hand and stood. Really, I needed to start getting ready for the party for Callum's relative tonight, but I had no problem with doing that with him in the room. Let him try to resist me while I was slipping on stockings under a robe.

Sheesh, I was burning up for the guy if I planned to seduce him while getting dressed, rather than undressed. I grinned to myself as I stretched out my spine. The session with his brothers had gone well. I felt buoyant.

"Wait, I need your help with the rig." Ally hopped up from his seat and made doe eyes at Callum. "It isn't finished. It'll take us half an hour. Swear to God. We can't lose this thing because of a little bit of effort."

"What's a rig?" I looked between them. "What thing will you lose?"

Ally's eyes lit up, compelling me to join in his excitement. Whatever this rig was, I instantly wanted to help him with it, too.

"It's the last event of Lachlan's Highland games. A raft race on his river. The river that runs all the way to our loch. The two estates have been having races forever, so we have to compete. The rivalry is epic."

"That sounds dangerous," I said.

"It's not a race down to the loch." Callum turned from me to his brother and palmed his shoulder, holding the boy still for a second and forcing him to pay attention. "They're only doing it across the river as part of Lachlan's birthday celebrations. It's cold and dark, and you'll stay in the limits of the floodlights or you'll not take part."

Ally slid a glance to his twin and winked, then grinned at Callum. "Aye, whatever. But we still have to smash it. You gave us permission so now you have to help us win."

Callum rolled his eyes to gaze on the rafters of the airy dining room. "I should've stuck to my guns and refused you. Why did I ever agree to this?"

"Because you'd been miserable without your lass and now you're happy?" Ally beamed.

"Who are you competing against?" I asked, trying to take the heat off Callum who'd dipped his chin and glowered. I loved it when he got flustered. I also loved the idea of him missing me and being grumpy for it. It was nice to know the effect I'd had on him, particularly as he was holding out on me now.

"Anyone who'll try me." Ally's smile held a wicked edge and, in his looks, further shades of Callum's stubbornness and determination shone through. Then he ducked his blond head and added, "You can help, too. If you like? If you can hold a hammer, you're in."

It was a kind offer, involving me in the family, and the warmth of the gesture surged down to my boots. I gave him a smile of genuine affection. "I need to go check on Beth, but I'm ready to admire the raft when it's finished."

"Deal," Ally said and bounded off.

The laird gazed at me for a moment. "Give me half an hour and I'll be up," he said to me, low and sweet, and then he marshalled his other brothers, and they took off through the great hall.

On my way through the bedroom wing, I passed my room and continued on to the next one. Earlier, James had sent a text to Callum saying both he and Beth were sick. James had a fever and Beth a sickness bug, and they were taking care of one another. I'd never known Beth ill before— she went to work every day regardless, so I wanted to check in on her, even if just to poke my head into the room. It sounded like they were doing fine without help, but I'd be a bad friend to not check.

I knocked lightly on Beth's door. It swung silently open in front of me, and James's face appeared on the other side. Dark shadows lined his eyes, and he blinked in the light of the hall. Behind him, the curtains were drawn, and Beth lay in the centre of a messy bed.

"Beth's ill," he said, worry clear on his face.

Automatically, I reached out and propped him back against the doorframe. His shoulder was hot. "I think you both are. Is she okay? Are you?"

"I'm perfectly well." With ruffled hair and wide eyes, he looked perfectly miserable.

"Shall I check on her?" I offered, but if he was here, taking care of her... I felt like I was intruding.

The young man pressed his lips together in a thin line. An imitation of a smile. "Please do. I'll go to the kitchens and get her something to eat."

"Get yourself something, too," I said to his retreating back then stepped into my friend's sick bay.

"Nng," Beth moaned as I sat on the edge of her bed. "Stay back. Quarantine zone. I feel fricking awful. Sick, sick, sick."

"I won't touch you. I just wanted to make sure you were okay."

She edged away, but even in the low light she was pale.

"Are things going well with Adam of the mountain?" she quipped, referencing the *Seven Brides* movie character. "This place rocks. You should totally marry him so you can get to be a Lady."

I chuckled, though after working through the plan for the future of this family, I felt invested. More than that, and far beyond righting the wrong of Storm Force's underpayment.

"So far, he hasn't asked," I replied lightly then changed the subject. "Bang goes your hookup plans for the weekend. Have you been sharing a bed all night?"

Beth huffed, a weak sound. "Yep. We've been friend zoned by illness. But he did kiss me before everything went to crap, so score one for me."

Ah. I'd wondered. "Better luck next time."

To my utter surprise, Beth gave a sob of frustration. "There won't be a next time. James only kissed me because he had a fever. He wouldn't have otherwise," she cried. "Have you seen him? Do you know what he is? He's so far out of my league I can't even see the start line."

"Beth, no!" Then I dragged in a breath, finally admitting a fact to myself. "If I could marry someone like Callum, why couldn't you find someone you wanted?"

"You and I are not the same. He's beautiful inside and out and no way is he meant for me." Her voice became tiny.

My heart panged. "This isn't just a hookup. You already liked him and now you're sharing a bed. Feelings are bound to happen. And that's good." Being in Callum's embrace like that would send me over the edge.

"I'm just ill," she countered.

"Listen, I can stay here tonight. If you need me." Callum intended for us to stay elsewhere, but I'd talk to him if she needed me.

"Don't. I'll be fine." Beth threw her arms over her head, her abundance of dark curls tangled over her pillow. "Go enjoy the party. I'll go home in the morning, and he'll forget I ever existed."

Her breathing slowed and, after a moment, it looked like she'd gone to sleep.

Tenderness filled me as I watched over my friend. In the same way I'd joked that Callum collected lame ducks, I had a strong instinct for helping people. Scarlet, Beth, and a substantial beginning of one for the McRae clan. Practicality might be my middle name, but I couldn't bear to think of people suffering. Boys missing a mother, a family unsupported, a man striving to be a good role model having never had one himself. Beth hurting had me wanting to weep. Sheesh, I was swimming with feelings.

And I knew exactly why.

He was nearly seven feet tall and sent my pulse skyward with every touch.

A noise came from behind me. A creak of the floorboards. James stood in the doorway. His silhouette waited, perfectly still.

Now, how long had he been there?

I stood quietly and retreated to the door. "I'm going to have to wake her. I forgot to mention work," I said. "She might need to cancel shifts. I'm not sure about her schedule."

"It's already in hand. We sorted it earlier. And you really don't have to worry. I won't leave her," he said and offered a polite smile on his worn, handsome face, but his gaze was on Beth. He moved to where I'd been sitting and placed his supplies on the bedside table. Crackers, water, a box of tablets.

"I really think I should stay." If Beth got worse I should be taking care of her. No matter how much James had it under control. What if he became sicker?

With a small groan, Beth turned and open her eyes. "Don't be daft. We're good. Go have fun. I insist."

"If you're sure," I answered, but neither of them looked at me.

With tender reverence, James took a curl of Beth's hair, moving it away from her face. As I closed the door, I thought I saw Beth reach out and drag him down to lay on the bed beside her.

I wandered back to my room, musing on risk. Beth and James were taking risks, whether they knew it or not. From what I could tell, their worlds were poles apart.

The McRae brothers were gambling on the future of their home, willing to trust me with all they held dear.

That left me.

If only I could work out how to take this step forward, I'd take a risk, too. One I badly needed.

18

PREPARE FOR A PARTY

*M*athilda

My phone had sat on my bedroom dressing table all day, and I returned to a further two missed calls from my father. With his voicemail received yesterday while I was on the flight, I couldn't ignore him for much longer. But one more night wouldn't make a difference. Right now, I needed to prepare for a party.

I took my dress from its garment bag and slipped it over brand-new underwear, the cool satin sliding over my limbs. I'd already curled my hair and applied my makeup, just needing to add the finishing touches of long earrings and my amazing shoes. They sat by my overnight bag, perched prettily on the floor and just waiting for my happy feet to step into them. The castle was a haven for tall people. Aside from Callum being a giant of a mountain man, all the men were above six-foot. The door heights were generous, and I could wear stilts and not bang my head. I'd walk tall tonight.

The floor-length mirror allowed me to evaluate my appearance, and I twisted to check my rear, the dress material shimmering.

I wanted to knock Callum's socks off.

A hammering shook my door.

There was only one person that could be. I swung it open, and Callum loomed in the frame. His gaze instantly heated as he took me in. He'd showered and shaved, and in a dark suit instead of his customary jeans, he was still rugged but dangerously sharp. I liked it. All of it. The sheer size of him.

"Hey."

"Hey yourself," he murmured.

All last night, I'd thought about the man. Wanting him to come to my room and clamber his weight onto my bed. Brace himself over me with those strong arms. Continue the hot and heavy kiss we'd shared. At the end of the hall outside, a set of stone stairs led up to his rooms. His solar, the suite was named. He'd pointed it out to me but hadn't taken me up there. I respected his boundaries, though in my imagination, I'd climbed those stairs to find him reclined on his bed, naked.

His long body heavily muscled, hard, and ready for me.

It had led to a somewhat disturbed sleep. I'd mangled my sheets.

"You're so handsome." I skimmed his features with my gaze. Smooth skin over a hard jaw. The curve of his mouth. So gorgeous.

"You're stunning. I'm the luckiest man alive to be your date tonight."

Pleased, I bit back my smile. "Aren't I *your* date? And I'm glad you like the dress."

"I liked you in the t-shirt you wore at my dining table, too. Thank you for that, by the way. For the hard work you've done."

"I want this plan to succeed."

The man of my dreams paused and watched my lips. His

gaze turned predatory. "You've already done your makeup. Pity I'm about to ruin it."

"Ruin away," I replied, entranced. Ready to jump him.

A clattering came from the hall. I peered over Callum's shoulder. The twins crossed the hall, dragging shirts over their heads and talking excitedly.

Neither of us had moved, yet we jumped apart. Callum shook his head, a wry grin on his face as he shut the door behind him.

"One of the reasons we're going elsewhere tonight." He turned the key in the lock, and the room seemed to shrink. "For all the size of this place, there's no privacy."

Elsewhere tonight. The idea gave me shivers. We needed to spend time alone and talk. I'd realised I hadn't told Callum my decision on Dominic's marriage proposal and, though he hadn't asked, it had to be bothering him. Maybe it was the reason he held back from me. I had no reason to play coy. Dominic's distasteful offer had no hope. Callum had stolen my heart. There was no two ways about it.

Even if I couldn't yet bring myself to acknowledge the extent of my emotions, Callum needed to know where I stood. For that matter, Dominic did, too. Not that he deserved the same care, but I'd call him this evening and set everything right. Start things with Callum on a clean slate.

The noise of the twins permeated into the room, and the laird stalked to a chair by the desk, the wood creaking under him as he sat. I padded across the room on my bare soles to perch on the desk in front of him. Two feet of the late afternoon's low light glowed between us.

"That's why I came to your room—to talk about this evening," he said.

"Shame that we have to go to the party first."

He inclined his head, lust still hanging heavy in the air. "No argument from me. We won't wait around after the boys have had their race. There is another objective, though. We need to talk to Lachlan." Callum had already mentioned the party was for his father's cousin, the chief of their clan. I got the impression they didn't get along. "I mean to ask the man for investment. Like Gordain said, money is an issue. No bank will lend us a penny, and Lachlan is an option if we're going to get this new business idea off the ground."

"Is he likely to offer the loan?"

As I spoke, the slit on my dress fell open over my knee, revealing my calf.

Callum swallowed, his attention travelling over my crossed legs. A shiver of delight ran through me at the weight of his stare, at the way he had to drag himself to look at my face.

"He and Da once quarrelled over a competition. Da claimed Lachlan owed him. If all else fails, I'll ask about that." Callum blew out a breath, pushing his shoulders back into his chair. "Lachlan and I are too similar. I'm my own liability as far as he is concerned. Last time we spoke, we argued, too. A pair of land agents have been snooping around, and Lachlan was considering selling up a parcel of his estate. Needless to say, I had an opinion or two I should've kept to myself."

It pleased me so much to hear him admit to a mistake. Because, a little devil in the back of my mind told me that Callum had one or two personality traits in common with my dad. His temper and full-frontal assault nature had given me pause, but overall the two men were so different. Callum was so open, he could never behave like my father.

"We'll reason with Lachlan. We can do this."

Callum's weighty gaze raised to mine. "You said 'we'. Do ye ken how my heart jumped to hear it?"

I shifted back on the desk, purposefully, and the slit in the blue satin of my dress opened farther. "I'm good at diplomacy."

"You could charm the birds from the trees." Callum reached out to grasp my ankle. He slid his other hand under my foot and drew it into his lap, beginning a slow massage. The room warmed.

"I interrupted you getting ready."

"You did."

His thumbs made firm circles into my insoles. *Heaven.* "Did you pack a bag?"

My eyelids now closed, I gestured to the bag by the door. "Are you taking me somewhere tonight to seduce me?"

His movements didn't stop. "Aye."

My eyes flew open.

"Just because I didnae leap on you like a starved wolf the moment I had you alone wasn't for the want of it."

With my kiss, I'd invited him to my bed last night. He'd refused. "You told me you were impulsive. Where was that when I wanted it?" I gasped as his massage took in my calf, his hand sliding to my knee before stopping. Retreating. Teasing. I wanted to spread my legs right there on the damn desk.

My lace underwear would be in front of his face.

"With you, I need to restrain myself." Callum wore a careful expression, though his heavier breathing told me how turned on he was. "If you only knew half the thoughts I'd had about you."

I wanted to hear his fantasies. I had my own. "Try me."

"No." He smiled as he began the same massage on my other leg, starting with my foot and gliding over my tensed calf muscle, stopped from going further by my crossed knees. I wanted his hands on my thighs. Higher. "Later. After the party. When we're alone and we have the time."

"We're alone now." No noise came from the hall.

I slid my leg to rest next to the other, my knees together. Boldness infused me.

"Later." Callum laid a soft kiss on my knee then stood and smiled wickedly. He walked backwards toward the door.

I groaned and rolled my head on my shoulders, desperately needing release from the pressure in my body. It was going to be a long evening, handling the difficult relative and waiting for our chance to get away. However invested I was in the wedding project, the heat that washed over my body needed to dissipate, and fast.

I returned my gaze to Callum. He stared over at me. The fire in his eyes could melt the very snow from his mountain.

"Give me promises for later," I whispered. I wanted a sure thing. My body needed it.

"You want to know how much I'm going to wear you out? I will, and you, my woman, will be begging for mercy. But there is something specific I need to ask you before we go further."

"What?"

"Are ye mine to want?"

He had been worrying. Beautiful, gentle man. The words were ready on my tongue. "Oh, Callum. I should have told you—" I started.

He raised a hand, halting me. "Don't go telling me anything now. Wait until later when we're alone. Get your shoes on and meet me downstairs. I've got teenagers to wrangle into cars and a raft to put on the roof. We've got the night to sort this out, and I intend to do things right."

"I'll be there," I croaked, but he'd already grabbed my bag and gone.

Leaving one very sexually charged and determined woman in his wake.

* * *

*E*very touch Callum gave me, handing me into the Land Rover, running his thumb over my knuckles while he drove, gave me shivers. On the journey to Castle Braithar, the tension in the car weighed on us so heavily that conversation was impossible.

Callum exhaled hard as we rolled into the floodlit car park, a kilted attendant ushering us into a space. "How am I ever going to get a word out when all I want to say is your name over and over?"

"You better whisk me out of here when we're done," was my only reply. In a matter of hours, we could have this conversation and we could leave for Callum's mystery venue. Finally get our hands on one another.

These would be the longest hours of my life.

My car door swung open. "Welcome," the young attendant said in a broad Scottish accent. She beamed at me and I climbed out. "Clan Chief McRae is glad to accept all-comers to his birthday celebrations. He extends open arms and the warmth of his fire. You've missed most of the Highland games, but there's still the raft race to come. The chief is in the hall, if you'd care to join the greetings line."

"Fucking hell, let's get this over with," Callum muttered and exited the car.

Alongside our vehicle, Gordain pulled up. The twins—who'd chosen Gordain's car after claims that Callum and I were giving off race-affecting pheromones—leapt out before the wheels stopped turning, hauling at the bungee ropes holding the raft on the roof. They had suits on, and I winced to imagine the state they'd be in by the end of the night. They'd mentioned wearing wetsuits for the race, but that still didn't make me feel better about either of the boys going into the water. For a calm night, it would still be freezing.

The four men manhandled the wooden raft to a lawn

leading down to the floodlit riverbank, bunting and lights strung up from a marque where an afternoon of games had taken place, and I took in Castle Braithar's four turrets. It was symmetrical, towers on each corner like a castle from a fairy story.

It might be nicely made, but it wasn't a patch on the mismatched walls of Callum's home.

"Pretty, isn't it?" Gordain arrived at my side and gazed up at the castle walls with undisguised awe. "I spent a lot of time here as a lad. Probably more than at home."

After Callum's story about the viciousness of their father, I could easily imagine why Gordain would stay away. "It's impressive, but I'm obliged to say I like Castle McRae better."

Gordain dragged his attention to me. "That's the right answer. You're definitely fitting in. Come see inside. The hall is gorgeous."

We joined Callum who was giving a list of orders to the twins on how not to drown in the river, but I'd snagged on Gordain's comment.

If I came back, if Callum and I became a thing, I wanted to manage their wedding business. To belong. I had a feeling that once I'd tasted Callum, taken him to bed, any other option than being his would be out of the question.

Which meant more rode on securing the investment than met the eye.

At the castle's arched entrance, a woman hollered my name then waved madly. It was Una, Callum's ex who I'd met on my last visit. "Oh, ye look fab, my lady. What a dress! See ye inside for a catch-up. We'll grab a wine or three," she called, like we were old friends.

I waved back and instantly felt a little better. At least I knew one other person here.

"What's the plan for tackling Lachlan?" Gordain addressed his brother. "I assume you'll ask him tonight?"

"Aye. I hate this, but it's our only real option. Mathilda, our mistress of diplomacy, is going to stamp on my foot if I say anything out of line," he joked. In a move that thrilled me, Callum dragged me in front of him and banded me in his arms, resting the side of his face against my temple. "Whatever he says, I can't hack Lachlan for that long. Boys, once we've seen him, and after you're safely to dry land, we're going. Obey Gordain, and we'll see you back at the castle tomorrow. We won't be home tonight."

"Sure. Lachlan's the reason you're running off," Ally quipped as we made our way into the grand entrance, blue and white balloons tied up in bunches either side. "Just don't make me an uncle yet, I'm too young."

Callum reached out and gently thwacked his brother's ear then kissed my cheek. I laughed off the awkward comment. Then we were there. Lachlan's lair. Here to slay the beast.

19

FUCKING LACHLAN

*C*allum
     The walls of Castle Braithar resounded with the
wail of bagpipes. In the hall festooned with clan banners,
groups in full tartan regalia danced reels.

Fucking Lachlan.

I scanned the thick crowd, Mathilda's hand gripped in
mine. What was the man playing at? We wore tartan for
weddings. Here, he'd thrown an ego party and had hung out
his Scottishness to dry.

For show, all of it, but for whose benefit?

Ahead, on a raised dais, the man sat surrounded by well-
wishers. A queue of guests waited to greet him, serving staff
offering drinks from trays.

"That's Lachlan," Mathilda guessed.

I grumbled and eyed the end of the queue. "The man
himself. On a stage. Christ on a bike."

"He looks like you."

As I stared over, taking in broad shoulders and a
strong jaw not dissimilar to mine and, Heaven forbid,
Da's, his gaze lit on our party, then clung to me. A

moment drew out before his wife elbowed him in the ribs, then the man thrust his chair back from the table and stood.

"Laird Callum McRae," he yelled, his voice booming over the musicians. Faces snapped our way. "At last you've come to pay homage to your chief. Jump the queue, boy. I've words to share with ye."

I'd been summoned.

* * *

*L*achlan didn't receive us at the high table, where we'd be like supplicants before his majesty's court. Instead, my relative stomped down and gestured us to follow him to the top of the hall. The crowd shifted, all eyes on us as we followed.

"For fuck's sake," I hissed, spotting where he was taking us. I should've expected something like this.

"What?" Mathilda whispered. She squeezed my hand.

"He means to put me on display."

Ahead, Lachlan reached a table and picked up a fist-sized ball of lead. A shot put. We'd come late—no way was I playing his Highland games—but the gleam in my relative's eye suggested differently. We reached the table, and a buzz came over the crowd. The music ceased.

"Your da and I used to go head to head. Every year. Do ye think you've got the balls to try me?" Lachlan hefted the shot put, a friendly smile on his face.

I did not return the expression. "I came here to talk."

"Ah, come on, Callum. Let's see your arm. It's only in fun, and half your kin are here." He gestured to the room then eyed me. "Maybe impress your lady?"

One thing Lachlan and I had in common was stubbornness. A glaring contest commenced. I'd never been his favourite—that was Gordain's claim—but I enjoyed his teachings and how he wore his pride.

At my other side, Alasdair yelled, "Do it, Cal. Show him who's boss." Then it became a free for all, the assembled partygoers joining in with catcalls and hoots. Many of my tenants were here. My kith and kin.

Fine. I had no choice but to indulge the man. I slid my jacket from my shoulders, handing it to the woman who I did actually want to impress, though by other means than heaving a bloody ball.

Lachlan beamed as I swung out a hand for the shot put, and the crowd cheered good-naturedly.

The game was on.

We took the match outside to the grass. Lachlan cleared a track leading to the river and took the first throw—a slow launch from his shoulder which landed with a thud under the yellow of a spotlight. He inspected his efforts. "Come on, lad. Best me if ye can."

I took the spot and rolled my shoulders.

My mind should have been on the game. On whether I should let Lachlan win for the sake of buttering him up, but my attention had one owner.

On the path, Mathilda waited, poised in my peripheral vision, and I cast a quick look her way. She'd sink into the soil in those heels so maybe she held back as she didn't want them dirtied. Later, behind closed doors, I'd have her keep them on. The dress could go, and I'd have the most beautiful woman up against the wall. Or bent over the bed frame, the heels placing her ass right where I wanted it.

With her cheeks reddening like she could read my thoughts, she drew her gaze up my body, resting on where my biceps strained my fitted shirt. I tested the weight of the ball, flexing more, and she blew out a breath.

She liked the view.

Oh fuck.

I'd spent much of the weekend trying to control being hard around her, but now I was on display, I had to stop my train of thought.

Down boy.

Tightening my muscles, I growled, using the energy and tossing the shot so far it flew past Lachlan's mark. And kept on going. It hit the river with a splash, and I dragged in a breath made of lust and pure want.

That woman was going to be the death of me.

My brothers crowed the win, and Mathilda's lips twitched in a smile. I stalked over and laid a kiss on her, not caring who watched.

"Well done," she said.

Behind, Lachlan called his congratulations, genuine humour in his voice, but my gaze didn't stray from Mathilda's.

"You liked that?"

She nodded blissfully.

"Strange, the things that work for you, woman," I said into her ear, and a shiver ran through her.

"I can't even explain it."

"Dinna try. I'll just be stealing that shot put and taking it home with us. Use it to impress you again." I winked, kissed her cheek, and we were swept up in the evening again, with Lachlan leading us back into the castle. His little exposure was over—though I'd won, he'd made his point and had me dance for him. Now, he'd give me the true audience I needed.

* * *

*I*n Lachlan's office, the man sat behind his wide desk and steepled his hands in a benevolent pose. He cocked his head as he looked us over one at a time.

Behind us, Wasp closed the door, the music, dancing, and undivided attention of the crowd muted.

"We appreciated the invite," I said stiffly. Trying to keep my manners despite the games. "This is Mathilda Storm, my date."

"It's a pleasure to meet you." Her smile was professional. "Happy birthday. We brought you a gift."

Gordain handed over a bottle of well-aged whisky from Castle McRae's cellars. Labelled with our logo—the castle and our family coat of arms on the other side.

"Aye, I'm glad to see you." Lachlan accepted the bottle and gave Gordain a pat on the hand, then looked Mathilda over. "It's nice to make your acquaintance, but it's even better to see this one attached." He pointed the bottle at me before he placed it on his desk. "It'll calm him down to have a woman. A couple of bairns' time, he'll be no trouble at all."

"Mind your assumptions," I snapped.

"Alasdair, William, you've grown like weeds." Lachlan ignored me and turned to the twins. "Fancy your chances in my rafting race? It's the last event now your brother has shown me his arm. Do you have your sights on the prize?"

"Aye, we'll win. There's no competition. Castle McRae always wins." Ally stepped forward, a swagger to his step.

Lachlan raised his eyebrows. "My stepgrandson is visiting. Brawny kid. I'd say you have a challenger. Braithar won't be found slacking."

I didn't like the gleam in Ally's eye. After the car-stealing stunt he'd pulled when I'd first met Mathilda, he needed no encouragement to be reckless.

Lachlan might enjoy messing with me, but my brothers were mine to manage. "Boys, ye said your greetings, now go on out and enjoy the party. You're here for the fun of it, remember that. The race doesnae matter. I'll see you out there."

The twins snickered, exiting the office, leaving Mathilda and I exchanging a glance as Lachlan congratulated Gordain on his new career.

"Deep breath," Mathilda mouthed, and I nodded, grateful.

Having to heed Lachlan—it was messing with my head. Being in control worked for me, but I was out of my comfort zone. My plan had been to stick to the facts and try to cut conversation short to avoid getting into an argument.

Right, I could do that.

After Lachlan came to an end of his praise to Gordain, I put my hands on my hips and exhaled hard. "Your guests will be missing you. You invited us here because you wanted to talk. I have a matter to discuss with you, so why don't we get on with it."

My chieftain tilted his head. "Aye? So talk, young Callum. What have you come to ask me?"

In brief statements, I outlined the wedding proposal. I gave a figure to Lachlan and ended with a blunt, "It's the investment we need. A business partner to buy in. Will you consider it?"

Lachlan stood and took up the bottle of whisky we'd given him, moved to a bar then poured himself a neat shot in a crystal glass. "No," he said.

Mathilda sucked in a breath.

I stared at the man. "No?"

"Are ye deaf, lad?"

My temper flared. "There's nothing wrong with my hearing, but there's something wrong with your memory. What about the debt you owed my da?"

"Whatever was between myself and Hamish is long in the past, and I'll thank you to forget it." Lachlan glared. "You can't get money from me, you can't get it from a bank. You're a bad investment. Why are you trying to hold on to the place like every inch of heather is worth its weight in gold? Take

164

the agents' offer and clear your debt, boy. It would set you up. Mine was highly generous."

I knew he'd had an offer, too. But only for a small plot. A chill ran down the tattoo on my back. "What do you mean?"

"I'm accepting." Lachlan threw back his whisky with a grimace. "The agents are outside enjoying the show."

"Accepting what? What agents?" Gordain asked, echoing my thoughts. My brother had mostly been silent. Now, he leaned forward like Lachlan's secret was of the utmost importance.

This couldn't be good. I braced myself.

Our relative sighed and put his glass on his desk with a knock, though he stayed on his feet. "It'll all be out soon enough, so you may as well know. Boys, I've decided to accept an offer on Braithar. I'm selling the place. Castle, land, title, and all."

* * *

With that, our audience was over.

Back in the hall, I flagged down the nearest waiter and grabbed three glasses from the tray, handing one to Mathilda and one to Gordain. My brother looked ill.

The news had hit us both like a ton of bricks.

"Fuck," Gordain swore. "He's going to sell up. I thought I had time."

The Champagne-piss nearly choked me as, across the room, I spotted the two businessmen—land agents—who'd tried their arm with me. One raised a glass to me, and I turned my back to him. "How can he? How could he give this up? How could he throw away the responsibility he has to the people who live here? Who rely on work and housing? To incomers who won't give a shite?" A century or two ago, the estate had been split into two, but it had always been owned by the McRae family. Our clan. A division, but one that had never felt divisive. It was why we'd never sorted the borders —there had been no need to.

"Do ye ken who made the offer?" Gordain bit out, his tone angry but his expression haunted.

"Aye, because they came knocking on our door. Acting for foreign investors." The place would become a holiday estate. Gordain didn't need to hear that now.

"You didnae mention it."

"Why would I? Like we'd ever sell. I laughed them out of town."

We both swore.

Mathilda watched wide-eyed. "And this person would become the chief of your clan?"

"No." Gordain spat. "Lachlan is talking out of his backside. He can't sell the title. That goes to Callum regardless. But the nerve of it."

Owning Braithar had long been Gordain's dream. Mine, too, for him. Two McRae brothers sharing the land. Side by side. No matter how impossible raising the money would be. I took hold of his shoulder. "It was always going to be tough—"

"Don't." Gordain swung back, and the set of his jaw told me how much he was hurting. I felt it to my bones. "Fuck him. We've done all we can. Let's watch our lads win the race and forget about the rest. My plans never mattered anyway."

"Aye they do," I said gently. My own strategy was in ruins, but at least I still had my home. For now, at least. He'd watch his dream get sold out from underneath him. We all would.

"I'm sorry," Mathilda uttered.

"I am, too." Gordain kissed Mathilda's cheek, thumped my shoulder, then took off into the crowd.

A moment passed between Mathilda and me.

"I need to make a phone call." She pressed my hand. "Can I find you in a minute?"

"I'll find the twins and tell them to win this damn race. We'll leave straight after. If you still want to?"

The room seemed to close in. My shirt grew tight at my neck, and I lifted my head for her response. To answer, Mathilda took my chin in her grip and kissed my lips like she owned me. Then she walked out of the hall, her shimmering dress filling my vision.

20

MY MOUNTAIN MAN

*M*athilda

The competitors floated their rafts, and an energy swept through the crowd, bets being taken and good-natured ribbing called between friends. Overhead, bright floodlights illuminated the dark, narrow river, and a boat waited in the middle. Still, anxiety dogged me, and I checked off a list of safety criteria I'd use at any standard event, scanning for guide ropes and sober marshals. All present. The event had been thought through, that was plain.

The kernel of worry in my gut didn't ease.

From the moment the starter pistol cracked, I kept my gaze glued to the blond heads of the twins. They crashed through the water, swift, uniform strokes of their paddles taking them into an easy lead. At my side, Callum and Gordain bellowed encouragement, swearing when another young man and his partner picked up speed. Lachlan's step-grandson, I gathered, the young man glaring at the twins as his raft inched to neck and neck with theirs.

Through the splashing, I strained my eyes to see the boys hit the other bank and sighed in relief at their clean moves,

168

turning the raft. Then they were straight back into battling the choppy water to return to the finish line.

They crossed the distance, the raft dipping and rising, even and fluid.

Until the rival leader's raft hit theirs. I yelped, then the rushing pulse of blood in my ears drowned out all other noise.

In the churning water, Ally lost grip on his paddle, a wave dragging it away from the raft.

Ally overextending himself to reach it. His body bowed over the edge of the raft.

My worst nightmare unfolded before my eyes. An inch more, and he'd be in the freezing water, the other rafts cutting over his head, the shadows and choppy waves concealing his position. We wouldn't be able to find him. He was too far out. Right in the middle of the water. How could the boat get there quickly enough?

"Haul. Him. In," Callum's bellow ordered, the loudness shocking me out of my frozen position.

In a miracle move, the raft tipped, Wasp's face contorted as he flung out an arm, grasping on to his twin's ankle and, with a heave, Ally landed safely on the wooden logs.

Like it was all a game, the boy let loose a howl, held up the paddle, and hacked at the water once more.

I squeezed Callum's hand mercilessly until the moment the twins' raft touched the wooden dock. Second. A heart-beat in it with Lachlan's boy taking first place.

Cheering and a loudspeaker announcement marked the win, and I took my first full breath in ten minutes. Then the boys scrambled onto the grass and stalked over to their competitors.

"Fuck," Gordain muttered and jogged into the melee. We followed.

"That the only way you could win?" Ally got into his

rival's face. He dragged his fingers through his soaked hair, water droplets flying.

"What's your problem?" The other boy sneered, puffing out his chest, his breath creating clouds in the air. "You lost control. Your mistake, not mine."

"You rammed us!"

"A tiny knock."

"Enough," Gordain cut in, inserting himself between his brother and the other boy.

"Not worth it." Wasp took position at his other shoulder.

"Agreed," Callum rumbled from behind me.

Ally swaggered back a step then shrugged, disappointment clear despite the bravado he wore. "Well, if that's the only way Braithar could claim first place, let them have it."

Gordain rolled his eyes as the boy stalked off, then turned to us. "Why don't you go. It's done and they're on dry land."

Callum's gaze tracked the boys. "Aye, it's over."

"We'll see ye both tomorrow." Gordain saluted and left.

Almost immediately, Callum was on me, pulling me with him over the grass. The race was done, and we were leaving.

"They're safe," I uttered, a strong maternal urge rising. I almost wanted to go and check them again. Make them change from their wetsuits and get them away from the water.

But I wanted Callum more. And from the searing look in his eyes, he felt exactly the same.

* * *

We drove in silence into the pitch black of the Highlands night. Callum set our route, speeding away from the castle, the grooves in his forehead deepening as he glared out of the windshield.

My body tingled in anticipation, even if I had no idea of

our destination. With no streetlights and no moon, all I could discern was when the maintained asphalt road gave way to a gravel track and the car began to climb.

Up and up we ascended, taking a winding route around what I guessed to be the mountainside. Eventually, snow crunched under our tyres, showing the height we'd risen Callum slowed the car, and I squinted to look about. Ahead, dark trees surrounded a low building, lights glowing at the windows.

"Ski lodge," he murmured. "Or log cabin, if you're inclined to be romantic."

I raised an eyebrow. "Aren't we inclined to be romantic tonight?"

I expected a smile, but Callum's frown only deepened. We trundled forward over the packed snow, then the car stopped, and Callum laid a hand on my forearm.

"Wait here a moment." He leapt out of the car, grabbed our bags from the back, and disappeared into the dark. The entrance to the lodge swung open, spilling light onto a wide porch. Two minutes later, my door popped open, and I was plucked from my seat.

I should have at least uttered a squeak at the surprise, but my heart was racing, and I clung on to Callum's neck as he held me close, his long strides transporting us over the frozen ground, my beautiful shoes suspended in the frigid air and my long dress hanging from my thighs. The cold, fresh mountain smelled like Callum had when I'd first met him.

My mountain man, bringing me deep into his territory.

Up the steps we went and into warmth and orange light. Across the room, a just-lit fire blazed into life, a rug spread before it. The polished frame of a large bed gleamed in the firelight, echoing the gleam in Callum's eyes. He carried me over to an armchair, gently placing me down before he paced back to the door and slammed it shut.

"Come here," I said, sliding my coat from my shoulders. Then I crossed my legs, reaching out to remove my shoe.

On the other side of the room, Callum lowered his gaze, and it scalded. "Not yet. Keep to your chair. Leave the heels on."

He tossed his smart jacket to the floor, but instead of coming to me, he sat on the bed. Then he removed his footwear, and slid out his silver cufflinks, all while I watched.

I liked the show too much to interrupt.

"I want ye, badly," Callum said, shifting his weight so his back hit the wide beams of the headboard. He stretched out his long legs on the bedspread. Cocked a knee. "If you still want me after what I have to say, I'm going to make you scream my name all night long."

There was nothing that could put me off him. Not now. Only my inbuilt manners had me holding back from jumping on him. "Talk, then," I managed.

Slowly, he undid his top button and dragged his shirt over his head.

I almost bit my tongue at the reveal of his manly, well-built frame. Limned in golden firelight, his bulging biceps stretched out as he shed the shirt, a broad chest dusted with rough-looking fair hair exposed. No manscaping here, but a body honed by hard work and nature.

A small groan escaped me.

Callum huffed a laugh. "Up here, Mathilda."

He pointed at his eyes, and I smiled at his game. His gaze fixed me into place, and the laughter was replaced with something else. A worried look that revealed the tender soul living within his huge frame.

"When we met, you talked about having a one-night stand to see if you could handle sex without love. Is that what I am? Another try? Because I can't do that."

A rush of feelings for Callum rose in me, swelling my

heart. I already liked him far beyond any person before, so much so the new sensation almost hurt.

"You think I'm going to sleep with you then leave you high and dry?"

"No. I think you like me more than you'd even admit to yourself. But I can't think. I need to know."

I stood, reaching behind me to lower the zip of my dress. Callum watched my approach like I was a dangerous creature.

"Wait," he said again, and I stopped my movements. "Dinna deprive me of what I've wanted to do all night. Anyway, I haven't finished stripping to persuade you yet."

He rose and unbuckled his belt. My knees weakened as he stripped off his suit trousers, leaving only his boxers in place.

Callum McRae reclined once more, almost nude. Glorious. With his legs apart, he took his huge bulge in hand, adjusting himself through the material of his boxers.

"Your persuasion is convincing."

"Then tell me you turned the man down."

I burned for him, *ached,* and my answer was ready. Turning Dominic down was the easiest thing I'd ever done.

I opened my mouth. "Of course I did. Before I came here, I'd already made the decision."

"Had you now?" A satisfied smirk pulled at his lips. He gave himself a lazy stroke, but his muscles were primed and his tone heated.

I didn't respect Dominic. I didn't care about his reputation and I hated how I would have been party to his affair. At the beginning, I thought I'd just be fixing his status and it would be a win/win, but the more I dwelt on it, the more I despised his actions. His lack of faithfulness, first, to someone else's wedding vows, then to ours. Whether I held them dear or not.

Callum would think it deeply wrong. I knew him well

enough now to see the honesty in him. The pride and the sheer heart of the man. Values I found I shared far and beyond my practical nature.

With Callum, I should have been clear. From the moment I'd got to the Highlands, he should have known where he stood. Even if embracing my fear felt like falling. I knew he'd catch me.

Just as he'd laid his body out before me, the message here wasn't subtle. *Be mine. Nobody else's.* And God, did I want to climb onto that bed, straddle his broad, warm form with my bare thighs, and fill the ache in the centre of my body. I wanted to use him, have him use me, and wake up tomorrow with something new between us. Something good and honest and true. It was all so new to me, sex—a relationship —with feelings attached, but I couldn't wait to try.

As he waited for my explanation, he caressed himself again.

I held up a trembling finger to pause his actions. "Stop trying to hypnotise me with that. I'm trying to explain it to you."

"How about you explain a wee bit faster." Another stroke.

On the porch of Castle Braithar, I'd called Dominic. Not out of respect to him, but because I wanted no confusion over the decision I'd made. But the call had gone to answerphone, and he'd been out of luck. Instead, he got my polite message. My thanks-but-no-thanks, crystal clear and final.

Leaving me free to jump on the man I was crazy about.

21

HOW WE STARTED

*C*allum

Mathilda stood, a vision in blue. "I rejected him. When he made the proposal, I had no real concept of what a loveless marriage might mean. I didn't think much of marriage at all." Then she held my gaze. "My parents' relationship was ruined by cheating, and my ex-boyfriend didn't think much of monogamy either."

My mouth dropped open. How could someone cheat on her? "I am a one-woman man. That woman is you. That's why I needed to know."

"I know." She bobbed her head. "My sister's happiness is everything to me, but that doesn't mean giving up my own. Which is why I decided that when I marry, it will be for love."

Again, her gaze briefly met mine, and holding my frame still had never been harder. Beyond being fired up and wanting this woman under me, against me, over me, her decision knocked me out. She was giving this up because she cared about me, but that was okay, because I was prepared to give her everything I had. This was how it started. How we started.

"I need to know who this man is, because the moment I touch you, you're mine. That means mine to protect."

Our gazes clung to each other's, and Mathilda swallowed, emotion plain on her face. "Is that so? Save the talking for the morning, McRae." She tapped her toe on the floor, and suddenly the mood shifted.

"Fine, but I know what you gave up for me. And why." I rolled up from the bed, the floorboards creaking under my bare feet as I advanced on her. Mathilda didn't back away. "You say you have a cool head, but your heart is just as warm as mine."

In response, she dragged the silver strap of her dress over one shoulder. It fell short of exposing her, but a wave of heat and adrenaline engulfed me.

I breathed out through my nose and commanded, "Get back on the chair."

Mathilda's lips parted but she did as I asked, perching on the edge of the ski lodge's curved armchair. Then I dropped to my knees in front of her and she squeaked.

"I've wanted you for such a long time," she confessed, reaching out a hand to trail over my shoulder. Mapping me.

I placed my palms on her knees then slid them up her thighs, taking her satin dress with me. Baring those long legs I'd obsessed over from the moment we'd met.

Finally, after weeks of denying myself thoughts like these, I let my eyes take their fill. Of smooth thighs, of the outline of the black lace I glimpsed where I pushed her dress higher.

Christ, I was ready to explode just from the sight of her underwear.

Mathilda cupped my chin and held it, forcing me to look at her. "Go slow." She glanced down to where my cock tented my boxers. "I'd wondered if every part of you was in proportion. I'm glad it's not just your castle that has an impressive tower."

I fought back a smile. "I'm glad to say I'm not lacking. Either in castle or cock."

With that, she leaned in and laid her sweet lips on mine.

This was meant to be my seduction, to tempt her away from worse options, and to have her fall for me like I'd fallen for her. But Mathilda Storm took control, and it was all I could do to hold on while she ravished my lips.

Not that I was a slouch.

We clashed, grabbing at one another. Her fervour took me by surprise, but I had weeks of pent-up frustration driving me. She licked my lips to gain access and slicked her tongue over mine. Then I dominated her right back, owning her mouth and laying my claim with my kiss.

She scratched her nails over my scalp, I groaned and dropped to kiss her neck, reaching around to tug on the zip of her dress.

The damn thing wouldn't shift. Any harder and I'd tear it off her.

"Stand up, will ye? I need you naked." I panted and sat back on my haunches.

Mathilda wobbled upright on those heels, her lips swollen from mine, then she undid the dress in a practiced motion. It fell from her form, pooling between us.

I looked up at a goddess. Rounded breasts, heavy in a black half-corset contraption, a swell to her belly and thighs that had my mouth watering.

On an inhale, she took off the bra and cast it aside.

Jesus Christ and all the saints.

Mathilda's body had me stunned almost to silence.

"You are the most beautiful woman who ever breathed," I managed, my voice tight with lust and admiration.

I reached up and ran a reverent hand over her full breast. She leaned into my touch, filling and overspilling my hand.

My cock swelled even more, so hard it was nearly painful.

I needed to see all of her. Taste her. Take this as far as it could go.

"These are in the way," I murmured to the final tiny scrap of lace covering her.

Leaning in, I snagged her underwear with my teeth and dragged downward, right over the part of her that had my senses going wild. Mathilda gave a little moan and gripped my hair, showing me exactly where she needed me most.

With gentle pressure, I pushed her back to sitting and finished the job of making her naked. Aside from her shoes. Because *fuck*. Then, my gaze holding hers, I pushed her knees apart and moved into the gap, using my body to open her thighs. Wide and inviting.

"Tell me you want me." I kissed her, taking her breasts in my hands as she gripped my shoulder muscles, sending me wild. I wanted to keep her here for days, learn every single inch of her and let her loose on me. I rolled her nipples, and she arched into me.

"Yes," she hissed, her exploration of my body bold. "All of you. To the hilt, McRae."

I laid open-mouthed kisses over her collarbone then down, until I sucked her nipple into my mouth. She cried out. My blood surged.

I hadn't planned to rush things, but I slowed, heeding a thought to savour this, and I pushed her shoulder so she reclined in the chair, slumped back and breathing hard.

"Take off your underwear," she demanded. "If you're going to do what I think you're going to do, after, I'll want you to fuck me hard, and I need to see what I'm dealing with."

"Jesus. I love it when you swear." I huffed a laugh and leapt up to dispose of my shorts.

"You make me like this." She pointed an accusatory finger,

her gaze glued to my crotch. "I've never been that bothered about sex, but you set me on fire. Do you have any idea how hot it is in here? That wood fire, your body. I'm about to melt."

"Do you have any idea how beautiful you look sprawled out there, ready and waiting for me?"

I whipped my underwear off, and my cock sprang free.

Mathilda gasped, her eyes widening. "Bring it here. Let me take a closer look."

"In a minute." I dropped down, clasped her thighs and, without warning, brought my mouth to the juncture of her body.

She was soaked and tasted like Heaven.

"Callum!" she screamed. I sucked hard on her.

I ran two fingers downwards then pushed slowly into the core of her.

So hot. So tight. So *mine*.

"Your lairdship will do. Or God. Call me that if ye like," I uttered against her flesh.

She wriggled under me and I thrusted slow, lifting her thigh with the other hand and loving her with my mouth, keeping up a slick, hot slide with my fingers.

Her legs wrapped around my shoulders, heels digging in. So fucking sexy.

If this wasn't the purest form of worship for the woman who held your dreams in her grasp, then nothing was.

She cursed me again as I added a third finger.

"Play with your nipples," I ordered, looking up her gleaming body. "Show me what you like. Make me crazy."

She did, palming her tits and tugging her nipples into peaks. I groaned at the sight. She watched my moves on her and alternated that with looking over my form. The approval gave me a surge of pride for my size, and I wanted to roll back and have her climb onto me. But not yet. I had to start this evening as I meant to go on.

It wasn't long before Mathilda moved her hips in time with my hand and mouth, and her yelps became a long, low moan.

"I'm close," she breathed. "Don't stop."

Like I would. I grunted acknowledgement, as words were beyond me now. My cock leaked for needing attention, and my world became Mathilda's pleasure.

I swirled my tongue then sucked hard, bringing her to a crest while my fingers hit the same spot over and again. With a cry, she pushed into my mouth then dropped down, half off the chair, her orgasm tightening around my fingers.

Thank fuck for that. I was close to dying, my entire being needing to join with her in the most primal of ways.

"Callum." Her voice trembled, and she pulled me up to kiss her.

I picked her up, her legs wrapping around my waist and shoes dropping to the floor, our kiss continuing as I found my way to the bed. "You're perfect. The sexiest creature I ever saw." I couldn't keep the wonder out of my voice.

"I need you inside me," she replied.

"You have me. In every way there is."

I knelt on the mattress and laid her out, snatched a condom from the box I'd thrown on the pillow earlier.

"Are you ready?" *Please, God, say yes.*

Mathilda drew a breath and sat up. Her cheeks flushed red, even in the orange firelight, and her tousled hair curled around her face in a cloud. "My turn to take charge."

A smile took over my lips. "Thought you wanted me to pound you."

"I changed my mind." She rose on her knees and grasped my shoulders, then pushed me backward to the bed. I went, willingly. "Hands behind your head."

She took the condom and rolled it over my painfully hard cock. I nearly died from the pressure.

"Don't say I can't touch you." That would kill me. If she was going to ride me, I wanted to grab on to her. Get handfuls of her hips. Grind her into me. Be able to push up and suck her tits into my mouth.

"Hands behind your head," she repeated.

I groaned, but I did it, gripping my fingers together like I wanted to break my own hands.

"Well done." She grinned, and I glowered at her. But the expression on her face meant I couldn't hold a frown for long.

She ran her gaze over me, from the bulge of my biceps, prominent either side of my head, almost lovingly over my features. Then she opened her mouth as if to say something, but then thought better of it. I needed to know what was on her mind, but my cock bobbed of its own accord, and Mathilda's gaze snagged on the movement.

She made a low humming sound then threw her leg over me, and I growled as she settled into position.

"You're the biggest man I've ever met, Callum McRae," she murmured, rubbing my cock against her, using me as a tool.

I'd lost the ability to speak, so focused was I on how her warm centre felt against my rigid flesh. *Fuck, fuck, fuck, dinna embarrass yourself, man.*

"Big in all ways. In your size," she gave my cock a squeeze, lining me up with her entrance, "in your heart, and in how much you care. You're beautiful, Callum."

I raised my head in surprise, but in a swift move, Mathilda sank onto me, taking half my length in one go.

"Yes!" we both yelled in unison. Then Mathilda followed with, "Oh my God," sinking lower, flexing her thighs, trying to take all of me.

"Slow," I managed, grinding out the word and jamming my shoulders into the quilt. If she moved, I was going to blow my top.

Sweat beaded on my forehead and chest as I stared at the sight. This gorgeous woman, backlit by firelight, with her head thrown back where she concentrated on fucking me. But I squeezed my eyes tight shut when she finally lowered herself the whole way.

The sensation alone was enough to have me insane.

"To the hilt," she uttered. Then she gave an experimental roll of her hips, my cock so deep inside her I saw stars.

"Let...me." I exhaled, needing to spin her over and take control, every instinct telling me to pound into her, to slam again and again and make her howl.

I'd howl myself at the wonder of it.

"Wait. Bring your hands back. Take mine," she commanded.

I offered my hands out, my muscles rigid. Mathilda used me as leverage and began to move.

"So big, but oh God." Her head lolled and I gave a tiny thrust up to meet her downward action. Her grip on my hands, my arms rigid, increased. "You're stretching me, and it feels so good. God. Do that again."

I did. With her thighs pressed into mine, as close as we could be, I thrust up, and Mathilda dragged in a breath.

And that was the last word either of us said that wasn't "yes", "oh fuck" or "more".

She clutched my hands, and I supported her ride, getting harder and my movements getting faster as her breathing sped up. She had to come again. And again, and again, before the night was out.

Mathilda chased her pleasure, working my length in and out of her. I watched her eyelids flutter, her breasts bounce, and her colour flush. When she was close, her movements slowed, so I took the initiative. Clamping our hands to her hips, I took over the action, fucking into her like I was motorised. My hips pistoned, and Mathilda moaned loud, arching back with her mouth open.

"Yes!" she yelled, and I was done.

Her second orgasm pulsed around my cock triggering my own. I dug my heels into the bed, my knees bowing out and my thrusts growing harder.

With a swift drag on her arms, I pulled her down and clamped her to me as I spun us over, then, with my woman underneath me, I let loose my desire. Mathilda groaned over and over, and I pounded into her, digging my fingers into her hips and pressing my knees into the bed so hard it creaked in complaint. Sweat dripped off me, and my jaw ached where I gritted my teeth.

I swore, the whole of my universe focused on the place we were joined. On the feeling of her around me.

I yelled her name. The most powerful orgasm I'd ever had surged through me.

The intensity knocked me out, and I dropped down, my hands white-knuckled, one still gripping Mathilda's perfect, round backside. I pulsed into her, my head at her neck, brilliant white light in my eyes.

Then I raised my face to hers to kiss out the last of my pleasure. The sparks in my body had me nearly shaking. Or maybe it was the blinding adoration in my heart. Then I realised Mathilda *was* shaking.

"What was that?" she breathed. "I mean, just… What?"

"Dinna ye ken?" It was what I'd known since I'd first seen her face. What everybody looked for and few could ever find. Because this was too big, too fucking everything for it to happen every day.

"It's what happens when it's right." I adjusted my weight so I didn't crush the lass. Then I hugged her hard, told her over and over that I wouldn't let her go, and sank into bliss with the future Lady McRae.

Maybe I'd leave it a wee while before I asked.

22

A PERMANENCE

*M*athilda
Callum slept, wrapped around my back with one hand splayed over my stomach and the other arm around my shoulders. Close, tight, and loving as we lay on our sides in the log cabin's big bed. He gave off heat like a furnace, and I luxuriated in the warmth.

We'd passed out after the mind-blowing sex, but from the illuminated clock across the room in the tiny kitchen area, only a couple of hours had passed before I'd awoken.

I had a problem, and it was keeping me from sleep.

The emotions in me had moved up another notch. I liked Callum. A life-changing amount. My whole being hurt with all the new feelings. The second biggest being a fear, and I shuddered for all the damage it could do.

Scarlet, my parents, Beth, my job, Callum's brothers... there were more than just mine and Callum's lives affected if we did this. What if it didn't work out?

Dad loved my mother so much it had destroyed a part of him when she'd cheated. The lesson I'd learned was that you didn't place too much of yourself into relationships as you'd have to sacrifice that part when it all went wrong.

I was giving Callum my everything, despite my worries. I had no choice. Even thinking of being without him... No. An unbearable thought. The safety of his arms spurred me on to face each of my other little fears in turn.

Maybe a long-distance relationship would work for a while, but his life was here. He had a family to support and people who relied on him. All of which he managed on his own. Would his brothers want me here? Could I bring my sister with me, if I found a way? I had a feeling they'd welcome her without question.

Scarlet was the only permanent fixture I had. I enjoyed my job but I'd happily give it up for the right opportunity. Living far from my parents was highly appealing. Then there was Beth. Moving out of our shared home—because my mind had terrifyingly leapt to me relocating to Castle McRae —would be a wrench, but Beth would move on eventually, too. We'd stay friends regardless and we could visit one another.

If Callum decided he truly wanted me in the same way, I could move to Scotland to be with him. I wanted it. Him.

My heart constricted, and I hugged his arm, wedging my bare leg tightly under his much larger, hairier one.

Callum made a small noise of contentment in his sleep, and his fingers caressed my stomach. Instinct had me wanting to hold back my little revelation, but I'd already held back too much.

I needed him, so I was going to make love to him, then we could talk it all out.

"What is it? Why are you breathing so hard?" came his drowsy murmur.

I didn't answer. Instead, I took his hand and ran it up to

my breast, then I massaged myself using his hand, coaxing my nipple to a hard peak.

Callum shifted at my back, pushing up on an elbow as he ducked his head to lay a sleepy, hot kiss on my skin. First my shoulder, then to my neck, his hand keeping up the kneading I'd initiated.

Against my ass, his dick hardened.

"Mathilda," Callum whispered, and I twisted my neck to kiss him.

The low fire washed him in amber, the light flickering over his skin. We kissed, and he clutched me to him, the hand at my belly possessive and the other leaving my breast to travel south. I whimpered into his kiss when he slid his rough fingers over my clit then to the core of me.

"So wet," he murmured then returned his attention to my clit, moving in small circles as I spread my legs, giving him access. So good.

He said my name again, and I reached back to bring his oversized dick between my thighs. Clumsily, I rubbed him against me, his rigid cock meeting my slick centre. His fingers gripped over mine, and together, we used him as a tool, readying me for him.

Then, he shifted his hand to circle my clit again, and I lined him up then pushed him inside me.

We both stilled.

I rolled my hips once, every nerve ending lighting up, blazing with sensation.

No condom.

Callum was bare inside me.

"Mathilda..."

"I know."

"Just need to..." He blew out a breath and reached over me to the bedside table, pushing farther into me at the same time. I mewled, and he made a sound like he was in pain, dropping back down, a condom packet in his hand.

"I've never done this before. Never tried it without—"

I rolled my hips. Another groan.

"I'm sorry," I managed to utter. "I'm clean."

"You're trying to kill me," he breathed, still not pulling out. "I am, too, but fuck."

"And I'm on the pill." There was a permanence to this. I'd always been safe. In every way. Sleeping with someone unprotected was the ultimate trust exercise. To be savoured. Saved for the one. We were almost there, except we hadn't talked this through.

"Christ, woman. Are ye sure?" At my moan, Callum lifted my leg and inched forward inside me. With his damp forehead on my shoulder, he pushed home.

"You have no idea how good this feels. How crazy I am for you." His voice was low and delicious. Strained with his fervour.

I slid my arm between my legs and stroked his thigh, then found his heavy balls. Pulled lightly, then ran my thumb between them. Callum's steady strokes stuttered, and his grip on me tightened, his fingers indenting the flesh of my hips.

"Touch yourself," he demanded.

"Go slow," I ordered right back.

I shifted my hand to my clit, and after a few minutes of his heavy, thick strokes, slow in the most delicious way, I was crying out and arching back. My orgasm hit me in stages: a slow pulse from deep inside, from the places he stretched and the magical spot he kept hitting, then a flurry of rising electricity from my fingers at my clit.

"Callum!"

"Yes, Mathilda," he growled in my ear. "Yell my name."

I did, over and over. I flopped onto the bed, sated, and

Callum reared up, no longer slow or gentle. With both hands, he rolled me to my front and dragged my hips up so my backside was in the air and my face down on the bed. He entered me in a single, hard thrust that caught the last vestiges of my orgasm and had me crying out, then he set a punishing pace, thrusting with a ruthless force.

The bed frame banged against the wall. The fire sparked. Callum's massive, powerful thighs stretched where he slammed into me again and again, then he bellowed, choking out my name as he came, pulsing hard deep inside.

His breathing ragged and his voice raw, Callum McRae never sounded more tender when he whispered words and collapsed down, taking care not to land on me before he rolled me into his arms. With soft, wet kisses, he told me I was beautiful, he said I meant the world to him.

The feeling was mutual.

I opened my eyes to a terrifying emotion in his eyes, and I knew it was in mine, too.

* * *

With the fire fed and burning brightly, Callum raided the cabin's small fridge and brought a midnight feast to the bed. I checked the time. Lachlan's party would still be in full swing. Callum had said it would go on until dawn.

It hadn't sat comfortably with me, his brothers going into the water, so I was glad we'd seen them safely out.

"You thought of everything." I eyed the small picnic with glee. Brie, crackers, and a jar of tomato tapenade.

"Not so. I only thought of you," he replied with a smile, offering me a bottle of water.

We consumed our midnight feast with the appetite of two

people who'd burned a whole lot of calories on passion. Callum watched me while he ate, a mixture of satisfaction and hunger on his face that I didn't think the snack was going to fulfil. I was blissed out, my body heavy and tingling. Aching. But still I wanted more. To maximise this time in the space he'd carved out for us.

As we talked, he shared a little more about his father and how he sought to be everything the man wasn't—a loyal family member, a valuable part of the community. Gentle, though a protector. Kind. Loving. I told him he was all of those things, and he rewarded me with the last bite. It was beyond intimate, it was…a beginning.

"You were holding out on me," I said. "We could've been doing this yesterday."

He shrugged, clearing the remnants of our picnic away. "You weren't ready."

"Huh?" I blinked at him. I absolutely had been.

"Fine, maybe I wasn't ready. This was never going to be casual for me. I needed to show you my life so you could choose if you wanted to be a part of it."

He said it as a matter of fact, but this was serious, and after the thoughts I'd had, a thrill ran through me at the implication.

"Not that I'm making any assumptions." He sat back on the bed dressed in only his black boxer shorts. I'd snagged his huge t-shirt, and it covered me to mid-thigh. Callum was comfortable in his skin in a way I never could be. Well, outside of sex. During, he made me feel beautiful.

"So telling me how I was yours over and over wasn't making assumptions?" I teased him and extended my leg, poking him with my toe.

Callum grabbed my ankle and dragged me to him, then he manoeuvred me onto his lap so he was holding me off the edge of the bed. With his hands gripping my waist and thigh, he kissed my hair. I giggled and tucked in against him.

"Maybe it was," he said. "Dinna tell me I'm wrong to have claimed you. My heart couldnae take the disappointment."

"You're not wrong." My heart thundered as I spoke, and I huddled closer, unable to look him in the eye, the sense of vulnerability too great. Only with Callum could I feel small. Protected by his arms alone. It hit me in a wave, and I fell harder for him and his magic touch.

"The twins are a lot to take. Always in some danger."

"I like them. They're your life."

"That they are. But only one part."

We sat there, him holding me quietly in the dimly lit space.

"Tell me what's happened with Scarlet." Callum shifted to move us to the top of the bed. He carried me with ease and leaned his back on the headboard, waiting while I settled against his chest. "You want her away from your da, but you never said why."

"She's been stealing." The words fell from my mouth. "She said it was to try to get a rise out of Dad, but keeping her away from temptation would be good."

"Away from the city, then," Callum mused. "I wonder where would be good for that."

I bit back a smile. "I'm going to talk to my dad again. There's something else he needs to know…" I took a breath.

We hadn't made a commitment, but we'd come close. I didn't want any secrets between us.

"The man who proposed to me is Dad's business partner. A man I think you met."

Callum stilled. "Who?"

"Dominic Hanswick." I hadn't meant to drop this like a bomb, but I wanted Callum to know. It was my business, the arrangement I'd considered, but Dominic's affair affected Callum's life. I had picked a side, and now I'd stick to it.

Around me, Callum's arms banded tight. I continued my explanation, needing to have it done. "Last year, Dominic was in the press for having an affair. He's single, but his girlfriend is married. She's a politician, so it made the papers."

Then I took a deep breath, readying the killer blow. "The publicity meant he lost investment. It's the reason why he can't pay his half of the Storm Force contracts."

I twisted around as Callum still hadn't said anything. His face tilted and he watched me, his forehead devoid of his usual frown, his expression unreadable.

"He'd have used you to cover up his affair?"

"That was the deal. Five years of my life. It didn't seem like anything. Scarlet had been caught stealing red-handed, and the tension at my parents' home was so awful for her. For everyone. Now, it seems like a life sentence."

Callum huffed a strange sort of laugh. "Aye, it would have been. But I get it. Your life for hers."

I shifted off his lap and looked at him properly, trying to get a read on where he was with this. "Exactly, but it was a bad decision based on how much I care for Scarlet and the lengths I'd go to for her. All of this was before I knew you existed. I'd do anything to help my sister, but now," I rubbed my forehead, "I think I was mad."

"There's nothing wrong with you. You put your family first. But Hanswick..." Callum sat up, breaking the connection between us. "That fucking man. He came here, walked around my distillery and shook my hand. Then he fucked over someone else's marriage, tossed a series of small businesses into turmoil, and went to you and tried to drag you into his mess. That self-interested bastard. Who does he think he is?"

A sense of guilt crept into me. Callum painted a bleak

picture. I'd thought if I accepted Dominic's offer I could only hurt myself. Now, a list of people flickered in front of my eyes. It might not have been me that had damaged them, but I'd have supported it.

Callum rolled up from the bed and crossed the floor. Emotion flitted over his features.

"I tried to see him. And your father. To tell them what they'd done. At least I know who to save my words for."

"My father hates Dominic's actions."

Understanding resonated on Callum's face. "Because of your mother's affair?"

I cringed at the casual way Mom and Dominic's actions were thrown together. This was where my cool head and my loyalties didn't match up. I'd never thought beyond Scarlet, but now the unsavoury nature of it all had me wincing.

Dad wouldn't like my plan, it would make things worse. All I'd done was try to navigate an out-of-the-blue offer and make it work for my sister, but instead I'd found myself involved in someone else's mess.

Callum jabbed his fingers into his hair. I waited for his judgment, unhappiness welling. And I hated it, because I judged myself, and I didn't like what I saw.

He'd change his view of me. I could almost see it happening.

A trilling sound rang out in the room. It came from Callum's rucksack.

"Damn," he said, ceasing his pacing to march over to the bag.

"What was that?"

"My emergency radio."

"For what?" I clutched my chest.

"The mountain rescue."

Callum threw out half the contents of his bag as he

located a device with a large aerial. He activated it and barked a call sign.

I stared and a staccato voice accosted the room. Teenager. Alasdair McRae. Missing in the Braithar River. Last seen heading downstream toward the loch at Castle McRae.

Ally was missing.

SHARP FEAR

Mathilda

Callum jammed his feet into his boots, his features tightly held and an air of controlled fear hanging over him. "Take the Rover to Braithar. Get Wasp. Can ye find your way in the dark?"

"Don't worry about me. Find your brother." I was on my feet, ready to help.

He leapt up, palmed my face, then kissed me like our almost-argument was a distant memory. Outside, the noise of a helicopter's rotor blades chopped up the air. It grew to a din as we reached the front door, and I half hid myself behind the frame. Callum stormed into the snow-covered field outside the cabin. The helicopter landed, he climbed on, then was gone.

Silence swelled. Freezing air swirled around me.

In minutes, everything had changed.

Happiness had shifted to sharp fear. As razor-edged as the sword tattoo I'd spotted inked down the centre of Callum's back before he'd dragged on his shirt. A reminder of who he had to protect?

Right. In a numb state, I dressed from my overnight bag, packed up our clothes and belongings, and found the keys to Callum's Land Rover. In the cold dark, I faced the night with a small degree of trepidation in driving the narrow, icy path. If I could help in any way with this, I would. I could retrieve Wasp and then find another way to be useful.

I needed Callum to see my decisions were usually sound. It hurt to consider what he must think of me now.

The car door creaked as I swung it open, slinging the bags inside. The metal was bitterly cold to the touch. The thought of Ally in the river somewhere nearly floored me and I hurried to the driver's side.

The water would be icy. The night pitch black.

I liked the boy so much. All of Callum's brothers were wonderful, but Ally...for all his size, he was a child, still. Lost, out in the cold. His brothers would be desperate. My heart hammered.

The Land Rover trundled forward under my careful, shaking hands, and I took the route back to Castle Braithar.

After a twenty-minute anxiety-inducing downhill slalom, I crossed the river to the castle. The place was a hive of activity with vehicles charging about. Though the evening I'd had with Callum had seemed to go on forever, we'd left the party early, and many guests were still here. Groups in suits and evening dresses gathered on the riverbank, torches in hand. Somewhere, the roar of the helicopter ripped through the air.

I dipped my lights and rolled off the road and onto the grass, searching the faces for anyone familiar. Then I spotted Una with Wasp at her side. Bringing the car to a halt, I half-fell as I ran over.

"Wasp!"

"Mathilda!" The boy lurched forward and wrapped his arms around me. I hugged him in return, placing my hand on the back of his head. Damp. His clothes were, too. The smell of river water was rich in his hair. He'd obviously been searching for his twin.

"Any news?" I asked.

Wasp dragged me a couple of steps. "No. Come on. Get back in the car. We need to join the search."

Una caught up with us, her pale face alarmed. "Gordain left William in my care. He's at risk of winding up in the river himself, trying to find Alasdair."

"I've got him. Thank you," I replied, snapping into management mode. I'd handled all kinds of emergencies before, though none had included missing boys. Family members. "Where's Gordain now?"

"Out on the rescue boat, heading down to the loch. The search party is going to convene at Castle McRae."

I gave her a grateful nod and continued to the car. Wasp threw himself into the passenger seat, and I stepped on the gas, propelling us away.

Along the dark road, a restless Wasp filled me in on the night's events. Ally had been goaded into a secret rematch by Lachlan's stepgrandson, a young man named Paulo. He'd taken the bait and not told Wasp or Gordain, but ten minutes after Paulo had reached the fast-flowing bend that was their end point, Ally still hadn't appeared. Paulo waited but eventually panicked, returned alone, and told the brothers.

So stupid.

In hindsight, so predictable.

The road followed the river, and lights occasionally flickered through the trees. Wasp jolted up at each one.

"Callum will find him," I said.

"Can we get out and look? I need to help. It was my fault. He always has to go that one step further, and I should've known he wouldn't be able to ignore that lad. All for a stupid challenge."

My heart hurt. "It isn't your fault, and he will be found. Your brothers are both trained in this, right? We'll find out more when we get to the castle."

Wasp stared into the dark night. The beam from the helicopter lit the clouds ahead like a star guiding us home.

"Check your phone," I suggested. "See if you have any messages."

The twins were permanently attached to their devices, and Wasp gripped his in his hand.

"Nothing," he muttered.

Ahead, the trees thinned and the night sky emerged. We were closing in on the downhill path to Castle McRae.

"Check mine." I rummaged in my bag tucked at my side, then handed the phone to Wasp. The boy took it and turned it on, the screen lighting up the Land Rover's cabin.

I glanced out of the corner of my eye. Message after message landed, scrolling up. Wasp looked through them but didn't speak. I knew I had notifications from Dad trying to get hold of me, but the screen kept moving.

"What?" I asked. "Is there news?"

"You…" Wasp pushed the messages up, reading through. The cold in the car seemed to dip the longer he paused. "They're not from Callum. These are all congratulation messages. And links to news sites. Who is Dominic Hanswick? Mattie, are you engaged?"

Shock had me snap my head around. "No!"

Had I thought the evening couldn't get any worse? It just had.

* * *

We pulled up outside Castle McRae at the same time the helicopter appeared overhead. Several things happened at once. Two support vehicles raced past us and down the slope to the path that led alongside the loch. People jumped out and waded into the water, their figures backlit by the powerful lamps on top of the cars. Angry vibrations shook the air around us as the helicopter hovered, readying to land. Then, finally, a rescue boat purred under the road bridge and coasted toward the waiting group.

Wasp and I took off to join the onlookers at the edge of the water. Alongside the uniformed emergency services, I recognised a number of estate workers huddled together, and the expression on their faces was identical to how I felt. Sheer terror at what the boat was bringing in.

"G!" Wasp yelled over the noise, his tone desperate and his hands clutching my arm.

Gordain's voice called back from the boat, resounding in the freezing air. "Got him. Cold but fine."

I nearly dropped to the rocky beach. Wasp grabbed me tighter, and we both gasped with relief. They'd found Ally. His twin left my side and staggered into the shallows.

"I'm alive," Ally's voice came. Though he sounded weak, his voice was music to my ears. Then the boat cruised in, and waiting hands moved to help the passengers with quiet efficiency.

Behind us on the grass, the helicopter had touched down, and heavy footsteps pounded down the track. Then Callum was crashing into the water, lifting his brother from Gordain's arms and turning back to shore. The look on his face was pure determination, and it melted as he held his brother to his chest and the young man threw an arm around his neck, holding the other out for his twin.

"Mathilda, keep close," Callum boomed, reaching the beach, and I jumped to follow. Gordain caught up and placed a hand on my back and, together, we moved into the castle.

The rescue was over, but I had a new battle to face. What

on Earth did all those messages on my phone mean, and how was I now engaged?

* * *

The last remaining visitors stood around the fire in Castle McRae's great hall. A paramedic had just concluded tending to Ally in his room, and the other parties began to disburse.

Playing host, I'd made hot drinks and directed people around the castle. Beth and James, still sick, had been ordered back to bed, and Callum and Gordain had carried out a rapid debrief but were taking care of their family upstairs.

As I understood it, Callum had spotted Ally by his frantic waving of his phone light. No signal in the rocky river valley to allow a rescue call. He'd been swept off his raft, submerged, much farther past the point Paulo had reached, but he'd managed to scramble to the river's steep bank. Then he'd sat and shivered until the boat reached him.

Despite the warmth from the fire, I trembled at the thought of how bad it could have been.

A knock came from the open castle door, and a new group of people entered, breaking my moment of reflection. It was Lachlan, a woman and young man with him. The boy Ally had raced.

"We won't stay long," Lachlan announced. "This is my wife, Marianne, and this wee idiot, Paulo, has something to say to the laird."

"Callum's with his brothers," I said, folding my arms and throwing a glance at the wooden staircase behind me. I didn't want to be rude, but the family needed their peace. Now was not the time.

"Please pass on my apologies to Ally. And to his brothers."

The dark-haired young man at Lachlan's side toed the flag-stones. His voice was thick with regret.

"Damn right you're sorry. You knew it wasn't safe to go downstream but you still went ahead with your challenge," Lachlan barked at the young man.

At a guess, I'd put him at seventeen or eighteen.

"But it was only to the third bend, before the rapids, then we were meant to walk back. I wrote it down and gave it to him at the start. Why did he go past the mark?"

The boy's words were lost by Lachlan's wife chastising her husband about family pride and winning at all costs. But I heard the implications. If he'd given the challenge in writing and Ally hadn't been able to read the end point, that explained why he'd carried on past.

He wouldn't have wanted to admit that he couldn't read easily.

Marianne turned back and gave me a firm smile. "Our boy should have known better, but rest assured he'll be punished appropriately. These idiot males with testosterone up to their eyeballs, it's a wonder they get anything done. We'll leave you in peace. Take care of the family and let us know if there's anything we can do."

As the woman marched Paulo out, Lachlan remained. He advanced on me slowly, a speculative look in his eye. "Congratulations on your engagement."

Oh Jesus. How did he know? In the past hour, I'd only managed a brief scan of my messages and concluded something ridiculous but true. Tonight, my engagement to Dominic had been announced by him at a dinner with his shareholders. Because of the link to his politician girlfriend, it had made the news. My name was barely mentioned, more focus on the association with my mother's previous fame and Dad's international business, but the press had camped outside the politician's family home to get the woman's reaction.

Abigail Price was her name. I'd paid no attention to her before, not even bothering to scan the articles on the affair after Dominic had made his request to me.

She had two young children, I knew that much. Now they'd be reminded of their mother's affair all over again.

More names on the list of those who'd gotten hurt.

"I'm not engaged. It's an error. It'll be corrected tomorrow." I dragged up a polite smile for Lachlan and resisted the urge to rub a hand over my face. Exhaustion had sunk its claws deep.

"Aye. I knew it was a lie. If anyone would know about false engagements, it's this family. Anyone who saw you and the laird together would know where you'd left your heart." Lachlan gave me a small smile, then left.

Damn. Damn, damn, damn.

With the great hall finally empty, I wobbled on weary feet to the main door and dragged it shut. Then I slid the bolt into place with a dull clunk of metal.

"What error will be corrected tomorrow?" Callum's voice sounded behind me, and I jumped. He emerged from the dark corridor at the top of the staircase and descended, shadows flitting over him.

I didn't want to hide anything from Callum anymore, but surely he'd already started to pass judgment on me earlier at the cabin. This would take the biscuit, wouldn't it?

"Apparently mine."

"How?" He dropped down the last few steps, the tiredness etched into his features morphing into curiosity. The man was practically sleepwalking. I advanced on him, my hands out.

"Tonight has already flattened everyone, so you have a choice," I said. "Either I can tell you the new drama, or it can wait until morning when we're rested and can think straight."

Callum moved closer and, without pause, slid his arms around me and held me tight. His cheek hit my forehead. "You choose. Do I need to know this right now? Because I'm not sure I'll act with reason. I know why Ally got into trouble —he told me about the note Lachlan's lad slipped him. I can't say I'm dealing with it well right now."

I considered it as I sank into his hug. There was nothing I could do about fixing this. Whatever story had been concocted, it was out there, regardless. Tomorrow, I'd travel to London, confront Dominic, and get a retraction issued. Then I'd see my father and handle him. I'd listened to the first of Dad's voicemails where he'd asked me why I hadn't told him I was dating Dominic—apparently the rat bastard had told him we were an item a couple of days ago. Then his other messages were more of the same.

I'd sent him a text saying I wasn't engaged and that I'd call him in the morning. My sister had sent me a picture of her face pulling a shocked expression, WTF added in large, pink letters, so I'd sent her a similar message as Dad. Then I'd turned the damn device off and tried to not panic as I'd returned to managing the people in the great hall.

Now, the panic flowed back in with a vengeance. But I was tired, still shaking from the search for Ally, and needing this hug. Callum needed it, too. His muscles corded around me, holding me as close to him as I could get. I already knew from the paramedic that Ally would make a full recovery, but the fear of what could have happened hit me in waves, and I struggled to speak.

"We'll talk tomorrow."

"Whatever you think best. I'm sorry our evening was ruined."

"I'm just glad you found him," I replied.

We stood in a silent stupor for a moment, the cool air of the castle enclosing us. Callum dragged in a breath. "I thought he was dead, ye ken? Dead, and it would be my fault. We flew a search pattern I've flown so many times before, but my mind kept telling me he'd be under the water so my searching was useless." He dragged in another breath that shook us both, and I held him closer. "I've been pushed to the edge. It would kill me to lose him. Any of them. Or you. Do you know that? If someone has hurt you—"

"Everything will be okay, I promise you. But right now? We're going to bed," I interrupted. He was so exhausted he could barely stand. "We'll talk it out when we wake. Make a plan."

"I trust you." Callum's blue eyes burned bright as I raised my head. "More than anyone, I think. We'll handle it together, aye?"

I nodded, taking him by the hand and leading him up the stairs. I wasn't sure at all of how Callum would react. My gut instinct, which was so much lower in importance than my logical mind, told me this was going to go badly wrong. And I only had myself to blame.

24

THE WORST VERSION OF MYSELF

*C*allum
        Dawn broke, and though I'd had only a few hours' sleep, the light flooding into my solar, plus my overactive brain, meant I was awake already. I'd left my rooms once in the night to check on Ally—I found Wasp sharing his bed, like they'd done when they were wee boys—and now I stared at Mathilda's sleeping profile.

Whatever had hurt her would face me. The edge of adrenaline and panic I'd been riding last night still held my muscles tight and, despite my rest, I was far from calm. My limbs tingled with the need to hunt for my boy. To run, shout, or fight.

I had the urge to wake Mathilda and bury my hard cock to the hilt in her heat. Take out my anguish and fury on her soft body. It would help, but I'd be rough, and I didn't want to use her like that. For her to think me an animal.

"Hey." Her lips parted in a yawn, then Mathilda's brown eyes opened. They widened as she saw my expression.

What I looked like, I had no idea, but she seemed to

understand my need perfectly because she reached out and found my hip at the same moment her lips touched mine.

She kissed me, hard, and I reared over her. Her hand slipped to grip the girth of my cock.

"I can't be gentle." I groaned into her neck, wanting to bite her, wanting to savage her body.

"I can take anything you've got," she answered, and I was done.

In a second, I had lined myself up, rubbing my cock over her already wet centre. Then in one thrust, I sheathed myself into her heat.

I took all my aggression, my guilt and hurt and fear and anger and channelled it into fucking Mathilda. And she gave as good as she got. Her nails clawed into my bucking back, her teeth bit my lip. Maybe she had emotion of her own to deal with. All I knew was this connection meant everything.

We fucked like we were fighting.

"Callum!" she yelled as my headboard nearly split against the wall, then I was coming. I grabbed handfuls of her thighs, crashing into her over and over, and I threw my head back, a bellow wrenching out of my throat. Then I stilled and pulsed hard, sweat pouring off me. My breathing ragged. My arms shaking. My need reduced, though not yet sated.

"So good," Mathilda mumbled, and she pulled me down around her. Kissing me until I lost my breath again.

"Thank Christ you came, because that was all animal. I'm sorry I lost control," I managed, but she only chuckled.

"I needed that, too. Not that it changes anything."

We caught our breath, and Mathilda dragged the blankets over her then sat up, holding her knees. "For the past few days, I've ignored messages from my dad. He's been trying to contact me."

"Aye?" I pulled on my boxers and sat at the end of the bed,

wildness still strained within me, exhaustion at the edge of my vision. Still, my attention was all hers.

"Last week, Dominic told my father we were dating. Despite me not giving him permission."

That fucker. I leapt up. "What the hell was he thinking? What a liberty to take."

Mathilda cringed and ushered me down. "Thin end of the wedge, Callum. It gets worse. He then announced our engagement to a party of their shareholders in a restaurant last night. One of them told the press who are having a field day over it."

Engaged.

To him.

How dare he? A wave of jealousy engulfed me. I couldn't speak.

Mathilda paled, and her fingers dug into my sheets. "Last night, when you came downstairs to Lachlan leaving, he'd heard about it on the radio. It's because the woman Dominic was having an affair with is so high-profile. Apparently, the press is pursuing her, assuming she's heartbroken. I checked a couple of the major news sites. My name is on the story along with commentary about a love triangle."

"The world thinks you're marrying that arsehole?" I managed, the fresh set of emotions turning my muscles to tight balls of energy again. I paced over to the window, my voice getting louder. "Lachlan does? Your name is out there being tossed around with his? For fuck's sake. That stupid deal he tried to trap you with. He had no right!"

An avalanche of selfish thoughts bore down, and I stared unseeing through the glass. If my relative had already heard, by breakfast time, it would be all over the estate. I loved my home, I fucking lived for the people of my clan, but the gossip, the small minds and old-fashioned ways, I despised.

Every single person I'd want to celebrate with us if she

accepted my proposal would now think of that arsehole first. I wanted to be the man with his name next to hers in the engagement columns. Dominic Hanswick had just taken that away.

What would they think about the relationship I had with her? That it was a fake? That I was a bit on the side? All while she lay naked in my bed.

My pride strained at the seams, too big for my frame to contain.

She was mine. Mine. I wanted her to have my name, be part of my family, belong to me as I belonged to her, but this had become messed up. I spun around, needing to get out of here before I made it worse by running my mouth. Like I'd done to James when he'd disappointed me. It hadn't been his fault either, and I'd learned a lesson.

Mathilda's features tightened. "It was a stupid deal, but I had good reasons."

"Aye, I know you did," I muttered, hating myself but unable to dampen the fire.

"Callum." Mathilda rose gracefully from the bed, my sheets around her like she needed to protect herself from me. Her expression was neutral now, and I knew I was fucking this up. She peered at me, waiting, but whatever she saw in my face brought a deceptive calm over her, masking her hurt.

Shame filled me. Disgust at my behaviour. That, added to my worry for Alasdair, and I was the worst version of myself I could be.

"I have to check on my boy."

Dragging on a pair of jeans, I stepped into my boots and snatched up a hoodie. Then I walked away because it was the only thing I could do.

* * *

I checked in on my wee brothers, my head in turmoil. Alasdair still slept, but William cracked open an eye. "He's okay. Warm enough. I've got him," he mumbled, then flung an arm behind his head and went back to sleep on top of his twin's bed.

Then I stomped on downstairs and found Gordain in the kitchen making coffee. No surprise he couldn't sleep either. Last night, we'd shared a grim look when he'd handed Ally to me from the boat. I knew the meaning behind it. He felt guilty for letting the rematch happen on his watch, and I felt it for leaving the boys to go to my night with Mathilda.

Neither Gordain or I would recover from this easily.

But in the kitchen, over the coffeepot, his look was entirely different. Indignant. His grey eyes burning. "Who the fuck is that English bawbag claiming Mathilda is marrying him?" He set his phone down with a clunk, the browser open with a news article. "Did she know about it? What is she going to do?"

"I can't even talk about it," I managed to reply through my clenched jaw. "But no, of course she didnae know."

"Let me know how we're going to go fix this. Whatever she needs, I'm there."

I loved the fact that my brother bristled on Mathilda's behalf. It told me he'd accepted her, though I'd expected that, given Gordain's easy-going nature. But I still couldn't talk. His reaction was what mine should have been. She was suffering now, and I needed to calm my bones to aid her.

I tried to be different to Da in every way, but controlling my overreactions had proved too hard. I had nothing of his violence or cruelty, but my jealousy and pride were instinctive.

"She needs me to pull my head out of my arse," I muttered to myself.

"I'll tell everyone I see that it's a lie," Gordain said, understanding, and he handed me a mug and let me stomp away.

In my miserable mood, I found myself in Da's office. In eight years, I'd never used this room, hating the memories of it being the place where my brothers had been hurt. But it was just a room, and either I was the laird, or I wasn't.

But I wasn't here to think about my business. I needed five minutes alone to work out how to make things right with Mathilda.

My phone rang. Patricia, the twins' mother, requesting an update as she drove to the castle. The second I hung up, it rang again with the Highland Rescue's regional chief wanting a report on the night's callout. I gritted my teeth and watched the clock, needing to get back upstairs.

An hour later, I'd finally got off the second call and was ready to tear my hair out. Going over the events had bile rising in my throat, and I was no closer to cooling off. If anything, my self-indulgent turmoil had deepened.

A composed if ashen-faced Mathilda appeared at the door.

"Thank Christ." I leapt up behind the ugly desk, gesturing her forward. "I was about to come find you."

"I'm packed. Beth and I are heading to the airport in ten minutes. James is driving us."

The bottom dropped out of my world. "No, don't. I can't have you go. Not like this."

Mathilda sighed and advanced in. Behind her, I spied her cases. "You're upset and hurt. So am I. We're better cooling off separately while I fix the problem with Dominic. I'm flying to London."

"Fucking Dominic," I muttered. "I want to be there with you."

She blinked for a second then shook her head. "Why? So

210

you can threaten him and stamp your claim on me? This is my problem, and I'm going to fix it."

"How about if I just wanted to be there to support you?" It was a unique concept for me to grasp, but the words came out of my mouth all the same. How could I be quiet in the same room as a man who'd lied and used her? I'd try to, though. For her.

Mathilda laughed, but her cheeks reddened. "Really? You blow up at the slightest provocation. I love how passionate you are, but right now? I need support, and all I'm getting is judgment. It was plain on your face. I made a mistake. I know that. I allowed myself to be used by a man who is trying to save his relationship but at the cost of so much else. Dominic can't see that, but I will make him, and I'll do it alone."

"And I'm nae judging you, I swear. That's so far from the truth. I'm selfish, Mathilda, and I hate that the world thinks you're in love with another man. It's killing me. I want to help you, but there's something you need to understand."

She was pulling away with every second that passed. I grabbed her hand. Clutched it to my chest.

"Feel that?" Her fingers gripped my shirt, and I made her look me in the eye. "That's the heartbeat of a man falling hard. This, you and me, it's real. That's why I'm so upset. Because I dinna love easily, but you're in my heart, and that will never change."

I wanted to fall to my knees at the expression on her face. Her mixed emotions. Outside, down the corridor to the great hall, a woman's voice yelled my name. For fuck's sake.

It spurred me on, desperation gripping me now. Blood rushed in my ears.

"Marry me, Mathilda."

Her eyes widened, and she dragged in a breath.

"I mean it. Be mine. Let me have the right to stand by you. To defend you."

"You...you're proposing? We're in the middle of an argument, and I'm about to leave the country. So you *propose*?"

"Then say yes!"

Fast heels clicked on the stone floor, nearing.

Mathilda threw her hands in the air. "No! It's ridiculous!"

"How is this any more ridiculous than you considering a man you cared nothing for?" Oh, shut the fuck up, my stupid mouth. Even in my overwrought state, I knew how bad that sounded.

Mathilda staggered back, her cheeks reddening. "A revenge proposal? Did Dominic piss on your territory, Callum? Is that what this is? A dent in your pride?"

"No! But you not taking me seriously is. Stay and be mine. I'm yours already, and that won't change. Listen to me, woman."

"I'm not listening because you're not making sense. It's like your suggestion for tackling my father. Your bullheaded approach only makes things worse. In both cases. You blow things up and hope they land right, but that doesn't work with people. You were wrong in that and you're wrong in this."

I copied her pose with my hands on my hips. "I'm not wrong. This has never been more right."

We glared at one another, both breathing hard. I wanted to kiss her, but she'd slap my damn face.

Patricia burst into the room, Lily, her baby, over her shoulder. "Callum! I wake up to fifty messages of how Alasdair nearly died! How did it happen this time?"

The interruption had me gritting my teeth, even if my father's second wife could get away with a lot in my book.

"He's alive. Did you go up to see him yet?"

"I'm going up there now, but neither of them is going to tell me the truth about what happened, so I came to you first."

"Christ, Patricia. Give me a minute and I'll come up, too. We're in the middle of something here."

The twins' mother rotated to Mathilda who'd turned pale. "I'm sorry to intrude. You must be Mathilda." She spun back to me. "Bring my daughter with you when you come up. I need both hands to throttle my son."

Patricia handed me Lily and hastened away. I hoisted the bairn over my shoulder, automatically patting her wee back as I returned to Mathilda. The babe mewled but settled. She knew me well enough and had slept on my shoulder once or twice before.

Quiet fell. Mathilda stared at Lily, and something deep inside me hurt when I registered her expression. Her longing echoed mine, and I felt a rip as my dream of life with Mathilda tore apart.

She dropped her hands to her sides. "I want children. I want love and marriage to someone who loves me. I never believed in happy marriages, never saw a good example of one working out, but now... Now I need to go and fix my mistakes on my own."

"I dinna want you to go." We'd both hushed our voices because of Lily, but I wanted to yell my proposal again. She hadn't believed it, and I could understand why. What had I said apart from that I'd fallen in love with her?

Which she hadn't said back.

My chest hurt, and I rubbed my knuckles over the ache.

"You have to stay, Callum." Her gaze touched the baby again, and she shook her head. "Just look at what you've got going on. Your family needs you, and this is my mess to fix. I'll...call you."

Then she was gone, and I was left alone. Holding the tiny babe. Rejected by the woman I loved. The responsible, too loud, too jealous family man who'd put his heart out there but said all the wrong things. Done it all wrong because I couldn't hold my emotions in check.

I wasn't sure Mathilda would be coming back.

With the heaviest of sighs, I sank into the chair at Da's desk and cursed my damn pride.

25

I OWN THE OUTCOME

Callum

By lunchtime, Patricia had settled herself into one of the spare bedrooms and was napping with her bairn, the twins were confined to the castle for the foreseeable future, and Gordain had driven off on his motorbike, heading back to barracks and his training.

Without knocking, James entered my study—I was claiming the fucking room, starting with chopping up Da's desk for firewood. My friend had been several hours taking the women to the airport, and I'd watched for his return as much as I watched my phone for a text from Mathilda. I'd sent her one, wishing her a safe journey. No reply had come back.

My friend ran his hand through his hair but didn't say a word as he dropped into the armchair next to the window. I knew something had happened between him and Beth this weekend, though I'd been so wrapped up in my own world I hadn't had time to talk to him. Plus they'd been sick and taking care of one another. We hadn't had a moment alone until now.

And alone we both were. Our women had left us. Though I wasn't sure Mathilda was mine anymore.

"You were a time." Sparkling conversation from yours truly.

"Mathilda's flight to Gatwick left first. Beth's to Bristol was later. I waited with her."

I rumbled an acknowledgement and rolled a pen over the desk.

Questions sprang up in my mind about how Mathilda had seemed before she'd got on the plane, but the man's face made me stop. James was hurting, too.

Adding 'bad friend' to 'bad boyfriend' was not happening today. I lumbered to my feet and made my way around the desk to join James in the chairs. Above his head and across the wall, the McRae coat of arms was painted in the corner of a huge map of the estate. A chest on the opposite side of the room held a bolt of our family tartan. I always assumed I'd wear it to my wedding, but that event seemed pretty remote now I'd driven the one woman I wanted away.

James glanced up at my approach then let out a rough exhale. "A couple of days ago, I received this from my uncle."

From his pocket, he extracted his phone, unlocked it, then handed it to me. On the screen was a picture of a woman. Young and attractive in a glossy magazine kind of way.

"Who's that?"

He stared at me, his fingers gripped together. "A dilemma. Can we talk?" At my nod, he continued, "I've shared little about my life with you despite how you opened your home to me and made me a part of your family. You've been an excellent mentor, Callum."

My heart squeezed. "And you've become my kin, James. Why do I get the impression you're about to say you're moving on?"

"I don't want to. I want to see our contract term out. But

I've been called home. My uncle is flying in tonight. He wants to discuss...the next phase of my life. Including me getting married."

I blinked then looked at the picture again. For months, I'd wanted James to open up to me, to trust me, but he wasn't making sense. "Since when are you getting married? What's this woman got to do with it?" I handed the phone back.

James slumped back in the chair. "In order to inherit, I have to get married by November. Before I turn twenty-one. I've always known this antiquated rule existed, but it's never been an issue before. My uncle has sent me profiles of women he thinks would be suitable, but it's never been real."

Fucking hell. "Until now."

He blew out his cheeks and stared out of the window. "Until now. Living here. Meeting Beth." To himself, he said, "Waking up."

I squinted at him, thinking of Mathilda's need to marry. I wanted to understand James's reasons in order to help him, but there was a sense of potent energy in the room. Of two men tied down, of bonds they needed to break. Opportunities slipping away.

My muscles tensed. The one at James's jaw ticked.

"Would you have done it? Married a stranger because you had to?" I asked.

"Yes. It would have made little difference to me."

"But you won't now." Please to God, I prayed he'd agree. With everything else falling down around my ears, I needed to hear that.

"I have never, ever gone against my uncle's word."

His statement was so final it stunned me. There I was, hoping beyond hope that he was about to tell me he'd come into his own. That he was going to stick it to his uncle and claim Beth, or some other woman he'd had the chance to fall for on his own. But no, I'd failed with him just the same as I'd

217

failed to keep the twins safe and failed to make myself into what Mathilda needed.

"I let Mathilda go because I'm an idiot with a loud mouth," I said. "You've got a chance now, and I'm damned if I'm going to let ye throw it away—"

"Throw it away? Callum! I'm trying to tell you exactly that. I'm not going to. Your mentoring has pushed me to think for myself at every stage. I've learned so much from you, but now it's over to me."

"What are you going to do?"

"I'm leaving for Belvedere this afternoon. I won't lie to my uncle like I wouldn't lie to Beth." He paused. "I have decisions to make, but whatever happens, I own the outcome."

"I'm proud of you, my friend. I'll be here. However you need me."

"I know." James looked around the room. Then he paused. "What are those papers?"

Three pieces of paper sat on the desk. In a line and equally spaced. A statement, an IOU, and an offer. Game changers, all of them.

"Problems and insults."

He squinted at me. "I'm not used to you being vague."

True. That wasn't like me. "One is a final bill for the installation at the distillery." He grunted in solidarity at the pain. Though James hadn't been living here when the Storm Force contract had been agreed, he'd been part of the efforts to get the product ready. My family knew well how it had cost us to lose out on that cash. Plus, I'd called the lawyer and instructed them to abandon the court case against Mathilda father's company. Whether the woman cared for me or not, I wouldn't make things harder for her.

"The second is an IOU I need to decide whether to collect." It had been written by Lachlan a long time ago. Found by me in Da's desk. He owed Da a debt after all, yet he'd lied to my face. It wasn't cash that I could use to save my home, but the man I'd idolised growing up, the big ox that was Lachlan, was very different in my eyes now. I should challenge him on this, too. But what was the point? I'd had enough of yelling at people to last a lifetime.

"And this?" James picked up the last, a formal letter on heavy, embossed paper. I let him read it. He'd been learning over my shoulder for six months so there was no imposition. It was good to have someone else know. "Another offer to buy your estate." His blue eyes darted up, bright and panicked. "You'd never sell."

"Put side by side with my bank accounts, it tells a story."

I was screwed. Worse than I'd imagined. Bills had come in, and only this morning I had tackled the last bundle, slicing angrily at the envelopes with Da's sword-shaped letter opener. My choices had narrowed, but I'd thought I had more time. Now I had to face reality.

James replaced the offer letter—sent by the same people who were buying Lachlan's estate and full of fancy language about honouring our traditions—and scowled. "Why didn't you tell me your debts were a problem?"

"Why would I?"

"In a matter of months, I'll receive my inheritance and be independent. What do you think I'm going to do with that money? Let me invest in the family McRae, like you all invested in me."

Warmth spread out from my heart, replacing the sluggish cold that had settled since Mathilda had left me. Though my options were slim and James would soon be one of the wealthiest men in England, I would never accept a loan from him. But the offer, and his affection, meant the world. "Aye, you would. But I want you as my friend, no strings attached. Money dirties things. I'll find a way on my own. I always have."

He smiled as if he knew there was no way I was taking his money. "A good prompt. I need to go and find my own way."

"And I'm going to find Mathilda."

It wasn't even a decision that I made in the moment. It was a fact carved in stone. Right now, Mathilda could be sitting in Dominic's office agreeing to go through with the engagement. She hadn't believed my proposal, and I didn't blame her. I had to make this right.

James held my gaze. "I'm not sure when I'll see you again."

"You'll call me, though," I ordered. This wasn't the last I'd see of the young Earl Fitzroy, I knew it. "I'm here for you, whatever you need. I mean it. Let me know what happens either way."

We both stood. I hugged my brothers all the time and had made sure to include James in the affection once he'd got over his unfamiliarity to touch. Now, as we hugged it out, he thumped my back just as hard as I did his.

"Go get Mathilda," he said, and I gave him a wide grin as I backed out of the door.

"Aye. I will. I'm away to London."

26

YOU FORCED MY HAND

*M*athilda

Dominic's secretary leapt up at my approach and rushed to open the sleek wooden door to the corner office.

"We're so happy to see you here. Congratulations. The office is buzzing with Mr Hanswick's news." The man beamed as he ushered me in. I'd met him before when I'd visited my dad, and if he'd simpered around me then, he was doubly obsequious now.

From his desk, Dominic glanced up, his phone in his hand. He murmured something to the caller, replaced the handset, and smiled at me.

Smiled. The nerve.

"I've been expecting you. Did you get your picture taken outside the building? It's been nothing but paparazzi hounding the reception all day." The door clicked closed behind me, and he continued, "Of course, they don't care about me. They want the scoop: either us in a passionate embrace or Abigail storming in to accuse me of breaking her heart."

He laughed like any of this was funny, then took a swallow from a glass of amber liquid.

"How dare you? You need to release a statement taking my name out of this." I was so mad my voice trembled.

I'd barely spoken to Beth or James at the airport, despite my friend offering to come with me to kick Dominic's ass, and I'd simmered in the slow-moving cab as we'd inched across the city. At the same time, I'd wanted to curl into a ball and protect myself.

I'd said I had to do this alone, but now it was the last thing I wanted. Mathilda the Island had finally made contact with land, and I missed Callum so much it felt like pieces of me were breaking off the farther I went from him. From his wonderful home and family.

Dominic rolled his eyes. "Don't be dramatic. You're not Scarlet with an excuse for a teenage tantrum. Besides, you brought this on yourself."

"What are you talking about?"

"I know you've got something going on with that McRae man—your voicemail last night told me enough. It's why I made my announcement over dinner. You forced my hand."

He was deranged. It was all I could do to stop myself from leaping over his too-tidy desk and strangling him with his ugly paisley tie.

"You have caused me no end of trouble, and now you tell me you did it despite knowing it was against my wishes?" I hissed. "I told you I didn't want this. I never really did. What gave you the right—"

"Without Storm Force," Dominic interrupted, raising his voice over mine. My attention gained, he quieted and continued, "Without this engagement, I cannot afford to pay the Storm Force contracts. At all. Not even the fifty percent I thought we could manage. The deal is a bust."

No. Callum needed that money desperately. Getting

nothing would force him to sell. "That isn't true. Dad is paying half."

"Your father withdrew his support. He accused me of seducing you for your influence with him. Like I'd need that. All I need"— as he stood, his lip curled into a sneer—"is to get this fucking investment secured. Don't you see? I had to do it this way for both our sakes. If I didn't, no contract means your precious boyfriend's business goes under."

He gentled his tone as I stood there, reeling from and absorbing the implications of what he had done. "If you won't do this for your sister, which I imagine is off the cards now your father has thrown a fit, do it for Callum McRae."

Dominic had used emotional blackmail when he'd first made his offer. Why was I surprised that he'd upped the ante? I cared about my sister, loved her, but Callum had so many people depending on him.

Before me lay two paths. The one I'd originally chosen, where I'd secure the happiness of someone I loved at the expense of my own, though now the person was Callum. Or, the route where I admitted how much I cared for one huge, overbearing, wonderful mountain of a man. Maybe even accept the marriage proposal blurted in anger, though I was pretty sure it was genuine.

But taking the second path meant the man I loved losing everything *he* loved.

Dad was already angry about what Dominic had done—my answerphone messages made that clear, so marrying him wouldn't get me Scarlet. Nor was I convinced it was the only option to save Storm Force. If only Dad would understand that Callum was an honourable and decent man, maybe I could get everything I wanted. Hope bloomed.

The choice was easy.

In careful, clear words, I informed Dominic of my decision. My head in a whirl, I left his office and hailed a cab, taking a moment before I climbed in to inform the waiting photographers of a news snippet they were clamouring to hear.

The taxi driver set out for my parents' home. Just one more dragon to slay, and everything would be all right.

* * *

*A*t a little after 4P.M., I bypassed the entry phone to the penthouse suite of Ashford House and let myself in with my keys.

"Dad?" I called as I placed my handbag down on the hall table. I'd left my luggage at Castle McRae, taking the two cases back to my room in a last-minute decision and bringing only what I needed for the day.

My heart and head were in a state, but I owed it to Callum to go back to him and finish what we'd started.

"Mathilda?" My mother's voice floated down the hall. "What are you doing here?"

Rounding the corner, I found her in the lounge, the big windows spilling London's grey light over her daybed perch. She must have been napping as she had a soft knitted blanket pulled up over her knees.

"Darling, it's so good to see you." She offered her cheek at my approach, and I bent to kiss it. "I'm home alone. Your father flew to New York two days ago. I know he wanted to speak to you, though. You should call him straight away."

No mention of my supposed engagement, but that was my mother. She probably thought it either a good idea or none of her concern. I dropped into the chair next to hers and closed my eyes for a second. "I'll do that."

"Wonderful. I'll have tea sent up." Mom picked up her tablet device to order from the maid service.

I grabbed my phone but paused before I dialled. "Mom?"

"Yes?" She moved her head as if listening, though her gaze stayed on the screen. Her hair was pulled back in a sleek chignon, even though she was the only person in the house and she obviously had nothing to do.

"Did you hear I'm engaged?"

My mother nodded, selecting an option and carefully tapping in a note. "Your father doesn't like it. He and Scarlet had a terrible row."

Oh, poor Scarlet. "But what do you think, Mom?"

"Dominic Hanswick? He won't give you any trouble."

Not even a hint that she'd been surprised I was marrying Dad's business partner. A man who no woman my age could genuinely be excited about.

"I'm not going ahead with it. It's fake. I only considered it so Dad would let me have Scarlet. I'm in love with someone else."

Mom finally met my gaze. "Oh, Mathilda, I am sorry."

I gaped at her. "What?"

Mom sighed. "Love is not a good enough reason to have a relationship. I've told you that all your life. At best, you have fun for a while before it goes and you have to carry along like before. At worst…"

I knew she was talking about her lover, not Dad whose love for her caged them both.

"At worst what?"

The air seemed to be sucked out of the room as she replied, "Love destroys."

Mom went back to staring at her tablet and, as she did, she cracked a packet in her pocket then slipped a white pill into her mouth. I recoiled and looked away, remembering how she'd done the same in the restaurant. Whatever she self-medicated with was partly responsible for her distance. I hated how broken she was and I hated how much it had affected me. I loved Callum. It had snuck up on me, but there it was, wedging my heart wide open. Nothing about it felt destructive. Transformative, maybe, but for the better.

Shaken, I called my dad.

The moment the dial tone sounded, Dad answered the call. "Mathilda! Now listen to me—"

"Wait, Dad, you need to hear me out first." I interrupted him for the first time in my life. "That news article—"

"That news article nearly gave me a heart attack. I want you to know two things. One, if you marry Dominic Hanswick I won't attend the wedding and I will never do business with him again. He's a cheat! Not only that, but he told me that he'd treat Scarlet well when she lived with you. The man is out of his mind if he thinks—"

Dad's voice got louder, and I held the phone away from my ear. Then he said something else that had me snapping it back. "Say that last bit again, Dad."

"I said I'll let her live with you but only if you do not marry that man."

"Scarlet can live with me if..." My mouth moved, but no more words came out. This was exactly what I wanted, and he'd offered it to me on a plate. I spluttered my next words. "All I want is for my family to be happy. For Scarlet to be out of the city and—"

"Out of the city? No, you misunderstand. I've rented the apartment downstairs. The one directly below ours. You think I'd let her move cities? You will live with her where I can keep an eye on you. Then," his tone changed from commanding to almost tender, "you'll join Storm Enterprises and run Storm Force for me."

"What?" My weak voice squeaked. "But I don't want to live in London."

"You will if your work is here. I'm buying Dominic out of the Storm Force contract. You can sell the Bristol house and buy in. We'll be co-investors."

Dominic had lied. Dad hadn't bowed out, he'd offered to *buy* him out.

"That house is mine to sell?"

"Consider it a trust fund. Your mother and I thought it better not to tell you until you needed the money for an investment."

"So I'd work for you, live in an apartment you've rented, give up...everything else?"

In my head, I swore a blue stream. A new option had landed on my table. The contracts would be paid. Callum would get his money and his family's stability. I would live with Scarlet but...

Give up everything else I cared about.

Didn't this solve all my problems? At least on paper it did. Callum supported so many people. How could I have got so swept up to think we could get everything we wanted and still have each other? Sacrifices had to be made. I'd always known that.

My hope died.

Then a door slammed in the apartment. Me and Mom jumped. "Scarlet must have gone out," Mom muttered, idly swiping at her screen. "Or maybe the maid. Is it Tuesday or Thursday?"

"Scarlet was here? But you said you were home alone!" My sister had heard me complain. No.

"I'm not sure when I last saw your sister."

"Dad, I'll call you back." I leapt up and ran to the door, ignoring Mom's comment about decorum. But the hall was empty outside, as were the stairs when I hung over the ornate banister.

I yelled my sister's name. No answer. Back in the penthouse, I flung open the door to her bedroom. Empty. Then I spied a folded piece of paper propped in the centre of her patchwork quilt.

It had my name on it.

Mattie,

So, newsflash: I've packed up and left Mom and Dad. You can tell them if you like. Photos or it didn't happen?

I can't get over what you were going to do for me. You're the best sister a girl could ever have. Go get your new boyfriend and don't worry for a second about moi. I've got a plan and I'm safe.

Scarlet xx

Oh no, no, no.

She knew about Dominic's proposal. But when had she left? A moment ago, or yesterday? Had she heard me complain to Dad? My sister was trying to save me the way I was trying to save her. But that wasn't her job. She was a child, and I wouldn't let her sacrifice anything for my happiness.

I needed help, ideally from someone well versed in finding lost siblings, and this time I wouldn't hesitate to ask.

27

SET THE RECORD STRAIGHT

*C*allum

A grey haze hung over the dirty city. I used to hate London, but a place had appeared for it in my heart. After all, I first met Mathilda here, and I intended to win her back here, too.

The line for taxis outside Gatwick Airport crept along, and I considered my plan.

It didn't help that I was hours behind her, but she'd told me where her parents lived, and I'd already been to her father's office on my last visit, so I had a place to start. My guess was she'd already have challenged Dominic so now would be with her kin.

And...I was going to barge right on in.

Fuck. Wasn't that exactly the bullheadedness she'd accused me of?

I slowed my feet. What was I doing chasing after her like this when she'd wanted space? Proving I couldn't listen.

Behind me, someone cleared their throat, and I blinked up from staring at the concrete. The line had moved on half a dozen feet, and I was next in the queue. Then the impatient fucker cleared it again, and I swung around. A lad in his twenties looked back at me, his hair punked up with red and green stripes. I glared. He recoiled.

"Sorry, man," he said.

I sucked in a breath, remembered my resolve. If I was going to support Mathilda and not run my mouth, I had to start now.

"My fault. I'm nae paying attention," I replied in the most reasonable tone that had ever come out of my mouth, and I got into the next waiting cab.

At the mansion Mathilda had once called home, I marched onto the fancy porch. Ready to go to battle, I took a breath and raised a finger to press the buzzer. Then a wee redheaded missile flew out of the door, nearly knocking into me.

"Oops, sorry." The girl righted herself, and I caught sight of her face as she hefted a rucksack on her shoulder. Tear-streaked and familiar. An accent with a hint of California. Wait a second...

"You wouldnae be Scarlet, would you?" I said. She had Mathilda's features, though she was as pale as a Scot.

The lass spun around, taking me in properly. "Who are you?"

"I'm friends with your sister. Mathilda."

Her narrowed gaze softened. "You're him. Callum McRae."

It wasn't surprising my name was familiar in that household. Her father had probably thrown it about enough. "Aye. For my sins."

"No! Your name has been a good thing," she said and took a step backward, glancing at the door as if anxious to get away. Maybe her father was on the warpath and that was why she'd escaped. My muscles tensed, readying for a fight.

"What's going on? Problems, aye?"

"Aye," she copied.

Such cheek. I already liked her. "Your family has issues."

Scarlet blinked. "No one ever sees it like that, aside from Mattie. They say I have an attitude problem."

I pointed a finger at her. "I'm not saying ye dinna, but it's not all on you."

Scarlet blew out a breath. "I have something to say to you. Can you wait a minute to see my sister?"

"She's here?"

"Yes, but I left before seeing her." The girl smiled through her tears. Then she said something which nearly had me falling to the floor. "She's in love with you but she won't tell you because I screwed everything up. It's all my fault."

In love with me? All of a sudden, a weight I'd been carrying fell away. "Mathilda said that?"

She glanced at the door again and made ushering motions. "We need to go! Come on, McRae. One foot in front of the other if you want to hear this story."

Teenagers and their drama were no strangers to me. But no way should I walk off with the lass. I was a stranger to her. On the other hand, she looked ready to fly, and I'd bet good money she was running away.

I scrubbed my fingers into my hair. Mathilda might be in the middle of an argument, maybe even over me, but her sister was about to disappear again. She'd want me to make the girl my priority, so I wouldn't let her out of my sight. "First, I need to let your sister know you're with me. I've brothers not far off your age so dinna give me any quarrel."

The girl rolled her eyes and gave me a sarcastic thumbs-up. "Fine. But talk fast, will you? I need to get away from here."

With a huff, I took her bag—almost as heavy as she was with all she'd stuffed in it—and slung it over my shoulder.

Then I pulled my phone from my pocket to text Mathilda. It buzzed in my hand, her name on the screen. I answered.

"Callum! Oh my God, Callum. I need your help—"

"Are you looking for a redheaded scrap, by any chance?"

She paused. "I... How did you know that?"

"Your sister is glaring right at me. She's just like you, same frown on her forehead."

"Where are you?"

"Nae far from you. But I've got a girl in need of a chat with me so I won't come up just yet."

"Scarlet is with you. You're in London." Mathilda floundered. "How... No, do you know, this is exactly why I called you. Because you fix things like this."

"A coincidence. I came for you," I murmured, vulnerability plain in my words.

"I'm so glad. And I was so worried about my sister. Is she okay?"

I eyed Scarlet. The girl had a defiant set to her chin, not liking my 'scrap' comment, I guessed, but she was folding in on herself, her hands jammed into her armpits. Whatever had happened, she was upset.

"I think so but I'll let you know. She has one or two things to share with me." Then I dropped my voice. "By the way, Mathilda?"

"Yes?"

"I heard you love me. I love you, too." With a chuckle at the stunned silence, I hung up the call.

* * *

My new friend Scarlet stepped down onto the pavement, and I went to follow, but something nagged at me besides walking away from the woman I'd flown hundreds of miles to chase. I glanced down the street. Ah, there they were. Two men had pulled up in a nondescript old banger, sneaking in behind a sleek Jaguar. Something flashed, reflecting the light. A camera?

"Why have we stopped?" Scarlet asked.

"Photographers," I muttered. I ushered the girl back to the porch and held up a finger to ask her to wait. I dialled Mathilda back.

"You've got company outside the house."

"Not the press again?" She groaned. "I already ran into a couple at Dominic's office. It's only Mom and me up here, but we could do without more hassle."

Dominic. Even his name had me seething. "Please tell me you punched him," I ground out.

"Do you mean Dominic?" Scarlet practically pogoed in front of me. "I'd love to punch him, too! I hate his smug face. Do you know my sister almost married him because of me?"

"I know." I smiled at her, and her eyes welled again. For a tough kid, she was having a hard time.

"I told Dominic where to shove his proposal and then I told the reporters it was a mistake. They wanted me to say it on camera, but I came right here," Mathilda said in my ear, her words shaking me more than I'd anticipated. She'd rejected him. Thank fuck for that. "Problem solved, or so I thought. What can they want with me now?"

Another car eased past the end of the side street and pulled up adjacent to Mathilda's home. Similar-looking guys inside. *Shite.*

"You need to grab your bags and get out of here."

"Now? Okay, but…" She blew out a breath. "My bags are still at yours. I was always going to come back." Then she paused. "I've got another call coming in. Dominic. I'll be right back."

I moved the phone from my ear, cursing inwardly.

"I can go talk to the reporters," Scarlet announced. "I'll

happily tell them how Hanswick played my sister. He's such a douche canoe. Do you know, he used to bring that politician to company dinners until she became famous and their affair was outed? Dad was furious when he found out. The guy is shameless."

"That's one word for him. We better get back inside." I wanted to talk to the reporters, too, but something was off, and I didn't like it. "Do ye have a taxi app on your phone?" She nodded, brandishing the device. "Order the nearest cab for as fast as it can get to the next road away."

Scarlet blinked at my instruction but hustled, opening the door to the mansion's entrance hall as she typed. We stepped into the cool and dark interior. "Five minutes until our getaway car gets here."

"Dominic, no. How dare you." Mathilda's voice sounded from inside the building, echoing down the stairwell.

I jogged down the hall and spied my woman descending the marble steps. She clutched the rail and glared as she ended the call.

My heart swelled, and I strode the final few metres then held my ground until she'd descended to the fourth step. She watched me the whole way, and her bottom lip moved, though no more words came out.

Oh Christ, I adored her.

With relief flooding me, I plucked her from the step and wrapped her in a bear hug that felt like home.

"Aw!" Scarlet crooned from behind.

"You said you love me," Mathilda whispered to my chest before she raised her gaze to meet mine. A rough desperation filled her eyes. "What are you even doing here, and why did you say that?"

"Because it's a fact. Ye ken it's true. Mathilda, I messed up, and I beg you to forgive me. I chased you down because I'm a stubborn fucker and I didnae want to let you go. But now I look at you, it's right there in your eyes. You still want me, aye?"

In my embrace, Mathilda trembled, her fingers gripping me like I might disappear at any second. I never would. I was hers for good. "For this sort of conversation, we should be back in that log cabin with the fire and romantic music."

"Gross," her sister whined from where she leaned against the wall, and I chuckled.

"We can do all that later. Right now, we need to get out of here before that fuckhead Dominic shows up. Come back to the castle with me. Bring your girl, and we'll work out what to do next."

Mathilda nodded, and Scarlet shrieked. "I'm going with you? Yeah! That's so much better than my plan."

"Which was?" Mathilda hugged me harder and then cast a baleful look at her sister.

"Joining the circus? I don't know, I didn't exactly think this through." Scarlet raised a shoulder and beamed.

Mathilda held out an arm, and her sister darted over and almost fell into her embrace.

With a squeeze, Mathilda released us both, though she kept my hand clamped in hers. She took a deep breath. "You said photographers are already here?"

"Aye, two of them outside, and two more just arrived. We might want to avoid them."

While waiting for my flight, I'd read the articles on Mathilda. Most were about the politician and her husband and family. Dominic's name came second, and Mathilda was barely mentioned. So why they'd pursued her here was a mystery.

"Dominic plans to make a scene. Reporters are pursuing his girlfriend, and he's desperate to lead them away by making this all about us. It's almost sad because he really loves this woman."

"What kind of scene?" I didn't share her sympathy.

Outside, shouting began, reverberating down the hall. "Mathilda!" the voice called. "Mathilda! Don't do this. It's all lies. I love you."

"What the hell? Is that him?" I barked.

"Mathilda!" the man continued. "Come out! Come back to me. Mathilda!"

For fuck's sake.

"Such an asshole," she whispered, gazing down the hall to the front door.

My temper flared afresh, heat flooding my veins. "He's saying he loves you?" No, no, no. No way was that making the news. *I* loved her. It would be nice to have one part of my relationship not muddied by that guy claiming it first.

"Mathilda, tell me what to do." I balled my hands into fists. "I came here to be calm and supportive, but the old me really wants to overstep the mark in a major way."

"I almost want you to," she said, her eyes wide in her ashen face. "He can't get away with this anymore. My mother is up in that apartment. If she comes down, they'll try to film her. She's too delicate for the drama."

"Tell me how to be," I ground out.

"Scarlet, wait here. Callum, come with me. We're going to set the record straight."

ENGAGED

*M*athilda
We exited the door to the main street with our arms tucked around one another, smiling like we hadn't a care in the world. Scarlet slipped out behind us to find the taxi and would wait there. Safe, though I didn't want to let her out of my sight.

Walking into the fray, I whispered to Callum, "Dominic offered me a deal on the phone. He said I could sleep with you all I liked and he wouldn't say a word as long as I kept pretending and married him. He said his girlfriend was devastated by the fact they couldn't see one another anymore, and I'd make everyone happy just by playing along."

"Whyever did he think you'd agree?" He faked a wide grin and planted a real kiss on my cheek.

Ahead, the photographers watched Dominic as he yelled up at the penthouse.

Callum trained his eyes on the man and made a low, aggressive sound. "It's only the second time I've met this little shite, and my knuckles are aching to make a closer acquaintance with his face."

My pulse quivered. Though we'd argued, I loved his wild side, even more now he was trying to contain it for me. "He was making a last-ditch attempt to appeal to my emotional side, which is dumb as I don't really have one." I shrugged then added, "Apart from when it comes to you."

"That's not a bit true. You care widely, I've seen it."

"You know? I think you're right."

This time, his kiss met my lips, and there was nothing fake about the passion.

A flurry of clicks broke our embrace. Footsteps scurried toward us.

"Gentlemen." I nodded to the photographers. "Nice to see you again."

I explained to Callum, "I met these two earlier at Mr Hanswick's office, when I'd visited to ask him to stop using my name." I tucked in closer to him. "Callum here is as confused as I am over this fuss, considering we became engaged this weekend."

At my side, Callum froze.

"Mathilda!" Dominic practically shrieked, his mouth an outraged 'O'.

"Mr Hanswick." With an expression of pity, I regarded the jerk. "Could you please stop shouting at my father's home? He isn't there for you to try to impress, and besides, I'm not sure it would change his mind."

"What...? No, I want to marry you." Dominic blinked, his tie askew. He glanced at Callum then wobbled and took a step backwards.

Callum was probably glowering, but he remained quiet. A wall at my back.

"Oh, knock it off," I replied. "If Dad won't work with you now, that's between you and him. But Callum and I are a couple, we're together, and you can't use me anymore. We're leaving."

I turned back to the photographers while my claim on Callum filled me with joy. One of the men had a video camera, so this was on film. Righting all the wrongs. "My previous statement still stands. Mr Hanswick and my father's business matters are between them and have nothing to do with my private life. I'm very happy in my relationship, and there's only one man for me. You can quote me on that. Callum? Let's go back to the castle."

* * *

*A*round the corner, the taxi waited. Instead of jumping straight in, Callum stopped me at the car door.

"What ye said..." He stumbled over his sentence.

I sighed. "I know. I should have thrown him to the wolves and shouted the truth about his girlfriend and let the press have their field day, but the thing about Dominic is he's just an idiot in love. He can't have the woman he wants because she won't ruin her career by leaving her husband. It's sad. He's sad. And as of now, he's no longer anything to me. I just left a nice vague business-related comment for the reporters to chew over."

"You have a heart the size of the moon, but... Not that. The other thing."

I cocked my head, my eyebrows pulling in.

"You said you'd marry me," he choked out.

My cheeks heated. "Oh, that. I did. But can't we do better than a proposal yelled in anger and an acceptance made in front of cameras while an idiot guy staggered around the shot?"

239

Then I smiled, and Callum let out his breath then crushed me to his chest.

"Aye, we can. I'll plan the kind of proposal you deserve, with rose petals and singing doves if it pleases ye."

With his gaze burning into mine, he laid a sweet kiss on my lips—a promise for later—and we got the heck out of London.

* * *

On the short hop back to Inverness, Scarlet peppered Callum with questions about his life and the castle. When she got too cheeky, he'd tut and put her in her place. And...it worked. She fawned over him with big eyes and a playful affection I couldn't ever remember seeing in her before.

Callum was a hit with my sister.

She'd confided in us both that she and Dad had an epic row before he'd left for the States. The usual subjects had come up, but finally—having never done it before—Scarlet had told Dad she wished he'd stop pretending to be her father if he couldn't do the job.

I couldn't see an easy way back for them, and Mom wasn't strong enough to help.

It was high time I stepped in and took control.

First, though, there was the small matter of the three little words Callum had said. *He loved me.* I bit my lip at the memory and rested my head on the plane's seat, letting my two favourite people chat over me.

I loved him, too. The feeling as clear as day. A wonderful, soul-filling sensation. And I loved how I'd shocked him by telling the photographers we were getting married. Most of all, I loved thoughts of decisions and conversations to come.

After Dad's revelation about my house in Bristol, I had only one plan for using the money.

Then the captain announced our descent into the Highlands, and I couldn't help the smile on my face. It felt like going home, and this time I was making plans to stay.

* * *

"You have to be fucking kidding me. Where's your mother? Please say either she or someone else drove you?" Callum smacked his hand to his forehead and bore down on Ally.

The boy beamed from the other side of the arrivals barrier. On his finger dangled the keys to Callum's Land Rover.

"Cool your britches. Ma's here, and Wasp is babysitting Lily. You were on the news, and Mattie said you were coming home, so we drove down to pick you up from the next flight." Ally appeared the picture of health, unaffected by his ordeal. He followed quickly with, "Ma drove. I needed some fresh air."

"Who's this?" My sister ran her gaze over the boy.

Ally's attention shot to my sister. His eyes widened. "More the point, lass, is who are you? Please tell me we're not related."

"This is Scarlet, Mathilda's sister, and she's fourteen. She'll be staying with us for a while, and for all intents and purposes, consider her your sister," Callum growled. "Now give me the car keys before I hang you upside down and shake them out of you."

"Bloody hell," Ally whispered, handing over the keys.

"I'm fifteen next week." Scarlet grinned and batted her eye lashes. I hauled her after a stomping Callum.

Teenagers. Suddenly I had three of them.

* * *

*W*e returned to the castle in the gathering dusk, and I settled Scarlet into my bedroom. With a meaningful glance, Callum collected my bags and carried them upstairs to his solar. Everything had shifted and settled into place. We'd decided how we were going to be, and that was that.

"Everything is going to be okay," I told my sister who'd plopped down onto the bed with a pair of headphones in. We'd talked as we'd unpacked her bag, and it had broken my heart to see the things she'd brought. The items she found important. No designer bags or expensive goods, but she had the teddy bear I'd bought her on a day out when she was four or five, and a family picture in a frame. Like she still didn't resent the family she'd been born into. "We'll work out what to do over dinner." I paused at the door. "I love you."

"Sure, I know. Go see to him." She waved a hand and rolled over. "That man has been looking at you like you're the saviour of his world since you came down the steps."

Oh shoot, he probably had. The feeling was mutual. With a soft smile, I closed her bedroom door and hurried along the hall to the stone spiral staircase, then ascended, my heart rate picking up with every step.

"Callum?" I called. The door at the top of the stairs opened into a wide room, the big windows showcasing thick cloud which cloaked the early evening sky. I set my path for the master bedroom.

Music met my ears.

I pushed the door open and walked into the centre of the room, yellow light spilling out from a single lamp. The tune played on, a soft ballad, distinctly romantic. Then the door closed behind me with a thud, and I jumped, spinning around. Callum stood against the frame.

"How long have we got?" he asked.

Over my shoulder, his enormous bed waited, and I backed over to it, kicking off my shoes.

"An hour." Not long enough.

Callum sank to one knee, and I stilled, pressed against the bed. "I'm an impatient man, Mathilda. If you need more time for this to happen, I will struggle with that but I'll bite my tongue. After everything, I dinna want to be in a half state with you. I have you here, with our family, and I never want you to leave again."

From the side table next to him, he collected a box. I sucked in a breath and curled my fingers into the bedspread.

"This was my mother's. Her wedding ring. I'll get ye your own for our engagement, but I haven't had the chance yet." He looked up from the box to where I hadn't moved an inch. "Let me propose properly before we take to the bed."

"I was going to plan something romantic for you." I stepped over to him, my toes sinking into the thick rug. "To make up for running away from you and not talking it out."

"Why, what did you want to say that you didnae already?" A mischievous look came over the big man's face. He adjusted his balance as I stopped in front of him. "That you're in love with me? I already told you that."

Arrogant Scot. "Do you want me to accept this proposal?"

The wide, teasing smile stayed on his face, and love gleamed in his eyes. "Aye, so get on with it, woman."

"Then let me say something. I've never been in love with anyone. I didn't even know what it meant. Then you came along, all seven feet of you."

"Six-ten." He rolled his eyes.

"And you swept me off my heels." A pressure in my chest threatened my composure, so I rushed on. "I am completely in love with you, Callum McRae. I love your family, your Highlands, and how you're this beautiful

243

shining star in the middle of it all. A pillar of strength to all around you."

His smile settled to being almost wistful. "I do what I must. But even pillars need support."

"I'll do more than that."

"Mathilda?" he asked, taking my hand in his.

My heart fluttered, and a happiness I'd never anticipated made itself complete inside me. I had everything I wanted, even things I had no idea existed.

"Marry me."

"Yes."

With a huff, Callum pulled me to him and kissed me, his hand on the back of my head, letting me know he was in charge now. I liked it so much, this powerful man, so used to ordering people around, managing a huge swathe of land, wanting desperately to dominate me, yet if I said one word, he'd leap to my command.

He owned my mouth, showing me just how hungry he was. Then he slowed. "Last thing," he said. "Before I forget."

The case displayed a beautiful old ring. Yellow gold with a delicate design, an oval diamond within the band. Callum plucked the ring out. "It's not exactly high fashion. It's was my mother's, and it means something to me."

I loved it, just like I loved him. "It's perfect."

Together, we slid it onto my finger.

Callum stared at the ring, his breathing slowing. In the background, the ballad came to an end, finishing on a drawn-out note. The lamplight glowed, and I couldn't have imagined a more perfect proposal from this man. In private, within the safe walls of his castle, after he'd just dropped everything to come for me. Our troubles weren't over, but we'd won the day.

"Will you tell me about her some time?" I guessed he was thinking about his mother.

He blinked. "Who, Ma? Is that where you thought my head was at? I'll tell you anything you want to know but I have to admit I was counting down the seconds to make this respectable enough before I carried you to my bed. Are we good? Because engagement sex has got to be amazing, aye?"

My laugh filled the room, and Callum leapt up and carried me to the bed. "I love you." He laid a soft kiss on my lips.

"I love you, too. Endlessly."

"How many bairns do you want?" His fingers feverishly worked the buttons of my shirt while he kissed my neck.

"Um, I don't know. Two?" We could fill the castle with babies if I got to have Callum for the rest of my days.

"Or five? Can we start now?" He dragged my top off and let his eager eyes take their fill of my breasts.

Heat consumed me. "Sure."

"I'm serious." Callum hauled down my bra cup with one hand and kissed his way to my nipple. He sucked hard, and I threw my head back and squirmed on the bed. A groan rumbled through him and he palmed and moulded me.

Then he brought his weight down between my legs, forcing my thighs wide to accommodate him. "How fast can you organise our wedding?" he said his breath warm on my skin.

I laughed all the more, and he set his attentions to my other breast, this time, his hand running down to lift my skirts.

"Jesus, you're soaking." Callum pulled my underwear aside and slowly sank two fingers into me.

"Oh God," I gasped. We'd had sex this morning, and I still ached from the size of him, but I needed him more than ever.

"How quick? A week?"

"Three months."

"No deal." He added a third finger and stretched me, readying my body to receive his.

I moaned, writhing, pleasure sparking across every nerve ending. Here, in the highest level of the castle, no one could hear me. There were stone floors and acres of space between us and our family. Callum was going to make me scream.

"Three weeks." Callum's belt rattled as he used his other hand to undo his jeans. A frantic note hastened his words. "I can't wait. I need you to have my name. I want everything with you and I want it yesterday."

"I need to organise invitations, caterers, choose a dress," I began, but Callum's cock sprang free, and he stroked his hard length twice before bringing it to the soft, welcoming centre of me. He circled my clit, and my jaw went slack. Oh, how good his actions felt.

Out-of-this-world incredible.

"Oh, fuck," he said, his booming voice dropping to a whisper. He slid his tip over my entrance. Pressing and testing but not slipping in. I wrapped my legs around his waist, so, so ready and impatiently waiting. "Fine. You can have a month, but I need to make love to you now."

"Tell me again." I screwed my eyes tight shut. So close already from his hands and mouth. Ready to explode with lust and love for my mountain man.

"Tell ye what?" he spluttered, almost vibrating with his need. Like we hadn't just agreed to marriage, babies, and a whole life together.

"That you love me."

Callum thrust once and filled me. He paused then jacked his hips, working every inch until our hips met. He rested his forehead on mine.

"Open your eyes," Callum commanded. He stared down at me and rolled his hips, making love. "I love you."

"How much?" I teased, gasping when he hit the spot.

There was no doubt left in me. Callum was pure heart and openness.

"With every part of me. Most of all, in this second only, this one." He thrust harder now, holding on to my hips, his fingers digging into my flesh. Long strokes, over and over. A wicked glint filled his eyes, and he halted and dragged his jeans down to his ankles, planted a knee on the bed, then grabbed my thighs and hauled me to the edge.

My skirt rucked up around my waist; we were too frantic to stop and strip.

We kissed, and he set a fast rhythm, slamming into me and demanding my love with his body. I gave him everything I had. In minutes, I was gasping for breath, the angle perfect and my emotions creating a whirlwind. I called his name. Raked his bulky shoulders through his shirt with my nails, and I clasped him to me, almost sobbing. Pleasure spiralled through me and electrified my body.

I came in glorious bursts of light, sparkling colours, and true love.

"I'm going to come." Callum gritted his teeth. "I can't wait."

"Do it."

He gave a ragged gasp then used those massive thighs for all they were worth, pounding and straining until the muscles of his neck stood out in stark relief and his forehead shone with earned sweat. Then he arched his spine and threw back his head. His cock pulsed, and I yelped at the sensation.

"You're mine," Callum choked out, gripping on to me like his life depended on it. "I'm yours," he added and dropped down, banding his arms around me so we were as close as close could be. He brought his demanding lips to mine, I ran my fingers into his damp hair and, as we cooled, I made him look at me.

"I can manage a wedding in a month."

"I can wait a wee while longer, if you'd prefer. But," Callum shifted his hips, moving his still-hard cock inside me, both of us groaning, "we dinna want to wait long. If we have bairns on their way, any dress you buy won't fit."

I grinned at the thought. Mathilda Storm, who planned everything to a finite degree, could end up not caring about the baby/wedding order. "I'll stop taking my pill, but you're awfully certain about yourself."

"Aye, and it'll be twins, too." He pulled out and dove down to kiss my belly, unzipping my skirt before he dragged it off.

I took my bra off and he removed the last of his clothes then settled once more on the bed.

We hugged, naked, Callum squeezing me to him, my soft body against his hard one.

"I want that," I whispered. "Or one, at least."

"You'll have everything you want. Always."

"We need to go downstairs in a minute. Sort the kids out."

"Aye, the world didn't stop turning just because we fell in love." He rolled onto his back and pulled me onto his broad chest.

I could stay there for days, just hearing his heartbeat and trusting him to care for me.

"Is it okay if I invite my father here tomorrow?" I asked, forming a plan on the spot. Dad would be having a fit right about now, assuming he'd spoken to Mom, but I would never again tiptoe around him. Not anymore.

"Mathilda," Callum replied, his voice lazy and sated in the best possible way. "Dinna ask for what you already have the rights to. Everything I own is yours. Bring the man here. Let another Storm hit my castle, and we'll quell that one, too."

29

WE HAVE A CASTLE, LET'S USE IT

Callum

We waited for the storm to break. Halfway through dinner—Mexican rice with steak and peppers, courtesy of Patricia—Wasp gave an almighty sigh. "Fine," he said to his twin, "but quit nudging me. I dinna see why you can't ask yourself."

The chatter ceased, and all eyes fell on him. Wasp raised two blond eyebrows at me.

"What?" I looked from one inquisitive grin to the next.

"Are you two getting married, then?"

Mathilda gripped my hand, my ring on her finger. Then she said, "How would you feel if we told you we were?"

"But are you?" the boys said in unison. Ally rolled his hands in front of him. "I mean, we'll be over the moon. Amazing news, congratulations, blah, blah, but…"

"But what?" she asked.

"We've got a bet going. I win a tenner if it's announced by the end of the night."

The beautiful sound of Mathilda laughing mingled with Patricia telling the twins off for gambling on family happiness. The boys crowed, and the meal descended into a typical McRae feeding-time chaos.

I sat back and watched my family. We weren't all here—Gordain was training to fly into war zones to extract injured servicemen, and James hadn't yet returned my messages, but they'd be back, and a new era at Castle McRae yawned.

In that second, I let it sink in. I was engaged. Content.

The change hit me like a missile. This, this right here, was what I'd strived to create. A happy family, free of violence and fear. So different to how we'd been as wee lads. I'd cared for my boys for long years, shouldering the burden and making every decision. Worrying and fretting, willing and able but so fucking alone.

No more.

I looked at Mathilda, and she brought her beautiful gaze to mine. "Want to confirm it?" she mouthed.

I leaned in and gave her a quick kiss. The boys yelled all the more.

"Aye, we are." I lost my battle with my grin, and applause and cheers rang loud. "But keep it to this room until I get a chance to speak to Gordain and James."

"And Beth," Mathilda added. "If she'd answer the phone."

"Funny, James isn't answering either." He'd be at Belvedere by now, if that was where he'd found his way.

Throughout the conversation, Scarlet had remained quiet. Now, the girl stood. She glanced between us, settling her gaze on her sister. "Would this have happened earlier? I mean, if it wasn't for me and the other plan you had."

At the head of the table alongside me, in the tall-backed chairs where lairds and ladies had sat together for generations, Mathilda smiled. "No. This has been a whirlwind. I'm lucky Callum persisted with me, otherwise I can hardly bear to think where I'd be now."

It was my turn to grip her fingers. "My stubbornness paid off. Thank fuck for that."

"Got to happen sometime." Ally winked.

"Dad won't like it. Just like he won't let me stay here." The girl's chin dropped and she slumped back into her chair. "He loves you so much but he'll be angry and he'll try to persuade you to come home. I'll have to go because he says so."

"Nobody is going anywhere," I growled in response, and my boys sat up.

Mathilda sighed. "Dad will be here in the morning, but this isn't a war."

"Aye, it is! And we have a castle, let's use it. Create a defence." Ally slammed a hand down, knocking his plate so it rattled. The atmosphere changed, and eating ceased. My brother pointed at the door. "If I understand this right, which I probably dinna, but what the fuck ever."

"Language," Patricia reprimanded, and he rolled his eyes.

"This lass wants to stay here, and nobody has the right to take her. She's Mathilda's sister, and when you two get married, our kin. We don't let anyone hurt our family."

"Well, aren't you and I going to be friends." Scarlet's grin sparkled at Ally.

He merely watched her, his mouth a firm line I'd never seen on the lad who almost always smiled.

"We're not going to let the man walk in here and take her." Ally sat, his arms folded.

I rubbed the back of my neck. "Whatever happens, it's for Mathilda and Scarlet to tell us what they need, aye?"

My darling woman twisted in her seat and patted my hand. "And that," she said, "is why I agreed to marry you. Even though I know how hard this must be, you're letting me take control."

What difference did it make sharing control? She already owned me.

After the meal, Mathilda and I called it a night.

I fucked her in the shower and made love to her on the bathroom floor before we found our way to my bed. Our bed. I had so much to say to her, to plan with her, and ask her opinion on, but my eyelids were lead-lined, and I fell asleep with her clamped to my side the moment our kisses slowed.

* * *

*D*reams, nightmares, really, invaded my peace. With monsters invading my land and trying to take everything I'd worked so hard to gain. Monsters shaped like Maximus Storm and an army of debt collectors.

Pent-up energy ate at me when I woke. No magic bullet could solve my problems, but I'd share the facts with Mathilda. Tell her all there was to know about my debts and ask her opinion. I owed her that, and I had the feeling it would be the last thing she'd expect me to do.

But she'd called me when she'd needed me. Showed me what it was to depend on someone. I could do that, too.

I'd considered my options. It broke my heart, but I'd sell the distillery. On paper, it was a good earner, but I carried the debt for the upgrading we did for Storm Force, and if I cleared that, we'd have space to breathe.

Mathilda's wedding venue plan had to go ahead. I needed to offer her a place in my life, so I couldn't take that away, but we'd have to start lower down the ranking for a few years. There was no money to front the costs, so we'd make do with what we could fix or build ourselves.

If she agreed to it all, we had a plan. If she didn't, we'd work another out together.

The ease with which I'd changed to fit her shook me. Who knew I could be so reasonable? I'd never had the chance to try.

My chores done, I glanced across the great hall to where Mathilda sat with her sister, perched on chairs by the big fireplace. Their father was on the warpath, having caught a flight back from wherever he'd been, and would be landing at Inverness soon.

In no uncertain terms, I'd told myself to keep my temper and let Mathilda handle her da. The logical choice was for me to leave for the morning. If the man raised his voice to either lass, I'd...

I straightened out my shoulders. No. I'd be a married man and maybe even a father myself one day. I couldn't keep letting my instincts rule. London had given me a taste of stepping back, even if it had been Mathilda's words that had stunned me to silence. I'd be in control around her father. I'd brain myself if I couldn't do it.

"Hey, Cal, do any of these work?" Ally hollered from across the hall. He pointed above his head to the old weapons displayed on the wall.

"No," I said and raised my gaze to the rafters. The swords were blunt and the guns decommissioned. And thank fuck for that.

"Ah, that's too bad." Ally huffed and strode off toward the cellar.

I rapidly cast my mind over any dangerous weapons that were stored down there and made a note to frisk my brother before Storm senior arrived. Better still, I'd send the twins out.

My phone rang in my pocket. Gordain. I could barely hear him over the chopping sound of a helicopter.

"Alasdair is claiming there's going to be some sort of trouble at the castle today. Do you need me home?"

"Callum." Scarlet waved.

I strode over to join the women at the seating area.

"No," I said to my brother as I moved. "Stand down, Serviceman. It's just Mathilda's father coming to pay a visit."

"Oh shite," he barked into the phone. "You'll be on your best behaviour. Can you hold your temper if he asks about your intentions to his daughters?"

I hated how it was so obvious that I was the liability. "Dinna even joke."

"Better have Mathilda tie you up and gag you and leave you in your room. Wait, that sounds kinky. I hear camomile tea is calming. Go boil up a vat of it." His chuckle mixed with the whirring rotor blades.

"Funny. There was I thinking Alasdair was the comedian."

"Well, ye ken where I am if you need me. I'll commandeer a heli to come and save the day. Let me know." Then Gordain was gone.

My family had gone mad.

Scarlet's gaze fixed on me. "Mattie said I could stay here for as long as I want. Aye or nae?"

I squatted next to Mathilda. "Aye. You're welcome to the room. But we'll need to work on your Scottish accent."

"Would I have chores?"

"Everyone earns their keep. The boys clean. They chop wood. They visit tenants, if needs be. Show visitors around." I eyed her. "Can ye drive?"

Scarlet snickered a laugh, and Mathilda pressed her lips together in a little smile, gratitude in her eyes. Earlier this morning, we'd talked through the implications of Scarlet staying. "Drive? No, what are you, nuts?"

"One of us will teach you. That will make you more useful. As for other chores, the twins are shite at laundry so you can have that, if you want it. You'll go to school in Inverness, and we'll work out the rest as we go. You'll make new friends, dinna worry."

Scarlet bit her lip. As fun as this place seemed, I bet she'd miss her home. Mathilda had told me about Scarlet's wide friendship group, how well she'd been doing at school.

The problem was Maximus Storm. The girl obviously loved him, but he couldn't get his head around being her da. The hard fact was, he needed to take responsibility here. No matter what a shite upbringing he'd had, and how the girl had come about was done and dusted, how they all went on together was up to him.

I felt for him, now I knew more about the man. My anger at how he'd treated me had shrunk. Still, I wished I'd had the chance to smack his business partner in the face. It rankled me that Dominic had gotten away with his behaviour.

"What time is your da's taxi getting here?" I asked Mathilda.

She checked her phone. "Thirty minutes. Lottie, are you ready? Did you decide what you want?"

The girl raised a shoulder. "For Dad to give a shit?"

"Callum, do you have time for a chat?" Mathilda pressed her sister's hand then turned to me, rising from the chair.

"I was about to ask you the same question."

"If that means adult time," Scarlet yawned, putting her dainty shoes up on the table, "nobody's fooled."

"Well, you can mind your own business, either way." Ally appeared at my shoulder. He frowned and thwacked Scarlet's feet from the surface.

I'd worried at his reaction to her in the airport—the lass dressed beyond her age and in a few years would be breaking hearts all over the place. Now, he looked at her with a wee wrinkle on his brow, like she was an irritating younger sister.

"Come on, you. Wasp and I are going to show you the beach. Chill you out before the battle starts."

For once, Scarlet gave no sass in her answer. Instead, she rose and smiled prettily at my brother then the two of them left the room, Wasp joining them at the door.

"Lead me, woman," I said, and Mathilda smiled, taking my hand.

"Always."

* * *

*W*e'd taken five steps down the corridor when a pounding came at the great hall's front door.

"Shit," Mathilda hissed and clutched my arm. "That'll be Dad. He's early. Oh God."

"We'll deal with him. We've got this."

"Do we? I don't know—"

I kissed her, stealing her words. After a moment, Mathilda smiled against my lips. "You are awfully good at distracting me like that."

"Mission accomplished. Now, let's go do this thing."

She took a deep breath and rolled her shoulders. Mathilda had dressed for the boardroom in a smooth black skirt and cream shirt. Later, when all this was done, those clothes would be on the bedroom floor. Except the stockings. I had something else in mind for those.

"Let's do it."

Together, we marched to the door.

But as I swung it open, my jaw rigid in a forced, polite smile, it wasn't Maximus Storm. Three people waited the other side.

Lachlan and the shiny-shoed land agents.

My resolve to be a calmer man strained at the seams.

"How can we help you, gentlemen?" Mathilda enquired, her recovery instant.

"Ah, Mathilda. Callum. How's the boy doing? Can we come in? There's a matter to be discussed." Lachlan inclined his head like he hadn't been a dickhead at his party.

"Ally's fine. We're expecting company, so I've no time for you now," I replied.

"Ah, come on. Dinna be like that." Lachlan grinned like I was an obstinate child. Behind him, thick grey clouds rolled by, heavy weighted and low. The wind had picked up and, down at the loch, choppy waves hit the beach. Rain would hit soon, but the twins knew the signs and would bring Scarlet back in time.

"We have twenty minutes." Mathilda slid her hand into mine. We stepped back and the men entered. "But I'm afraid that's all as we really do have plans. My father is visiting."

"Nae problem. This won't take long."

Mathilda led us through the great hall and down the corridor to my father's office. Inside, she ushered for me to sit at Da's desk then stood at my side while we waited for the others to shuffle in.

"Mr McRae," the first land agent began, opening a briefcase.

"Laird McRae to you." Mathilda frowned at the man and, inwardly, I beamed at her defence.

"I beg your pardon. *Laird* McRae. Regarding the precarious state of your finances, and assuming this is getting worse rather than better, we're in a position to renew our offer to purchase Castle McRae, the estate, and holdings. Of course, the offer isn't as good as—"

"Wait!" Lachlan exclaimed at the same time as Mathilda uttered, "Hold on a moment!"

The eyes of the room switched to her.

"What do you think you know of my fiancé's private affairs?"

"Business accounts are available online. The state of Castle McRae's accounts is public knowledge, Miss...?"

"Mathilda Storm." She stared the man down. "And put your assumptions aside. You know nothing."

Knives of shame slew me. No way did I want my dirty laundry aired like this. I put my hand to the small of Mathilda's back and stood. "Lachlan, what the hell are ye doing bringing these vultures here?"

"We'd agreed to discuss land borders, not this," Lachlan spluttered.

"Well, that's another thing to be finalised." The land agent raised his eyebrows. Then he extracted a pen and piece of paper from his briefcase. "The state of your legal situation is going to take months if not years to unpick, but that isn't the point of this visit. Mr McRae, I'm going to write down a number—"

"No, you're not." Mathilda reached out and neatly took his expensive-looking pen. She pointed it to the door. "Gentlemen, please give us the room. Callum and I need to talk."

"Aye, we'll go to the great hall." With a dark expression, Lachlan led the men out.

Mathilda followed then slammed the office door behind them.

"I might need to hear them out." With an ache in my heart, I dragged my gaze to meet hers and forced my lips to move. "I told you I inherited debt, aye? It hasn't got easier. Fact is, I'm drowning in it."

"Show me your accounts."

She tapped the pen on her hand, and I grabbed my phone from my pocket, opening the spreadsheet I used to track every line of income, each bill and loan repayment.

All the lines were in the red. All overdue.

I handed it over and watched her face, crushing the instinct to snatch it back. No one had ever seen the extent to which Da had left us in trouble. The measures I'd taken hadn't fixed our problems, not after my gamble with Storm Force had failed.

I trusted Mathilda completely, but it still hurt to share my failure. "I know it looks bad. I've been treading water, but my plan is—"

"Your plan is our plan, now. I'm investing. I have money, I think, and I've never been so sure about anything in my life."

"Wait," I interrupted, but she pressed a finger to my lips, determination in her eyes.

"No, I won't. Now you sit there and put your pride aside for one minute, and damn you, Callum, you listen to me."

God help me, I shut my mouth, retook my chair, and let Mathilda in.

30

MAXIMUS STORM

Mathilda

I paced the office floor, Callum's gaze tracking me. He wouldn't agree to this without another fight, but with Dad coming and the land agents baying for blood, we needed the issue sorted.

"My house in Bristol... Dad told me he bought it as an investment for me. A trust fund which he anticipated me using to invest in a business. I have two choices now and I'm asking your opinion. But this decision is mine and, if you value your balls, you'll let me make it."

With no shred of apprehension, I waited, and he blinked. Then he made a gesture. "Go on."

"I want to feel part of this family. Fully invested. Look at what you bring to the table versus what I bring. You'd give me this incredible home on a plate—"

Callum waved a hand and interrupted the start of my rant. "Give me the options, woman. If I'm meant to keep my trap closed, you aren't going to downplay your value on my watch. Move this along."

"Fine." Then I told him how much the little house

was worth. The neighbours had sold up a couple of months ago, and their sale price was listed online, so a simple search had reinforced my plan. His eyes grew wide.

"Now, I could buy Dominic out of Storm Force and go into business with Dad. It would make him happy and it's what he intended for me to do with the money. More importantly, you'd get your full contract paid."

Callum flicked his gaze to the wall, to a huge map of the estate. "Buy in to Storm Enterprises? You'd need to travel, aye? To leave here."

My own gaze trailed from what looked like the border with Braithar, over the mountain, and down to the farthest farm. "Yes. I'd need to spend part of my week in the London office."

Callum made a 'fuck that' expression. "What's the other option?"

"I invest in Castle McRae and use my money to start a business. I pay off the debts to create a clean slate, a safe starting place, and then carry out the renovations needed to run beautiful weddings. Bigger than we discussed. I mean the works. We could use the castle as a venue, but I'd also look further afield and act as the agent for other places. I'd hire coordinators and seize the corner of the market that wants a destination wedding in the Highlands, regardless of the budget."

I drew a breath between the ideas flowing out of me, still half-formed but beautiful and shining. This was my dream career, my very own company. Before, I'd had no idea how to start it, and I couldn't do it alone, but if he'd only say yes and not let his pride derail this...

I swallowed and said, "It would need a lot of time invested, more than I'd asked for from you."

Callum shook his head, and my heart sank. "Mathilda, I'll

261

give you everything I have, but nae that. My debts are not yours to take on, and that's no way to start a business."

A knock came at the office door. "Mathilda?" Lachlan's voice interrupted. "There's a man here to see ye. Looks like you. I'd hazard a guess and say he's your da."

Callum and I looked at one another.

"To be continued," he murmured.

Then we were on our way to the front door. A new battle to face.

* * *

*D*ad stood on the rain-damp steps outside the castle, deep lines in his dark skin around his eyes, and his expression one of bewilderment and worry. I launched myself at him, throwing my arms around his waist. His coat smelled of cigar smoke and airports.

The worst thing, the very worst thing, would have been if he'd stayed away. But he'd come. We had something to work with.

No matter how bombastic Dad was, no matter how controlling and dictatorial he tried to be, at the heart of it, he was a scared little boy trying to find his family. At points in my childhood, he'd been the best father I could have wished for. I had wonderful memories of the parties he'd thrown for my birthdays and of when he'd taught me to ride a bike. He'd shown me how to be ambitious and to go after what I wanted, and right now, the very best outcome was he could be that same kind of father to my sister.

I meant to make that happen. If it hurt, so be it.

Fat rain drops hit his thick, short hair. "Mathilda," Dad said, and he hugged me right back.

"I'll give you two a minute." I heard Callum step away and I lingered for a moment before I broke off the hug.

"I'm glad you're here," I said.

"You know, I never met him. Dominic handled all the distillery and site visits." Dad watched Callum remove himself to a polite distance. "He's bloody big, isn't he?"

"His heart is huge, Dad."

Dad gave me a querying look, and we followed Callum into the great hall. "All the way here, Dominic left me messages, spinning wild stories about you and this laird. How he's manipulating you, using you. But I know my daughter. Come. Tell me the facts. Why are you here?"

I would, but this was my show, and Dad was on my territory. "First, you need to meet him."

I led Dad to Callum who tipped his head in silent question. I placed my hand in Callum's and took my position at his side.

"Dad, this is Callum McRae. My fiancé."

"Maximus Storm," Dad clipped out.

Callum reached out and took my father's hand. "I'm glad to meet you. Welcome to my home."

Dad's jaw dropped. Over a slow handshake, his brown eyes expressed a dozen emotions. "Fiancé?"

"Uh huh," I confirmed calmly. "We became engaged yesterday, but you've been traveling so you wouldn't have heard. But you can share your congratulations later. That's not why you're here. We have a more important topic to cover."

Dad switched his gaze to me but didn't say another word. Rarely had I seen him stunned to silence like this. The moment drew out, but I wasn't about to let this get awkward. Nobody could be prouder of their partner than I was in Callum, and if Dad had allowed his judgement to be clouded, that was his problem.

I needed him onside for Scarlet, and for my investment plan, but his opinion on Callum made no difference. I was a woman in love, fighting for my family. Dad would always be part of that but in a new form, whatever that might be.

"I'll see what I can do about getting rid of these men." Callum cleared his throat then beat a strategic retreat, joining Lachlan and the land agents at the fireplace.

Dad gazed around the cavernous room. "Mathilda? What is going on?"

"This isn't about me."

"I know." Dad shook his head, and I gestured to the den. The battered green couches were as good a place for this conversation as any, and I had high hopes. Dad hadn't come with anger holding his muscles tight, or calculation in his eye. He appeared worn. Battered. Maybe he'd come here to face the music. God knew it was overdue.

And if Scarlet remained absent a little longer, I might have enough leverage to work on him. Bring him to my way of thinking.

But before we cleared the room, a crack of thunder sounded overhead, and the great hall's door crashed open once again. Lightning ushered a laughing duo through the door. As she stumbled inside, my sister threw her head back, crowing in delight at something Alasdair said. His hoodie, and his arm, wrapped over her shoulders as he guided her in, Wasp absent now but the scene friendly to my eyes. Brotherly. The two of them dripped with the heavy spring rain.

"Scarlet," Dad announced under his breath and, somehow, across the open space, she heard it.

Her gaze found his, her smile dropped, and the storm shook the room.

* * *

"Hey, Dad, how was your flight?" Scarlet enquired as she tripped lightly across the great hall. She swept past us, and Dad and I followed her into the den.

"Which one? The one I took into New York City to try to secure the future of Storm Force, or the two I suffered to get to this far-flung corner of the kingdom to collect you?"

We sat on the battered green couches, and silence held. Scarlet and I had agreed that first, she needed to tell Dad how he made her feel, and I'd only step in if she became overwhelmed.

"I left home," Scarlet began. "Because—"

"Scaring your mother half to death," Dad cut in.

"No. Mom barely notices anything these days. You have no idea what's been going on."

Our father blinked at my sister. "Your mother is fine."

I couldn't miss the wince on Scarlet's face and I jumped in. "I called Mom while we travelled back here. After Scarlet ran away from home. Her painkillers are making her into a zombie as all she could worry about was you and your reaction. Even then her speech was slow, and she barely asked about Scarlet. Our family is falling apart, and we need to fix this. Mom needs help. We all do."

He squinted at me in disbelief. "Painkillers? She takes pills for her anxiety, but…"

Scarlet and I had compared notes during our little chat in her bedroom. She knew exactly what Mom was taking. All my fears had been confirmed.

"Dad. Scarlet and I love you, but we need to set a few things straight." I had to get this out before I lost my nerve. "We're both your daughters, regardless of heritage. Scarlet needs you more than ever, but if you can't give her what she needs, she's staying here with us."

"Because somehow you're engaged. Tell me, daughter—"

"Oh Jesus, Dad." Scarlet leapt to her feet, and our father's gaze darted to her. "Don't you know what you're doing? Stop trying to control Mathilda! She nearly married that man Dominic just so you'd let her take me in. Do you know that?"

"What?" Dad's voice sounded as I slapped my hand over my eyes.

I wasn't planning to tell Dad about Dominic just yet because I felt fool enough as it was.

Scarlet's eyes reddened as she continued, "All Mom and Mathilda ever do is creep around you, but you're hurting them! You hurt me! We never talk about it, but what the hell does it matter that you're not my bio dad? How does that give you an excuse to be such a shit father?"

The echoes of her final words rang.

Something enormous shifted, just by naming the beast.

Dad swallowed. "I'm sorry, Scarlet. I've never given you the opportunity to meet your real father as I didn't want to hurt your mother. If you want to—"

"You're my real father. Come on!"

He blinked.

"I think what Scarlet means is that she wants you to step up, Dad."

With tiny movements, realisation dawned on our father's face, and he looked stricken. Broken.

"All this time, I thought you'd reject me—" he began, but his voice hitched, and my heart lurched.

I stood, because my sister was openly crying, and this time it wasn't for me to comfort her. I had so much to say, about how many years he'd missed, about the hurt she'd suffered when he'd turned her away, about the desperation we'd all seen whenever she'd tried to get him to notice her.

But when it came down to it, my sister just needed a hug from her dad.

Dad stood, too. As I walked out of the den door, I glanced back. He'd sat in my vacated seat, right next to Scarlet.

Then he reached out a fatherly arm and pulled her in.

THE FIRST WEDDING I PLAN

*C*allum

The sight of Mathilda's tears tore a hole right through me, and I stormed across the great hall to where she'd emerged from the den.

"It's okay, nothing's wrong," she sobbed, and my own eyes heated. I dragged her into my arms.

"They're talking?" I kept my voice low and kissed her on the cheek. Kissed her tears away.

"He's hugging her, Callum." My cool and calm Mathilda buried her head in my chest and shuddered as she controlled herself. "After all this time."

"Look at what you did." I drew her head back and smiled at her tearstained eyes. "You should be so proud."

"We should. This was partially your idea, except Scarlet did the yelling, not me."

"Just proves what an excellent team we are."

Across the great hall, someone cleared their throat. Loudly. Pulling my head back, I gritted my teeth and eyed the source of the irritation.

"McRae, you need to listen," said the smaller of the land

agents who for some reason still crowded my home. "You can't keep ignoring this. You're only making things harder for yourself and your family."

At the same time that Mathilda had reconciled her family, I'd come to an agreement with Lachlan about the land borders while point blank ignoring the two morons at his side. Having a broad back to turn had its advantages. We'd just got to the main point I wanted to ask Lachlan and Mathilda had emerged.

Actually, there were two points, but first I needed to get rid of the infestation of blowhards. I murmured to Mathilda to give me a moment when a war howl erupted from the top of the stairs.

"Think you can take our land? You've got another think coming, southerner." From the landing, the twins appeared. Armed, of all things, with an array of colourful water balloons.

"Jesus." Mathilda clutched her hand to her mouth.

A chuckle rose in me, but I forced it back.

"What?" Alasdair raised his eyebrows at me, the Devil in his eyes. "You said no weapons. These won't leave any permanent damage."

Behind us, the den door swung open, and Scarlet and Maximus appeared. "What was... Oh my God," Scarlet drawled. "They're really going to do it. You were meant to be the target, Dad, but I talked them out of it."

"Thank you," Maximus replied faintly, his gaze moving from the twins to the land agents, who'd taken a step back.

"Lads, it's been no pleasure talking to you, but I think you'd better run." I folded my arms and faced the men, letting them know where I stood. With my family and never bowing to them. "I'll fix my problems myself, and in no way will that involve giving up one inch of what's mine. Boys?" I gestured to the twins, and their eyes widened.

I guessed my brothers had assumed I wouldn't allow this. But fuck it. Today had already been wild, and a little cleansing with water would do these two the world of good.

"You aren't seriously going to let them—" the first land agent uttered, then a balloon flew through the air and landed directly in front of him. Water droplets exploded out, soaking the man's legs. He staggered back with a huff, clutching his briefcase.

"My brother told you to leave. What are you waiting for?" Wasp tossed a balloon, then another quickly followed.

"Laird McRae!" The men shrieked and made for the door, balloons raining down on them. "Chief!"

"Run, pal, run!" the boys chanted and kept up their tirade. Explosions of water surrounded the fleeing men and decorated the flagstone floor in wet splodges.

Beside me, Lachlan let out an almighty guffaw and bent double at the waist. "Oh Christ. Another, lads!"

More flew. Scarlet cheered, and I swore even her father chuckled. The door to the great hall slammed behind the two arseholes, and my wee brothers hung over the bannisters, their faces as pleased as punch.

"How did you know who those two were?" I planted my hands on my hips.

"Gordain told us about the sale, so we knew they were about. And it would've been a shame to waste the water." Wasp wiped his brow. "Lachlan, you have to know Gordain's cut up about your plans."

He had a point. I turned to our relative. "Aye, Lachlan. We'll need to talk. Can you wait a minute or do you have to go after them?"

"Ah, let them get wetter. They can walk to Braithar in an hour."

"Not so fast, Callum." Mathilda crossed the great hall, her heels clicking on the floor, the echoes sounding to the rafters. She bent at the knee and collected an unexploded balloon.

"What are you doing?" I eyed her hand as she straightened.

"Before all the excitement, you and I were having a little chat. But as I recall, you seemed to be stuck on a pretty major point."

Right. That. "Mathilda. You can create a business here, that's fine, invest in prettying the place up, that's all yours. But—"

With a flick of the wrist, she threw and caught the balloon. If she was aiming for menacing, I adored her enough to consider pretending to be afraid.

"Dinna you even think about it, lass. I'm the laird here."

"And I'll be the lady, correct? Equals, remember? Wedding vows tend to include lines about being richer or poorer."

"Aye, but nowhere in that is a vow to bring you down with a sinking ship." My words came automatically, built on pride and years of coping alone, but I wasn't sure I meant them. Mathilda's proposal would save my home, offer security to my brothers. Why was I arguing?

We eyed one another, and I readied myself to force back my pride.

Mathilda's menacing look became speculative, and she squeezed the balloon. "Is this how our marriage is going to be? You bark and I obey? Because you're going to have to think again."

"There is nae chance that you'll soak me with that balloon." Not in front of our family. I knew it... At least I thought I did.

She tensed her arm.

Shite.

I moved to the balls of my feet, readying to dodge.

At the top of the stairs, the twins gave a yell of encouragement. Traitors.

"I don't seem to recall," her father stepped forward, "anybody asking me for my daughter's hand."

We both stopped.

He was right. No matter how antiquated a tradition that was, I had the feeling it would mean a lot to him. But first, "Would you like that?" I addressed Mathilda.

She loosened her shoulders and popped her hand to her hip, the balloon still readied. Then she gave me a little nod. "Actually, I would. I'd like everything to be perfect."

"Then, sir, I'd like to formally ask for your beautiful daughter's hand in marriage."

Maximus Storm paused, and the room fell silent. "Mathilda, I told you Dominic made a claim that Callum was manipulating you."

She stared. "And?"

With a sober expression, he regarded me. "I travelled to Manhattan this past weekend to secure an investor for Storm Force, should my daughter choose not to join my business. I had good reason to suspect she'd made plans elsewhere. I gained a good deal with a new partner and am now in a position to pay the contract to you as promised. Does this make a difference in your offer to Mathilda?"

"Dad!" Mathilda and Scarlet shouted in unison.

The money would be paid in full. A wide beam spread over my face. "Not one bit." Then I bit my tongue to stop from making a remark to the man who'd be my father-in-law, who was just doing right by his family. Finally. "But I think you've just prevented me getting soaked."

"I think you just might have." Mathilda dropped the balloon to the floor and moved in on her father for a hug. Then she came to me. "Don't think I wouldn't have done that, McRae," she mumbled.

JOLIE VINES

I held on to the woman I loved and let my joy overflow. "Aye, I'm starting to realise just how dangerous you are."

* * *

*W*ith Maximus asking Mathilda about her business plan, and providing good advice from what I'd overheard, I snagged Lachlan before he left the castle.

"A moment." I jerked my head toward the fire, and we took opposite seats. "You never told me your motivation for selling. I know your daughters dinna want the place, and your lady has her own businesses to think of, but why now?"

My relative heaved a sigh and stuck one booted foot on the opposite knee. "He'll never be able to afford it."

Gordain's want for Braithar was no secret, and Lachlan knew exactly where I was taking this.

"Give us time. We might be able to work something out."

"You have an idea of the offer price, aye? For Christ's sake. He earns an officer's salary, your father pissed away any inheritance he might have claimed. What do you want me to do, Callum? I can't give it to him. That isn't fair to my lasses."

"On that…" From my back pocket, I extracted the piece of paper I'd found in Da's office. The IOU. Brandishing it like a weapon, I passed it to Lachlan.

The older man took it, and his eyes widened.

Then he laughed.

"I'd forgotten all about this. Where did you find it? Wait, let me look at the date." He scanned the note. "Callum, this is a quarter of a century old. A relic from before you were even on the planet. Christ, I remember it now. It was from a competition. We'd quarrelled over Marianne, my bride. He took the IOU for Braithar to hold over my head."

"I wanted to remind you of how close our families are. You are my chief—"

"I know." Lachlan shifted in his seat. "You and I should be closer, and I'm sorry we aren't. It's my fault. Mine and my memories. We were like the twins, your da and I. Always together, always into mischief. Then he inherited sooner than I did, and the pressure broke him. After he lost your ma, it was all over."

With a sigh, he dropped the hand with the paper to his knee. "He wasn't always a drunk. But—"

I cut in. "But sometimes people make the wrong choices. It doesn't mean those who come after and suffer for it need to forgive them. You and I can try harder."

"And on that, I agree. I'm glad to know you'll never claim the same fate. You might look like the man, but you could hold the weight of the world on those shoulders, my lad."

Lachlan rose from his chair, and I stood, too. Beating him for height and in bulk. "I'll give you this. Three years. If the boy can come up with a deposit, I'll sell to him. If not, the agents of doom get it. I'll write it into the contract."

"Thank ye." In my heart, I still didn't believe Gordain had a hope, but I wanted it. To make good on his childhood. To keep the estate together and in McRae hands and not developed into a Highlands theme park.

Three years gave us time to work out a plan. And work we would. I'd even consider talking to James about it, should he ever call me back.

"Congratulations." He walked away, indicating across the room to Mathilda, her patient expression holding as her father pontificated and her sister rolled her eyes. The lass interjected with a smile and her hand on her da's shoulder. It warmed my heart to see them together. "I'll be waiting on my wedding invite."

With a nod, he left me, and I dropped back into the hard, wooden seat, closed my eyes. Happy, finally.

* * *

*I*n the dark of our room, Mathilda trailed her fingers over my bare back, finding the outline of my sword tattoo.

"Dad and Scarlet go home tomorrow. They are going to take a holiday with Mom. Work on how to live with one another without fighting."

"They are welcome to come here. Anytime."

"I know. Scarlet will come by herself, more likely. Mom and Dad need to work on rebuilding themselves, and that will be the harder part. Mom needs therapy, and a lot of it. Dad, too."

She rounded my shoulder then trailed her fingers up my throat and over my chin until she found my lips. I kissed the tips.

"I have a question." With a swift roll, I pulled Mathilda onto my chest and reclined. "How quickly can you quit your job?"

"My contract is up in two weeks, but they like me there. If I want, it'll be extended for another three months."

My heart seized. In idle conversation, she'd mentioned being out of contract soon. "Do ye…want that?"

Every fibre in me wanted to demand she quit and start her business here. But I'd learned my lesson.

Mathilda dipped her head and found my lips. She kissed me like the first time when she'd laid her lips on mine in Inverness airport. Where she'd knocked me out in the stormy Highlands rain. I'd never been the same since.

I slid my hands to her hips and adjusted our naked bodies into alignment, my hard cock snug against her. We'd been in our solar for an hour already so this wasn't the first or last time tonight we'd be celebrating our engagement.

"I already quit, and with the holiday they owe me, I don't actually need to work another day. So, I booked a consultation with my friend, a wedding planner, who will help me get my business off the ground. She'll be here next week, then we can start looking at a plan for the works needed. Really, Callum. Did you think I'd leave you?" With a clever movement, Mathilda sheathed me inside her, and I bucked my hips, sliding home.

"You're staying."

"I am."

"And you're mine."

"All yours. But more importantly, Callum McRae, you're mine. And the first wedding I plan will be ours."

EPILOGUE

Callum

"Show me again?" For once, my youngest brother's face held a serious expression, his gaze taking in everything Gordain was doing. He copied the kilt adjustments and straightened his so the centre point in the tartan lay correctly down the middle of his body. By some form of miracle, the twins were dressed on time, their formal Highland attire transforming them into smart young men. My groomsmen.

A wave of emotion had me turning in my Ghillie Brogues to stare out of the tower's narrow windows. Not only was I torn up from seeing my brothers as boys no more, and from having us wear McRae tartan, but for the overwhelming fact that today, I would be wed.

There was also another far bigger reason, but I had nae idea how to handle it. It required delicacy, and God knew I had little of that.

"Now for your kilt pin. Right hand corner, through the top layer and pointing down. That's it. Dinna stab yourself." I glanced back to see Gordain supervising the finishing touches. He caught my eye and grinned, but I couldn't return the smile. My mind was away with the fairies.

"Done. Why don't you two go check on the guests? I can hear cars arriving, and you'll look a handsome pair waiting on the steps." He dismissed the twins who took off at a clatter down the stone stairs.

From the moment I'd delivered them to the seamstress for measurements, I'd expected whining, but through the whole of the wedding preparations, they'd shone with pride.

Gordain appeared at my shoulder. "Want to talk about it?" he asked, scrubbing a hand through his hair as he regarded the view.

I blew out a breath. "If ye had the choice to ask a question, and get an answer that might send you either wild with delight or down in the dumps, which would you choose?"

"Depends on how much rides on knowing there and then." He watched me. "Can I help? Go find out something for ye?"

I turned and clapped him on the shoulder. "Nae. But I appreciate the offer. I need to get my head on straight. This thing starts in under an hour, and I'm a wreck."

Gordain's gaze turned speculative. "How about a dram? If we're going full traditional, we should be well on our way to merry by now."

"Aye to that." We had more than a few wedding traditions to the McRae name, many of which centred around getting blind drunk. Gordain and I had chosen one or two, but most had been discounted because I wouldn't make it to the altar in one piece.

The boys had threatened me with one in particular—a hazing of the groom right after the vows, but I'd made enough of a fash to make them change their minds. At least, I prayed so.

My brother led me to a wee door embedded in the wall of

his living room, then extracted a bottle and two glasses. We knocked back the shot—our own fine whisky made right here on McRae land—both grimacing.

"However was Da addicted to this stuff? I can't imagine putting a bottle of that away. How would ye get anything done?" Gordain placed the bottle back. Neither of us drank often, so the thought was a strange one.

"He didn't," I said, and Gordain hummed in agreement.

Fortified, we moved to the door. "Ye ken, I'm not sure the boys and I ever thanked you," Gordain said, dragging it open, the sound of wedding preparations echoing up.

"Thanked me for what?"

"You held the family together in the hardest of times. I hate to imagine what would've happened if you hadnae stepped up. The castle would have been sold off long ago. We'd have all been living separately. Now you're getting married, starting a family of your own. I just want you to know how proud we all are."

"Don't, man. The twins have already laid it on thick this morning." With my emotions peaking, I shoved him away. He stumbled into the stairwell and caught himself on the curved stone wall before he jogged down the steps, chuckling. I followed, my thoughts even more scattered.

At the bottom, James waited.

"Fitz. Got any words of wisdom for our groom?" Gordain asked. "We're trying to make him weep like a babe. It's tradition."

Our friend gave me a mischievous smile and straightened his collar. Not being a McRae, he didn't wear a kilt of our tartan, but I'd had a cravat made for him from the same bolt of material. He wore it with pride.

"I'd say listen to your wife. More importantly, because she wants to see you now."

"She can't!"

The two men blinked at my protest.

"It would be bad luck," I added, but then again, I'd be able to ask her the question that had been bugging me all night.

Ever since I'd found the receipt for a pregnancy test on the dresser. Three kits, to be exact.

"She insisted, but you don't have long. People are arriving, and we'll need to get in position." James ushered me forward.

"Christ," I muttered, but I jogged after him, my sporran banging against my nether regions with every step.

We crossed the rear of the great hall, and I raised a hand to the relatives hollering my name. James led me into the kitchens, bustling with caterers, then up the back steps to the bedroom hall. At the staircase to my solar, he stopped.

"She's upstairs, alone. Here, put on this blindfold when you get to the top." James handed me a length of cloth. "And good luck."

"Wait." I grabbed his arm. "I'm glad you came back. I know your own family is your priority now, but I want you to know you're as much my brother as my own blood."

Since he'd left us, life for James had turned a sharp corner, with no end of legal issues and high drama. Half an hour ago, as we'd dressed for the wedding, I'd caught sight of his scarred skin, and my heart hurt for all he'd been through. Yet, despite everything, he'd turned into one of the best people I knew.

And he'd shown up for me today. The love I felt for my boys welled.

"I wouldn't have missed this for the world. You've been the best of friends to me, and I'm so proud to stand at your side."

He dragged me into a hard hug, and I swallowed yet more emotion. We both laughed as we separated, and I eyed the stairs, ready to go.

"You know what this is about, don't you?"

A smile broached his face. "Go. Find out."

Then he left, and I was alone, my blood warming at the thought of being near Mathilda again. A single night of being apart and I'd missed her more than I could bear. I'd hated it. Gordain had bolted the tower door to stop me breaking my own rules.

I leapt the stairs in long steps, rushed to tie the blindfold, then knocked on the door. "Only enter if you're devastatingly handsome and unable to see me," my woman's voice called through the wood.

I swung open the door and strode in, immediately smacking my shin into a piece of furniture. Must have been moved by the bridal party; I knew this place like the back of my hand.

"Oof." I winced and closed the door behind me. "Where are ye, lass?"

"Here. On the sofa."

Her voice came from right ahead. With care, I moved forward. "Can ye see me?"

"No. I didn't want bad luck for either of us, but I couldn't wait to see you. Well, be near you."

I dragged in a breath, detecting her perfume over the standard castle scent of old wood and even older stone. "Can I hold you? I need to feel you. I hated sleeping alone last night."

"I did, too. Let's never do it again."

Material rustled, then a tentative hand touched my shoulder. I grasped it and pulled my bride into my arms. A rush of love and happiness flooded me right then, and my cock woke up and started paying attention. "God, I've missed you."

Mathilda nestled her face into my chest then drew back. "Are you wearing your kilt?" Her voice held mischief.

"Aye."

"Do you have anything on underneath?"

I found her hand and dragged it over my knee. "Find out for yourself."

Her laughter rang loud in the room, but she didn't explore further. "There's time for that later. I have something to tell you first. Two things, actually."

My smile dropped. "What is it?"

In the short time we'd been living together, my sole aim, beside making her happier than she knew possible, was to get Mathilda pregnant. She wanted babies, so did I. It had become an obsession.

Silence met my ears. Then, "We did it."

My jaw dropped. "You mean…"

"Three tests. This morning. Little pink crosses or double blue lines on all."

Like a felled Scots Pine, I crashed to my knees. "You're sure."

"Completely," she said with a laugh.

"You've made me the happiest man alive. Do you think it's twins? Aye, it'll be two boys. Brawny and strong, both of them. Though Heaven help you if they're the size I was as a newborn."

She giggled all the more as I wrapped careful arms around her waist and kissed her belly through the silky material of her wedding dress.

"I don't think twins follow the male line. Besides, what if they are girls?"

"I'd be ecstatic, but it won't happen. My family only has boys."

"Mine only has girls. No boy cousins."

She ran her fingers into my hair, and we held one another close, mutual joy radiating from us.

"I want to tell everyone," I murmured, so fucking over the

moon. Also, still horny. "I can't keep secrets. My brothers will know the second they see me."

"Maybe, but you have to wait."

"I also really want you right now. One night away from you was torture." I found the edge of her skirts and lifted them, finding her smooth thighs and, oh Christ, a garter belt.

"Should we wait? I want you begging for it by the time the ceremony is over."

I groaned and stood. "Do we have to do all that? Let's stay here."

"Callum McRae," she admonished. "I've spent weeks putting this wedding together. I want people to admire the arrangements and coo over how beautiful it all is."

"They're getting free food and alcohol, they'll be admiring and cooing either way." I ran my hand to her face and tilted her chin. Then I kissed her. "I love you."

"I love you, too. Maybe we could have a quickie right now."

Our kiss heated. Her hands skimmed my thighs, I grabbed her backside, and she squeaked. Right at that second, a knock rattled the door.

"Mattie, time's up," Beth called.

"Fifteen minutes," Mathilda mumbled back. "We're busy."

"Ten would do it." I grinned, kissing down her neck. "Eight, if we're bargaining."

"Everyone is seated. Your dad's ready to walk you down the aisle. It's kind of important you both come down."

Mathilda groaned and straightened. "Fine, I'm coming out." With a sigh, she gave me a final kiss. "Want the other news?"

"What could beat this?"

"Earlier, Dad showed me the post-launch sales for Storm Force. It's a success. A huge success. McRae whisky is blowing the competition out of the water. They are going to double the order."

The security I'd dreamed about, worked so hard for, fell into place. Mathilda's business could take flight now, without having to repay my debt. My brothers would never know the worry of losing their home. I hugged her carefully. "My home is safe, and all I want to do is take you to bed."

"You have a one-track mind, my soon-to-be laird."

"See you at the altar, my lady."

* * *

*M*athilda
At the front of the castle, my bridesmaids —including Una's two little girls, dressed in white—moved into position. The twins, handsome in their blue-and-grey tartan, hollered a greeting, and Dad beamed. The sun shone on the collection of my friends and relatives and warmed my heart, too.

From the doorway, Gordain gave a cocky whistle of approval then cracked open the door. He signalled to someone inside then gestured for the twins to take their places.

Inside the great hall, Callum waited. My Highland laird.

Butterflies took flight in my stomach, and anticipation left me breathless. I brushed my hands over the ivory satin of my gown.

"Deep inhales, slow exhales," Beth, my maid of honour, whispered.

Like me, this morning, she'd been fussed over and primped to within an inch of her life by a team of makeup artists and hairdressers. Her thick curls had been tamed into a sophisticated twist, and she looked elegant. Regal, even.

"According to all these traditions, I'm meant to buy you a tea set. Did you know that?" she added.

"I saw a gift from you on the pile. It wasn't crockery shaped. What did you get us?"

My best friend grinned. "I made you a newlyweds survival kit. Vitamins, energy bars, body lotion. Earplugs, for everyone else."

I snorted a laugh and hushed her, some of the stress leaving me. "Thank you. We'll open that in private."

Ahead, James exited the door, sharing his best man duties with Gordain. I glanced at Beth.

She sighed and tilted her head, watching him, her gaze gentle. More than I'd ever seen her be before. "Would you look at him in that suit? So aristocratic and beautiful. I told you he was too good for me."

Then she sucked in a breath, and I glanced back to see James watching her, too. Studying her. Taking in the sleek dress and her form within it. He looked like he was in pain.

The whir of bagpipes commenced, distracting everyone, and my stomach seized again. Oh heck. This was it.

In pairs, my bridesmaids and the groomsmen moved off until it was just Dad and me. Then we, too, were on our way. The wedding had begun.

At our first step into the great hall, the music rousing, flowers and lights strung over the walls, a gasp rose from the crowd. Heads turned. Family, clan, and locals peered. Mom dabbed at her eyes as I passed her chair, but all I truly saw, all I knew, was Callum, waiting at the end of the aisle.

He was a vision, a true and powerful Highlander, in his kilt, waistcoat, and jacket, but it was the expression on his face that faltered my footsteps. He'd once told me he wore his heart on his sleeve, but it was plain to anyone who owned his soul.

He stared at me like he hadn't seen me in months, like

284

every detail of my face was rare and needed memorising. An intensity to his gaze that drew me in, enveloping me in bliss.

Much the same way as I saw him.

Dad squeezed my arm.

Then I was at my fiancé's side, and if the castle fell down around us, I couldn't have moved away.

"You're beautiful," he mouthed, his eyes shining as he took me in. Then he dragged in a lungful of air, steadying himself like he could finally breathe.

"You're magnificent," I whispered and was rewarded with a quirk of his lips. Like he could doubt the impact he made.

"Dearly beloved," the celebrant welcomed the guests, commencing the ceremony.

Throughout, Callum only glanced away when demanded by the proceedings. He made his declaration, his *I do* to accept me as his bride, and his voice boomed to the great hall's rafters, his soft brogue wrapping around the words.

When we moved to the vows, his warm hands encased mine.

James brought the rings, and Callum slid mine onto my finger.

"I take thee, Mathilda Victoria Storm, as my lawful wedded wife. I pledge my love, life, a joyful home, and everything I own to ye. I swear to be faithful and true. I'll care for ye and cherish ye so long as my heart beats. This is my pledge."

I placed my ring on his finger, and my voice trembled when I spoke. "I take thee, Callum Hamish McRae, as my lawful wedded husband." I repeated the vows—his family's vows—and the words made a place for themselves inside me.

A pensive silence filled the great hall, and I lost myself for a moment in the overwhelming love that bound me to my Highland laird. To Callum. To the adoration on his face, and the feeling in my heart as we became man and wife. Callum

McRae was everything I'd dreamed about. My childhood fantasy come to life, though better as, instead of him solving all my problems, he supported me in doing so myself. We had a beautiful future ahead of us, and I couldn't wait to start it.

"By the power vested in me, I now pronounce you husband and wife. You may now kiss the bride," the celebrant announced, breaking my reverie, and a cheer ran through the room.

"At last." Callum took my waist and gently dipped me backward. He laid his lips on mine, and we shared our first kiss as a married couple.

The cheer became a roar with stamping feet and applause.

"I am wildly, crazily in love with you," I murmured. We turned and faced the room, him towering over me, making me feel so safe and protected.

"And I, wife, am wild about getting you upstairs."

We stifled a laugh, leaning on each other, and I loved the glint in his eye.

"All hail Laird and Lady McRae," Gordain bellowed, and our names resounded.

A happy scene met us, with people lining up to take photos and smiles on every face. Everyone had words to say, hands to shake, cheeks to kiss.

It was going to take forever just to walk the aisle.

Callum leaned into his brother as we passed and murmured low, "Stall them, will ye? We need half an hour. Or as long as you can get."

A wicked smile touched Gordain's lips. "I'd say it was nae bother, the dancing can wait, but there are one or two lads who have a different idea. You won't sneak out on your own."

Callum wheeled around, glaring and looking for the twins. "They better not even think about it."

"Congratulations!" called the people standing nearest.

The bagpipes swelled and wailed.

"Think about what?" Instinctively, I moved in front of my husband. The twins had threatened Callum with all manner of mischief on his stag do, but he'd stayed sober enough to evade their tricks.

Across the room, the boys appeared, leading the piper, calling on the crowd to line up in a dance. Gordain chuckled.

"Nae, it's no trick. They are causing a distraction so you can get away. Go. Take as a long as you need. The party will wait."

Callum huffed, then, in easy moves, swept me into his arms. I grasped his neck and laughed while he took off along the aisle then up the stairs. The sound of a ruckus followed us, but we were away.

At the top of the stairs, we paused in the hall, kissing. Callum stumbled, hitting a bedroom door with his shoulder. It swung open, revealing Beth inside the room beyond. She stood in the centre of the floor, but she wasn't alone. James had his fingers jammed into her now loose hair, and they attacked each other's mouth, furious passion in the air.

They didn't even notice us. We exchanged a glance, stifled our grins, and Callum swiftly shut them in once more.

Well!

In our solar, Callum stormed to the bed. He placed me down with reverent care, then got busy lifting my skirts. I grabbed at his smart jacket, but he batted my hands away.

"No time. It'll take too long to get dressed again, and I'm nae wasting a minute."

"We're married." I beamed at him. So handsome. So strong.

"And you're finally going to find out what I have on under this kilt," my Scot said with a grin.

I did.

THE END

*T*hank you for reading the first novel in my series featuring the men of Castle McRae. Another lass has fallen for my hot Scots.

Read on for a sneak peek of Love Most, Say Least (Marry the Scot, #2) or buy now: mybook.to/LoveMostSayLeast

You can get a glimpse of Callum and Mathilda in the future (plus Beth and James) in my exclusive newsletter subscriber **free bonus epilogue.** Note: this is for both book one and two's couples together, so it's better read after *Love Most, Say Least.*

The complete *Marry the Scot* series is now available to order plus the next generation *Wild Scots* spin off series of standalones. Find all the titles on my Amazon page here: amazon.com/author/jolievines

ACKNOWLEDGMENTS

First, I need to thank you, my lovely reader, for picking up *Storm the Castle (Marry the Scot, #1)*. I hope you loved reading it as much as I loved writing it.

Laird Callum McRae, and his family and friends, have been part of my world for several years now, so to finally have their names in print is a dream come true. These characters have come a long way since I first dreamed about their lives. As have I!

It's easy to see my inspiration - I adore the Highlands, its gorgeous scenery, lochs and castles, and of course, the brawny Scots that reside there. I'll let you into a little secret - I married a half-Scot myself, so perhaps some aspects of this series are true to life.

As a new and independent author, I am so excited with every new reader that finds me. I love to talk books. See the links over the page to find me on social media.

Reviews are my lifeblood as it helps other readers find my books. If you enjoy my stories, please leave a review on Amazon and Goodreads.

Even a brief "I loved it" is wonderful. I am truly grateful for each and every person who reads my words.

Huge thanks and big hugs go out to my critique partners, Zoe Ashwood and Elle Thorpe. Despite living oceans apart, we've been a great team for years now, and your drive and unending support have made my journey to publishing so much smoother and my books a thousand times better.

My beta readers: Becky - your gut feel for stories is spot on and your support is so wonderful; Tara Watson, your advice is perfect and your fangirling made me fall in love with the story all over again, despite being in my third round of edits; Brenda, you gave me such helpful comments and your fan art (and your poetry!) is just gorgeous; Katie, I'll thank you in babysitting hours.

Last, but not least, to Emmy Ellis at Studio ENP for your perfect edits, and to Natasha Snow for your knockout covers.

I owe you all wee dram.

Jolie x

ALSO BY JOLIE VINES

Race You: An Office-Based Enemies-to-Lovers Romance

Fight For Us: a Second-Chance Military Romantic Suspense

Visit and follow my Amazon page for all new releases amazon.com/author/jolievines

Add yourself to my insider list to make sure you don't miss my publishing news https://www.jolievines.com/newsletter

LOVE MOST, SAY LEAST
MARRY THE SCOT #2

SNEAK PEEK

CHAPTER ONE
A WOMAN

*J*ames

It was a strange kind of winter's morning that had me, a man who couldn't talk with ease, waiting on a woman I'd never met before.

I made balls with my fists, clenching them tight and jamming them under my armpits against the chilly February dawn, all the while staring down the dark city road.

To my left, Callum spoke in low, urgent tones to the woman he'd met last night. And had fallen head over heels for. He wanted to see her again and, by the sound of things, he was having some success persuading her.

I moved a few steps away, giving them privacy.

My mentor and I were leaving London today, heading home. But first, we were waiting for Mathilda's—his new friend's—ride. Leaving couldn't come soon enough for me. Even on the hotel's deserted back road, I couldn't settle.

I rolled my shoulders, my muscles aching from a hard workout this morning in the hotel gym, but it wasn't that which had me edgy. Something bothered me. A sense of foreboding, or perhaps anticipation. But of what?

From the end of the road, a red car sped towards us.

I tensed, monitoring it as it neared. It drew to a halt alongside, and a woman—with thick brown curls, and big eyes on a pretty face—sat back in the driver's seat. She grinned, then called out a greeting to Mathilda, and cast an appreciative eye over Callum and me.

"You didn't say there were men here. Whoa, mama."

"Beth," Mathilda said. Her tone held a warning.

"Be right back," the driver replied, and she accelerated away.

"Gentlemen, meet Beth. Don't be alarmed," Mathilda said.

Alarmed? Why should I be? Where was she going? My sense of unease grew, a wariness descending over me.

At the end of the road, the woman—Beth—performed a neat U-turn. She revved the powerful engine, and I stood taller, my attention fully on the car.

With a roar, the vehicle punched forward.

"I—" I started, my throat tight. Callum grabbed hold of my arm, keeping me still. "What is she—?" I tried again. Then I stopped.

She reached us, too fast. Far too fast.

Fear clawed its way up my throat. A shout came out as nothing but a choked-off cry.

The car spun in the road, bright lights, brakes squealing. It was coming right for us. A one-eighty turn. Nearly on top of us. About to crash. And then…

It stopped, rocking. Engine off. Neatly and perfectly parked in the narrow gap.

I gaped.

But it wasn't the woman I saw beaming out of the window. I saw red. Tasted blood. Heard the crunch of tearing metal. My skin slashed, the scars burning with the memory. The grating cries—

"What in God's name— What the hell did you do?" I

295

yelled, my voice a surprise to me, the ease with which I spoke.

Callum muttered something from beside me, his grip firm, but I couldn't hear. White noise filled my ears.

Then the woman was approaching me, her features twisted in regret, but I couldn't...

I just couldn't.

Like a bereft child, I turned and fled.

The automatic lobby doors opened onto the dark interior of the hotel. I paced inside, heading to the coffee shop. Locked inside my head, my torment sent image after image of all I'd tried to forget. My skin crawled, and my breathing shuddered on the inhale. But the farther I walked, the more my sheer fright from the flashback melted, instead morphing into embarrassment.

I hated being like this. Damaged inside and out.

Light footsteps drummed behind me. "Wait. Hey! Stop a second."

I turned, already feeling irrational. Overdramatic. Beth arrived beside me. I raised my chin to the woman, trying to summon words.

Her gaze took me in. "I'm sorry. About the stunt? I've done that a million times and it's so safe. Just a haul on the handbrake, floor the gas, spin the wheel, and bam." She winced. "Not bam. I mean, a nicely parked car, facing the right way."

She dropped her gaze, and I took a deep breath, forcing myself to calm. To remember how to make my mouth work. "It's fine," I forced out.

The woman dragged her fingers through her hair, sweeping it over her head, revealing a shaved side, hidden under the weight of curls. "It isn't. I didn't think. I just saw two big, handsome men, and I got all stupid."

Handsome?

The panic receded further, and a new, unexpected emotion replaced it. A twist of something...more. A warmth in my veins.

"You're not to blame for my behaviour. You knew your own skill. I was ignorant of it." My voice came easier this time. I blew out a breath. Tried to force the stiffness from my limbs.

Then the woman raised her eyes, and our gazes met.

Collided.

The warmth in me flickered, a flame trying to ignite.

"I, er... God, let me start over. I apologise. I'll never do that again," she said, her brown eyes wide, a stunned expression on her face. "You have really beautiful eyes." Then she gave an awkward laugh and took a step back. "Shut up, Beth," she muttered to herself.

My strange feeling...it was desire. The woman in front of me was striking. Very much so. Her features, animated in her embarrassment, fascinated me. The flush on her cheeks had me thinking words like *adorable* and *charming*.

Why, I had no idea.

"Want a coffee?" she asked, changing the subject.

I blinked then swung my gaze to the bemused-looking barista waiting behind the counter a few feet away. "Yes. I could, I mean, if you wanted..."

"Great." Beth cocked her head to one side. "I'm buying. Call it an apology."

She grinned at the barista. "Americano, please. Black. Nothing fancy for me. Something sweet for him. He needs it for the shock of meeting me."

I wanted to laugh, but that was a step too far. My life had many complications, and no matter how I readied myself to face them, nothing had prepared me for this—the confusion that went with attraction to a hot-blooded woman. It didn't mix with the irritation still grating on my memories.

Drinks in hand, we left the hotel, emerging back into the light.

Beth stumbled at the door, her Americano sloshing. I caught her, earning a beaming smile from her red lips.

Then she hugged me.

I'd been hugged before. Callum and his brothers were a physical family. A punch to the arm for a job well done. A bear hug after time apart. That was nothing like this.

Beth's hair smelled good, and the way she lingered, holding me sweetly, soothed the rough edges of my nerves. Arresting in the sense of peace I gained. It was...enjoyable.

But just as I relaxed a tiny degree into it, it was over. Beth darted to the car, got in, waved, and drove away. All in the space of time it had taken me to touch the place on my chest where she'd laid her head.

Callum loomed over me, a grin transforming his hard exterior. I was far more used to him being stern. Grumpy, even.

"Women, eh?" he said with a laugh, then slung an arm over my shoulder, leading me to the concierge so we could check out.

Women.

"Good luck with that," I replied, brushing off the thoughts, even if I could still feel her touch. I had no time to sort through the mess relationships brought, the hassle Callum seemed to be seeking. Besides, it wasn't for me, this way of finding a partner.

My path had long been laid out. No shock to the system was going to change anything. No lass with dark eyes and dark hair and attention-seeking habits.

I stuffed the new sensations into the back of mind and got on with my day.

CHAPTER TWO
HOT LETTER WRITER

*B*eth The letter burned a hole in my pocket. Jammed into my hand by Mattie, my housemate, on my way out of the door, it had become weightier the longer my shift dragged on. Not least due to the extremely hot letter writer and my curiosity over what he had to say.

Who wrote letters anymore?

Particularly to a woman who'd almost ran them over.

I'd had no chance to sneak a look. Despite it being a Monday, miserable Kendra, the supervisor at The Corkscrew, had filled my section with a large party of diners. But my waitressing shift had ended ten minutes ago, and I was out of here. I ought to be tired. My feet ached like a mother flipper, but my brain was wired, and I set my sights on the exit with two things on my mind.

Reading the letter, obviously, because the anticipation was killing me, and getting into my car and hitting the open road. The need to drive zinged in my veins.

The door slid open, and the cold spring night flooded in.

Almost free.

JOLIE VINES

"Beth." Kendra's voice rang out through the empty restaurant. "A word, please."

With her expression set somewhere between caustic and dour, Kendra strode over, barging through the cleared tables. In the corner of my vision, one of the barmen, a new guy, pulled an 'ouch' face in sympathy. I plastered on a smile and met the manager halfway.

"I need to change your shifts this week. Two people are out, so I need you tomorrow five until eleven-thirty, then the same on Wednesday but covering lunch as well. Then I'm cancelling your Friday and Saturday—"

Shit. That wouldn't work. I had two jobs, study, and a full week lined up. "Wait. I can't change my shifts, I've got other commitments."

"What commitments?"

I toed the sticky floor. "Shifts at the multiplex. I'm there Tuesday—"

"Cancel." She folded her arms and rested a hip on a blue-painted table. "We need you here."

Aw, this was horrible. I hated saying no, mainly because I needed the money, and pissing off my employers was not good for my bank balance. "I really can't. I already agreed to the shifts, and they're set weekly. It's too late to cancel."

Kendra heaved a sigh like I'd personally destroyed her hopes and dreams. I braced myself for fireworks.

"We don't appreciate the lack of loyalty. Your refusal has been noted," she snipped, then spun on her heel and stomped back to the kitchen.

"I'm sorry?" I called at the logo of a corkscrew emblazoned across her retreating back, though I wasn't truly. Work was work, and I kept my word. But the doors to the kitchen flapped closed, and she was gone.

"She's a real ball-buster, huh?" the new bar guy said, and I twisted around to look at him. He stacked a glass on the high shelf then wiped his hands on his company shirt. "I'm looking for more hours. I'll offer to cover. That'll take the heat off you."

He swept his gaze over me, something overeager in his attention, lingering on the undercut I had shaved on the left side of my head. I knew what was coming. He'd been hitting on women all night.

"Cool hair. Wait around. I'll take you for a drink."

Not tonight, sunshine. "Knock yourself out with the shifts, but sorry, no can do with the drink, I've got somewhere I need to be..." I paused to let him fill in the name blank.

His lips thinned. "Stan. I introduced myself at the beginning of my shift."

Oh. "Stan. Right. See you later in the week."

Then I was out the door and tripping my way down the rain-splattered road to where I'd parked the Audi. Not *my* Audi, obviously. Like I could ever afford a luxury car. Mattie was the owner. She hated driving, and her father had bought her the top-end model for her birthday. As long as I chauffeured her around, she didn't mind me taking it out for a night ride every now and again.

The cost of fuel was my one extravagance. I needed this freedom or I'd go insane.

The door made a neat clunk as I closed it, and I settled into the cosy interior. Then, with my fingers itching, I extracted the letter from my bag.

Beth, it said on the front in a neat scrawl.

I tore into the envelope, and my buzz of excitement grew as a folded white sheet plopped onto my lap. My stomach flipped, and I began to read.

Beth,

You might not remember me...

Yeah, right. You didn't see a man like him and forget in a hurry.

...but our friends are friends, and I wanted to ask a favour.

I was pretty sure our friends were more than that. Mattie had travelled all the way to Scotland just for the day to see the letter writer's housemate, hence how she'd received the mail. If they weren't knocking boots already, they soon would be. I read on, forcing myself to take it slow.

I'm buying a new car, and I recall your expertise in that area. Would you give me a call? I'd be grateful for your advice.

Yours, James Fitzroy

The windows fogged from my breathing, and I punched the button for the heat.

It was a line, right? The car thing?

He barely knew me, so he couldn't have any idea about my driving pedigree. I snorted at my word choice. *Pedigree.* Cars were in my blood, but my family history was nothing but criminal. Then again, what did I care about his motivation? I'd thought about James more than once since the single time we'd met last month. Not only due to how he looked, because *hot damn*, but because I'd scared the living crap out of the guy, and the guilt had eaten me up.

I didn't know what made me do it, the stunt, but the moment I'd seen Mattie outside that hotel with two hot guys beside her, I'd decided to show off.

There was space. It was a quiet road. I'd thought I was safe.

Well, maybe thinking hadn't been top of my agenda.

In a satisfying roar of engine meeting fuel, I'd executed the neatest trick to park the Audi, sliding it into the space next to the kerb. Mattie had barely blinked, used to my shit after living with me for a year, but James, he of the gorgeous face, had freaked.

Kind of killed the mood.

I'd found him and apologised, and he'd apologised in return—an educated accent coming from his lips with the hint of a Scottish brogue. *So sexy.* Then I did something weird, even by my standards.

I hugged him, right there in the hotel lobby. Flung my arms around this perfect stranger, found myself all hot because he smelled good, and his big, hard body tensed under my touch. I inhaled him, liked it far too much, then fled to the car. I'd blame the adrenaline on the stunt, but it had barely got my blood up.

Nothing like hugging James had done.

I thought about it to death. His overreaction. The honesty in his apology. The way my stupid, impulsive behaviour hurt him. It gnawed at me.

Being a former foster kid, I knew trauma when I saw it, and whatever he had going on made him undeniably fascinating. I hadn't forgotten him one bit.

I tapped the letter on the steering wheel and eyed the empty road, street lights creating shadows on the deserted city centre. Maybe he really did need car help. Whatever it was, having someone to talk to tonight wasn't the worst idea. I needed a distraction.

I whipped out my phone, saving James's number as a new contact. Then I typed a quick message, my fingers flying. I really needed to drive.

Hey, it's Beth. Give me a call, and we'll talk. I figure I owe you.

Then I dragged in a breath, threw the car into first, and sped out to find some peace.

* * *

*T*hank you for the reply. When can I call? James Fitzroy

His formal response came in just before I hit the on-ramp for the motorway. The M5 took me south on a long, straight path through dark countryside. Beautiful by day but empty at night. More than enough driving time to stop me obsessing over my problems.

A smooth transition, and the car sang in blessed fifth gear, then I merged into the light traffic and let the Audi fly, weaving over to the fast lane and opening up the engine with a purr of absolute bliss. The car's, not mine. Though soon, hopefully, I'd get my sense of escape.

Popping in my headphones, I dictated a text message to my phone.

Now's good, I'm free.

My phone buzzed a few seconds later. Him, calling.

"Beth's Auto Shop, how can I help?" I grinned at my own joke. Like any garage would employ me, a five-foot-nothing woman with no qualifications in—well, anything. Let alone the other black marks against my name.

There was a pause on the line, and I chuckled. "James, it's Beth. I'm just messing around. How are you doing?"

The soft sound of his deep almost-laugh had me push my earbud in farther.

"I'm well, thank you."

Then nothing. A fresh squall of rain from the grey-and-black sky hit the windscreen, and the wipers started automatically. "Um, so, your letter. What did you want to talk about?"

"I'm buying a new car. I wanted to ask you a question. But it's late," he said, stating the obvious, and I tried to picture him, wherever he was. I knew he lived with Callum, and Mattie had mentioned the guy owned a castle. Like that was a normal thing.

James was probably sprawled on his bed in a turret room in Scotland.

Long limbs on nice sheets.

Well, hello imagination.

"That's true. But I'll be up for a couple of hours at least. I only just finished work." The road bowed right, and I inched the steering wheel around in a perfect arc, dead centre in my lane. This car had such nice handling.

"You've been working? But it's nearly midnight."

"I work most nights. And days for that matter. Or I study. I don't sleep all that much."

James made a tutting sound. "My request can wait until you're rested."

"No! Don't go. This is the most interesting thing to happen to me in weeks." It wasn't a lie. All I ever did was work. "Talk. Cars are my thing. But be warned, once I start, it'll be hard to shut me up."

A moment of quiet, then he relented. "I've been driving an old Land Rover of Callum's, but safety is my priority. When we met… Well, when it came to buying my own car, I thought of you."

Up ahead, orange lights flashed, reflecting onto the wet road. An emergency sign? I squinted at it. "Hang on a sec. My lane is closing. I need to pay attention to the signs."

I signalled left and slid the Audi in behind a column of cars, filtering into one long queue. *Fuck.* This wasn't in the plan. I needed speed and the open road. My knee jiggled. I slowed to a crawl.

"You're driving?" James's voice sounded strained.

"It helps when my mind is busy," I replied, distracted by the growing traffic.

Behind, someone blared a horn.

"You…? I can't…" The line went dead.

He hung up on me?

A quick glance at my phone confirmed it. *Call ended.* Well, fuck.

Twenty minutes later, and I'd inched into the motorway services. A check on a traffic update website told me the motorway was closed and my night of easy driving dissolved.

With my hyperactive mind mulling over roadworks, my manager's expression as she'd left, and people hanging up on me, I dialled James back.

He didn't answer.

I hard-tapped out a text message.

I've stopped driving. It's safe.

Nothing.

I sat in the dark warmth of the car, stewing. It wasn't his fault my night was messed up. That my teetering pile of worries, about the money I needed for my foster mother, about the future I wanted but was always out of reach, kept my mind from settling. But James had done something he hadn't intended. He'd given me a fun idea to dwell on when the rest of my time was spent on problems. Then he'd hung up on me and taken it away.

In a fit of petulance, I muttered "Jerk" to his letter, rolled my shoulders, and set tracks for home.

*T*hank you for reading the preview! Buy Love Most, Say Least (Marry the Scot, #2) now: mybook.to/LoveMostSayLeast

ABOUT THE AUTHOR

JOLIE VINES is a romance novelist who lives in the South West of England with her husband and toddler son.

From an early age, Jolie lived in a fantasy world and is never happier than when plot dreaming.

Jolie loves her heroes to be one-woman guys. Whether they are a huge Highlander, a touch-starved earl, or a brooding pilot, they will adore their loved one until the end of time.

Her favourite pastime is wrecking emotions then making up for it by giving her characters deep and meaningful happy ever afters.

Want to be the first to hear Jolie's book news, access giveaways and bonus content? Subscribe to her newsletter.

Want to contact Jolie? She loves hearing from her readers. Drop her a line at jolie@jolievines.com, find her on Instagram, and join her Facebook group

www.ingramcontent.com/pod-product-compliance
Lightning Source LLC
Chambersburg PA
CBHW051123190726
48290CB00006B/1665